HOMUNCULUS

Hugh Paxton

MACMILLAN NEW WRITING

First published 2006 by Macmillan New Writing,
an imprint of Macmillan Publishers Ltd
Brunel Road, Basingstoke RG21 6XS
Associated companies throughout the world
www.macnewwriting.com

ISBN-13: 978–0230–00049–0 hardback
ISBN-10: 0230–00049–5 hardback
ISBN-13: 978–0230–00736–9 paperback
ISBN-10: 0230–00736–8 paperback

1 3 5 7 9 8 6 4 2

A CIP catalogue record for this book is available from
the British Library.

Typeset by Heronwood Press
Printed and bound in Great Britain by Biddles Ltd, King's Lynn, Norfolk

For Annabel, Nushi, Michaela, Tim and Robin.
Your first book dedication. Just don't
read it until you are a LOT older!

CHAPTER ONE

Small Beginnings

Sierra Leone. Recently.

The first man encountered on the road to Lalapanzi was not a man. Not really. He was a boy, a kid, wearing nothing but a pair of large, shabby sneakers and holding an AK 47.

Like his regional commander, General Butt Naked, the teenaged Revolutionary United Front (RUF) rebel was – apart from his sneakers – butt naked.

He also had a hand bag.

Christiaan Rindert, twice the sentry's size, three times the sentry's age, watched him through scarred Leica binoculars, then scanned the dusty scrub on either side of the road-block for signs that the kid was not alone. As road-blocks went this was a singularly sad effort; two ancient wheel-less prams with a banana tree propped between them partially transecting the rutted dirt track. Wouldn't stop a bicycle, thought Rindert with contempt. Beside it a pile of beer bottles (empty), a sheet of blue plastic with the UNHCR logo on it writ large, and a broken white chair marked the sentry's bivouac. Flies seethed behind it. The RUF hadn't bothered to dig a latrine.

Par for the course.

He brought the binoculars back to bear on the rebel.

From the way he was wobbling Rindert reckoned the RUF sentry was utterly, numbingly, dead-on-his-feet stoned.

Wobbling kid excepted, nothing was moving. The scrub was

hot. Dry. Green and very still. Crickets whirred listlessly. More to the point, Rindert could see laughing doves pecking for seeds. The birds were skittish. If more rebs were there in ambush the doves would fly.

The doves just pecked away, cautious eyes watching for everything.

Behind Rindert as he bird-watched, were fifteen pro-government Kamajor militiamen. They had more clothes than the RUF sentry, but they had also been firing up bushweed since dawn. It would keep them moving for hours; it dulled hunger and banished fear. All three were fine by Rindert. Sober pro-government soldiers, particularly over-dressed oddballs like his, were prone to running away. The down-side to the drug was that it prompted outbursts of psychotic rage.

Not always an asset.

Behind the militia, emotionlessly videoing the impending murder of the RUF boy soldier on a Sony handycam through the windows of their Toyota Hi-Lux, were Rindert's two Japanese clients.

He loathed them; thought them both repulsive and ridiculous with their sour breath and sweat-shiny, heat-mottled faces. Both men had bottle-thick glasses, and wore leopard-patterned safari jackets and zebra-striped bush-hats.

If their dress was an attempt to blend in, look African, it was pathetic. If it was an attempt to look like safari tourists it was spectacularly misguided. Tourism in Sierra Leone wasn't dead. It hadn't been born. Who'd want to come? To see this?

The names the Japanese had given Rindert when they contracted him as bodyguard and escort in Sierra Leone's capital, Freetown, were Sato and Suzuki – the Japanese equivalents of Smith and Jones. Both Sato and Suzuki claimed that they were doctors, here to capture the Ebola virus and find a cure. This, too, Rindert suspected was a lie.

They might be here for Ebola. And if they were, they weren't the first.

Word on the West African "security consultant" circuit was that the Aum Shinrikyo Buddhist sect that had Sarin-gassed the Tokyo subway in '95 (killing twelve and injuring 5,500) had sent some of its people into neighbouring Liberia probing for Ebola. They'd been escorted by a Russian: some hardcase ex-Spetsnaz freelancer with a bad rep for impatience, named Koransky. The Aum expedition had failed in circumstances that were still obscure.

Sato and Suzuki, in Rindert's opinion, were more of the same – virus hunters. There'd be fun and games in Tokyo should Sato and Suzuki succeed in their quest. That was Rindert's guess.

"Is it just the one, Commander?" whispered the militia corporal, Benjamin Franklin. Eighteen-years-old, best-dressed, least-stoned, Franklin was Rindert's temporary right-hand man. Even if he was wearing a purple top hat decorated with a skull and crossbones.

Rindert nodded, tried to overlook the man's hat, tucked his binoculars away, and with practised ease raised his rifle for a leg shot.

The temptation was to raise the sights and blow the RUF kid's head off. It was a temptation that Rindert resisted.

He'd need to question the boy about RUF patrol activity in the area and needed him disabled but not dead. It was unusual, no, *it was highly unusual*, for only one person to man a RUF road-block, even a crummy one like this. As a rule, the child soldiers were pack animals, preying on the wretched detritus of broken refugees which, without hope, trudged the roads. Seeking sanctuary from a civil war of nine years' standing.

"Kapow!" said Benjamin Franklin.

"Kapow," agreed Rindert.

He squeezed the trigger.

The shot startled the doves. They scattered with a rattle of wings.

The RUF sentry for his part span around, then flopped and writhed, flopped, writhed, in the reddening dust.

Hoots and jeers from the militia accompanied his collapse. Rindert banged a heavy sunburned hand on the roof of the Bedford's cab. At the signal the driver refired the engine. The party advanced. Some of the men around him, Rindert noted with bored disgust, were panting. Tongues out. Mouths open. That bushweed really fuelled the atavistic flames. Or maybe they were just hot. The Japanese video whirred steadily away. The Japanese doctors didn't seem to need bushweed.

Watching was enough. He glanced at them. They didn't seem perturbed by the shooting. One was licking his lips.

If they were bigger, Rindert might even have found them threatening. But size here counted, and Rindert was the biggest. He was also the best and he could kill the entire party he escorted in a minute or less if he felt so inclined.

So no problem.

The RUF sentry Rindert had shot precisely through the left knee was in a sorry state. Not just stoned and shot. Sick. There were boils all over his nose and neck. Something awful was going on in the blood vessels of his left arm. "Not pretty," Rindert thought. Something of an understatement.

There were flecks of blood all over him and they had not come from the gunshot. They were dry.

The wounded kid's AK, when Rindert checked it, had a jammed magazine. That was clever. Jamming an AK's magazine took real initiative. It was a giant step from youthful incompetence. Almost an act of will.

There was also earth in the barrel. Also a very colourful stone. How had the kid got a stone that size wedged there? Getting it out looked more trouble than it was worth. Guns here were one commodity not in short supply. Next to the gun was a panga, its notched blade crusted with dried blood.

While the Kamajor militia fanned out, or more accurately

wandered, into the bush, shouting obscene expletives at an enemy they knew wasn't there, Rindert checked the kid's hand bag.

While he did so, he kept an eye on the kid who was rolling listlessly in the dust, not even paying regard to his broken leg. Very sick indeed. Not Ebola though. Rindert was no doctor, but just a glance told him the kid was one nasty but very common little cocktail of parasites and malnutrition; maybe with a shot of what the East Africans called 'Slim' added for light relief.

There were six hands in the bag: two pitifully small; two adult female, their nails smudged with the ancient ghosts of mauve polish; two adult male, all recently parted from their owners but already flyblown. Taking hands was a long-standing RUF initiative to discourage voting in UN supervised elections. The logic behind it was that amputees would be unable to register their democratic objections to the current status quo by putting an X or even a fingerprint on the ballot papers.

General Butt Naked was a keen proponent of "the RUF handshake" or "chopping" as it was also known. Rewards and promotion were offered in return for hands. Though quite what promotion meant in a guerilla army where generals such as Butt Naked were nineteen, and General Murder fifteen, Rindert couldn't figure. Didn't even bother to try. Just killed them when he saw them. But tried to see as little of them as possible.

Hey ho! Back to the hand bag!

Judging from the freshness of the hands, the people who'd been chopped were not far away. But they could have staggered in any direction. Conceivably this stoned kid's comrades could be grilling them back at camp. That might explain why the kid was alone.

"Not a party," Rindert said. Meaning, to Rindert at least, there was no point in looking for the handless.

Or, as Rindert had told a drunken Reuters journalist in Freetown, practically the only people in Sierra Leone to be successfully disarmed since peace negotiations between the warring factions collapsed. The journalist had subsequently plagiarised the quote. It had then been edited out on the grounds of bad taste.

Rindert tossed the hands into the bush. Christ but it was hot! Rindert tried to ignore the stench of human waste and disease and the rusty, dusty odour of unwashed skin. He waved droning, bloated blowflies from his face. Asked the kid questions. The kid attempted to spit at Rindert. That was the last thing Rindert needed – some HIV-infested spit in the eye. He thumped his gun down into the contorted face. Strangely, Rindert, albeit in a far-away way, felt a sudden pang for the kid as his pug, boil-swollen nose cracked.

He was unquestionably a brutal little sociopath and, as the hand bag's contents eloquently demonstrated, was responsible for atrocities, but he was the product of his environment and about to die naked and alone. The rope for sure. If the militia felt like it, a stake up the kid's rear end for good measure. A squalid life. A squalid end. Waste, waste, waste.

The kid had stopped spitting.

Rindert, crouching now, scolded the kid in a paternal tone. Admonished him for his discourtesy to a person older than himself. Weirdly the kid apologized, his voice indistinct and squeaky. Rindert asked the kid some more questions. Got some mumbled, increasingly humble replies as the kid softened, perhaps began to think that he wasn't going to be shot or chopped (chopping was a practice not confined entirely to the RUF). Rindert rumbled on, like a kindly uncle, asking his questions.

The kid started spilling.

The main RUF unit had been recalled by General Butt Naked to celebrate the opening of a new RUF radio station. He was guarding the road in case the monsters came back.

Rindert ignored the reference to monsters. The idea of General Butt Naked running a radio station was appalling enough. *Butt Naked the DJ!* The mind boggled at the prospect.

The kid said he'd been left behind. Alone.

Why alone?

He'd been too stoned to move, so they'd left him. Left him for the monsters.

Rindert forged on.

Yes, the kid admitted, he had taken the hands of a family. The RUF had promised three American dollars for each hand.

The kid said his name was Corporal Punishment.

"No," Rindert murmured soothingly, "that's a clever name but what's your real name, the name you were given by your mammy?"

"Abraham Lincoln."

"Ah."

Lincoln thought he was twelve. Could the commander – he meant Rindert – take him to see his grandmammy? He didn't want to be left alone for the monsters.

Rindert said no he couldn't and even if he could he wouldn't. Because, Rindert explained, this "take me to my grandmammy" bullshine was just a ploy to avoid consequences. He didn't even bother to pursue the monsters issue. That was, in Rindert's opinion, drug-related.

"Abraham," he said, "what you need to understand is that if you chop people's hands off then you are behaving in a way that is not so nice. You must be held accountable for this."

"I ate my mammy," confided the kid who didn't appear to have been listening. "General Butt Naked made me eat ... her ..."

The kid faltered.

Rindert decided it was time to move things along. He really didn't want to hear which bits of his mammy Abraham had had to eat. This whole eating people business made him depressed. Jonny "The Cat" Bouchard had told him that he'd busted in on a funeral in southern Uganda. But not before the Lord's Resistance Army had busted in first. The LRA maniacs, whose credo was the establishment of a Christian state ruled by the Ten Commandments, had, for reasons obscure, forced the villagers to cook the deceased with maize porridge.

Then eat him.

Bouchard had thought that this was about as good a story to come out of Africa as had ever been told and had expected at least a few laughs and a round of pastis. But The Cat had only just arrived in Sierra Leone. When he'd smugly challenged the other drinkers in the squalid chop-shop (local parlance for a bar and eating shack) to "top that, *mes amis!*" the other drinkers, all of whom had been in Sierra Leone four months or more, had had no difficulty.

Fats Dupree, a pig-ugly brute from Marseilles who was hired gun for two Belgian *diamantaires*, had recounted an incident involving him finding half of a lower jaw-bone at the bottom of a soup cauldron, complete with fillings.

The fillings bit was the important part of the anecdote, as Dupree had explained. Everyone knew niggers ate each other and where was the harm in that? But the fillings meant that the stew was probably made of expatriate white meat, Sierra Leone not being particularly well-known for its abundance of orthodontists. Dupree even thought he knew who he'd eaten. Jo Jo Lafayette, a perky, earnest ex-Médicins Sans Frontières volunteer nurse. She'd been working on AIDS awareness, loosely associated with Freetown's long-suffering Connaught Hospital. Then she'd died – of AIDS – and someone had pinched her body from the remains of the Connaught Hospital's routinely overcrowded morgue.

Dupree added that the cook had used far too much curry powder and that it had given him the shits.

Dupree had then looked suddenly concerned.

Rindert remembered feeling an abrupt, peculiar, childish hope as he watched the awful hoggish face rumple in thought and worry. *Dupree had discovered a conscience*! He'd eaten a nurse, but that wasn't his fault. He hadn't ordered her. She'd just been served up as *plat du jour* smothered in onions and too much curry powder.

The point was, that Dupree had realized he was making a joke out of it, and Dupree had suddenly realized that he was *wrong to do so*.

If there was hope for Dupree, Rindert had thought exultantly, there was hope for humanity!

Dupree had then said, "Can you catch AIDS from eating somebody?"

"Not if the meat's been cooked," someone had said.

"Thank Christ for that!" Dupree had announced, relief showing bright-as-a-flare on his flushed face. "Can recommend the place then. It's bloody cheap. Good honest French food. And there are big servings."

There were gusts of laughter; roaring gusts of laughter.

There wasn't hope for humanity, Rindert had decided, and ordered another drink. Something poisonously strong.

Rindert shook his head to clear the memory and returned to the business in hand. God curse these flies. "Benjamin!" he bellowed. "Stop horsing around with that RPG. You're looking like you've never seen one before. Here man, now! Kill these flies. They're driving me bloody crazy."

"There are monsters in Lalapanzi," Abraham Lincoln said, back on the monster thing, eating his mammy apparently forgotten.

"There's monsters everywhere, Abraham," said Rindert. "You're a monster. I mean, why? *Why*? Why are you chopping these ..." Rindert pointed at the hands. Suddenly he wanted to impress upon this maimed, boil-covered, psychopathic shit the implications of cutting off hands. "People need hands. If they don't have hands they can't write."

"*I* can't write," mumbled Abraham Lincoln.

Dear Christ, thought Rindert. Of course you can't write. You probably shot your English teacher.

Lincoln's eyes were rolling. He was going into shock. His scrawny, ugly body was shaking. If it was one of his own men Rindert would have wrapped him in a blanket, but Rindert didn't want to foul one of his blankets on this diseased RUF mess. No point. Blankets were a luxury, and Lincoln was most definitely on the way out.

The boy soldier's voice rose to a frightened wail.

"Real monsters, Commander. Zombies. Porroh! And I've seen one with green smoke coming out of its nose." He was now clutching Rindert's leg. Babbling. Babbling. "The priest's killing everyone with them. Everyone knows the Ebola gets you. You dead. All the nuns dead of the Ebola. Just the priest left and Papa Det. I saw Papa Det. He was like mist. The monsters are coming. It's the end of the world. Am I OK?"

The kid's out to lunch, thought Rindert. Enough time-wasting. Time to make an example; time to leave General Butt Naked's boys a message.

"Bring the rope and the board!" Rindert shouted.

The board said "DONT JOIN THE RUF! EMBRACE LOVIN JEZUS!" The Jesus stuff was the idea of Benjamin Franklin, who professed to be a Baptist. That was unusual for a Kamajor. Most were, or, more accurately, thought or claimed they were, hunter-magicians.

The board went around Abraham Lincoln's neck, as did the rope. It then went over a tree limb.

"Up you go, son," Rindert said, pulling the rope taught and the whimpering, bulge-eyed RUF soldier free of the ground. Light as a bloody feather, Rindert thought, tying the rope secure around a branch. For a moment he considered pulling the RUF kid's legs, breaking his neck cleanly, but then he remembered the hands. The little one he'd chopped couldn't have been more than a toddler. Toddlers don't vote. No, that handshake had just been viciously gratuitous. Three bucks a hand. Hanging Lincoln slowly was evil, Rindert knew that, but it was necessary. The RUF recruits would – *might* – get the message. Might not reach so readily for the pangas next time they caught a family. Evil. Yes. But a necessary evil.

"As you sow, so shall you reap," intoned Benjamin Franklin perhaps trying to rationalize the ongoing atrocity. He'd removed his top hat and stopped swatting flies. He looked unhappy.

"Some fucking harvest," said Rindert, his eyes equally mournful.

The other pro-government troops had no such qualms. They came scrambling excitedly out of the bush and gave each other high fives. They squabbled over the dangling kid's stinking sneakers, then brought out the stake; which they thrust into Abraham Lincoln's rectum as he hung there fighting for air that was all around him but impossible to breathe; a little boy very much lost, twitching and turning beneath vast, blue African skies.

Rindert's thoughts were. Very deliberately. Elsewhere.

That was the first man met on the road as Rindert's small convoy continued its cautious progress towards the village of Lalapanzi. It was also the last. Rumours of Ebola seemed to have cleared the area of combatants. Perversely it took a viral haemorrhagic fever that made the human body erupt blood from every orifice to stop the fighting here.

Or maybe it was the monsters.

As they continued their advance Rindert pondered the complexities of Ebola the peacemaker – another necessary evil? – and wondered what sort of programming General Butt Naked had lined up for his new radio station.

Mostly though, Rindert thought about what an utter relief it would be to leave this wretched country, live somewhere peaceful. Orderly. Sane. Clean, starched sheets. A nice little game farm in Kwazulu or the Free State. No General Murders, no Corporal Punishments, no little monsters to worry about.

Somewhere where he could find peace, quiet. Peace. Quiet.

The column reached Lalapanzi in the late afternoon. And that's when things got seriously weird. Weird even by Rindert's standards and God knew he'd seen more than his fair share of the capital Weird in his fifteen years freelance soldiering in Africa.

CHAPTER TWO

Welcome to Britain

"Name?"

"Derek Campbell," murmured Rindert. That was what it said in his Freetown-forged Zimbabwean passport.

"Occupation?"

"Tobacco farmer. At least," Rindert's voice hitched brokenly, "at least, I was."

The British immigration official's expression softened. He'd been following the Zimbabwe war veterans' invasions of white-owned farms on the BBC. A bad business, the immigration official thought, a bad, bad business. Bad for Africa. Bad for Zimbabwe – what was it? Two thirds of the population now in poverty and Zimbabwe once one of the richest countries in the region?

This poor devil – Jim rechecked the passport – this poor devil Campbell had no doubt lost land that had been in his family for generations. Maybe even had family members slain. No compensation offered by the ruling ZANU PF party that masterminded the land invasions. Just because an ageing totalitarian president didn't know that it was possible to retire with dignity.

And now Campbell had a new life to build in a country that was foreign to him.

A hell of a wrench.

The immigration official was black but felt himself British to the core. Hell, his family had caught the boat some time back in the 1800s. Every time he watched the latest African lunacy on the BBC he thanked them for that.

He suspected this white immigrant was African to the core. In this suspicion he was also right.

"Jim," said a colleague slipping neatly over from her desk. "We've got an A1."

This wasn't an official code. It was private. Several of Heathrow's staff had been abjectly humiliated by a robotic, obnoxious series of immigration officials on a recent group trip to New York. The appalling rudeness of the airport Americans had grated beyond belief and soured the entire jolly excursion.

It was payback time. They'd got a Yank on holiday at desk three who worked for US immigration New York JFK and had worked the La Guardia desks. Guilty as hell.

"Can't be too careful, Carol," said Jim on behalf of UK immigration. "Must maintain international standards. Give her the US checks. Has she any association with Nazi Germany and its allies? Has she ever been denied entry to the United Kingdom? Is she a criminal, habitual drug abuser, guilty of gross moral turpitude, de dah, de dah."

"She's got pepper spray in her handbag."

"Has she no respect for our laws?"

"Not yet."

"Duty calls me strongly to the next booth, Mr Campbell," said Jim, redirecting his gaze to the destitute white farmer who was beginning to wonder what the hell was going on.

"Welcome to Britain. I hope it works out for you here, Mr Campbell," the official added with such feeling that Rindert half expected Jim was going to give him a five pound note to help him rebuild his life. More pressing, though, was the A1. Jim hustled off in the direction of Three.

A shrill voice rose in protest from desk three. "This ain't right!" It's horrid nasal whine was pure aggrieved New York immigration official.

"Thank you, UK," said Derek Campbell, mustering a brave and grateful smile as he wandered broken-backed and destitute through customs into the country that would offer him succour for, hopefully, just three days.

Assuming all went well.

It didn't. Rindert headed for the Speedlink to Paddington. But tiredness was beginning to show. On arrival in Paddington Rindert took a wrong turn. He was jet-lagged and bemused by the bustle and size of the place. He always felt slightly inadequate when he visited Europe, particularly London. Just so many damn people. It set him on edge. He'd read somewhere that just walking through Piccadily underground one inhaled sufficient discarded skin cells to coat an entire human body.

He was thinking about how many human skin cells he might have involuntarily inhaled on the Speedlink and was hoping that there weren't too many ones with eczema when he took the wrong turn.

The wrong turn took him into a Dickensian alley. Slimed cobbles. Piled and leaking sacks of rubbish. Shadows. Victorian London. Yech.

"Wrong turn," muttered Rindert. The alley smelled old, rancid and unkind. Bleak, windowless walls of brick rose sheer above him. A nation of chimney pots, someone had said, or words to that effect. Rindert felt a sudden pang and a yearning for the wide clean skies of Africa.

"Wrong turn's right, white boy," said a large black man emerging from behind the rubbish bags. A second runty man with bad teeth followed him out.

"Dear heaven, is there no end to it?" Rindert thought, reaching instinctively for a pistol that wasn't there.

"Are you political?" he asked. Rindert had in times past followed orders. In a number of ugly campaigns. If these people were political he might have a serious fight on his hands. It wasn't likely, he realized. Not likely at all. He relaxed.

The two men laughed. Laughed like apes! All mouth, teeth, nervous eyes. Jumpy as hell.

"Never touch politics, mate. We're into honest living. We two here are muggers. So you hand over your valuables, white boy, or I'll cut you." The man produced a switchblade and began to flick it about.

No, not political, thought Rindert. Just poorly armed. And rude. White boy! He wasn't going to take that.

The mugger continued to flick his knife.

"What are you planning to do with that thing, man? Butter me?"

"Funny," said the large mugger, the one with the muscles and the Snoop Doggy Dogg T-shirt. "But we're here on business."

The smaller one laughed and looked increasingly mean. Always watch the small ones, thought Rindert; they've so much more to prove.

"Look, man," Rindert said, "I don't want nonsense." He didn't. He really didn't.

"You're fucking South African," said the small one, finally placing the accent. "You racist bastard!"

"You called me white boy! What's that? Affirmative action?" said Rindert. "No, it is not affirmative action. It's fucking racist. One, I'm not a boy. Two, I'm not white. I'm red. It's called fucking sunburn! And three, if you two kaffirs don't get out of the way right now, I'll stamp you out."

The big guy was now looking doubtful. This wasn't proving to be an easy hit and he'd heard bad things about South Africans. But the little guy wouldn't let the matter drop. He twitched with energy.

Rindert sighed, placed his suitcase on the grime of the cobbles, suggested that they come and get it. When they came to get it, he gave it to them. Little one first. The big bastard made a run for it when he saw what had happened to his partner-in-crime. Rindert used a rugby tackle then slammed the guy's head into the wall. Bricks were dislodged.

He then searched their pockets, where he found an extraordinary £310 in notes and a huge number of coins, as well as materials wrapped in plastic that were obviously drugs, and a sharpened screwdriver that was no longer any use as a screwdriver.

"You see, what gets me down is the way this sort of nonsense never stops," Rindert told the two semi-conscious muggers who were, unwisely, beginning to pout and sputter obscenities. "You've got all this money, you're well nourished, you've got plenty of drugs, why the hell don't you count your blessings? Drive a train or some damn thing, work in a bank? There's decent, honest people in Africa with nothing. Nothing!"

In a sudden fury Rindert stamped on the two muggers' reproductive organs.

The stamps were too hard and too punishing to produce howls or commotion on the part of the stamped. Just gagging and nausea. Rindert then launched a volley of kicks that rendered them insensible. He then beat the little guy a bit more. "You racist little kaffir shit!" was the parting verdict.

Rindert liked black people. When they were good they were the best. When they misbehaved, like anyone from white to brown to Eskimo, they deserved a vigorous kicking. That was his philosophy.

The two bodies he buried among bulging black rubbish bags.

"Damn nonsense never stops," he muttered as he took their money, drugs, sharpened screwdriver and coins.

Still, every cloud ... Rindert thought, as he left the alley, took the right turn and approached the rank of phones. £310 plus change wasn't a bad return on three minutes' work.

And with his newly acquired coins he wouldn't need to waste time queuing at WH Smiths to break a note for the call he intended to make.

* * *

It was August, high summer in Japan, and the humidity was thick enough to scrape off your cheek and flick into the corner where it would land with a splat. Tokyo was choking in car fumes beneath low, jaundiced clouds. The typhoon season was just close enough to excite hopes for a crack in the skies, but not nearly close enough to do any good.

In a stifling room with a claustrophobically low ceiling, above a computer sales shop in the Tokyo electronics district of Akihabara, four damp men were sitting wreathed in cigarette smoke, listlessly sipping bitter green tea. Sweat stained their shirts. The room, charitably stated, stank.

The men were all members of Aum Shinrikyo's "government". They were waiting for the Science Minister. And what they had to tell him was not going to make the Science Minister happy.

It had been a mixed year for Aum Shinrikyo (now renamed Aleph). The computer business that sustained the cult was thriving despite the current recession and recent media outrage following the revelation that government ministries, including the Defence Agency, had been unwittingly using Aum's software. Recruitment, which had dropped to a trickle in the aftermath of the Sarin gas attack, was once more up, with some 1,500 members for life in twenty-six centres nationwide.

But with the cult guru Shoko Asahara facing a death sentence (or, if he was extremely lucky, a life sentence of solitary in Abashiri), there was a perceptible lack of direction creeping in. What was needed was a morale boost. A success.

And success was not what was waiting to greet the Science Minister.

On the table were news clippings from the Asahi Shimbun, the Mainichi Shimbun, the Yomiuri Shimbun, and several local papers. Also video clips from broadcasts on NHK, the Japanese national media service. The news that two Japanese humanitarian aid workers in Sierra Leone had been killed by a landmine had just broken in Japan. Now the media had their teeth in the story and had flown correspondents into Freetown from Nairobi. There was every indication that there was going to be a press feeding frenzy.

Hardly surprising, given the ingredients of the story, and the death of any Japanese overseas routinely prompted media hysteria.

No-one had linked the two brave deceased doctors to Aum or Aleph.

Yet.

The door opened. In stepped the Aum Science Minister, Hidekazu Chubachi, graduate of the illustrious Todai University, twenty-eight years old, face round, smooth as a peach, and, even by Aum's consistently ambitious standards, a very disturbing man.

"Summarise," said Chubachi brusquely as soon as the ritual bowing was complete and more green tea had been poured.

Aum's Minister of Transport, who had been responsible for the Sierra Leone expedition logistics, and the Minister for Health and Welfare who, along with the Science Ministry, was responsible for developing the covert biological weapons programme necessary for the *Saishu Sen* – the Final Apocalyptic War – exchanged uneasy glances. The Minister of Trade merely looked blank. Ending the world wasn't his brief. His job was to sell computer programmes.

It was the fourth man, the Minister of Media and Telecommunications, who spoke. He had a square, threatening face, with thin lips and brutishly thick eyebrows.

"The two doctors' vehicle is reported to have hit a landmine in the destination village," he said without a trace of emotion in his voice. "Media states variously that they were UN volunteers, or working with the Japanese Organisation to Consider and Counter the Problem of Poverty and Child Welfare in Africa. Two papers have got the country wrong, one placing the incident in neighbouring Liberia, the second placing the incident in Sierra Gabon. Sierra Gabon is not a country at all. The error is typical of Mainichi Shimbun reporting."

The Science Minister snorted impatiently.

"All the papers state that the two doctors had been partially cannibalized and had body parts removed. One paper says that a local radio station covered the story. The radio station is reported as being named Radio Butt Naked. I presume that this is an error. No-one in his right mind would call a radio station Butt Naked."

"Stick to the point," snapped the Science Minister. "Did our researchers make contact with this priest, this Father Jack?"

"We have no information. It might be assumed that they hit the mine prior to making contact. It might conversely be assumed that they met their deaths leaving after a successful contact. The details are unclear."

"What happened to the mercenary? Linda?"

"Linda?"

"Linda, the mercenary."

"Oh, you mean Rindert. We have no definite information. He might have been killed as well. He has not been in contact with us. He was retained by our team in Freetown. To all intents and purposes he has disappeared."

"It could be suggested that not only has Linda disappeared, but that also all the funds that our researchers were carrying have disappeared. We do not know whether our researchers contacted the priest. Have we contacted the priest?"

"We have attempted to resume contact by email but have received no response."

"The priest was offering Ebola," said the Minister of Health and Welfare. "He was also offering additional biological weapons but was vague."

"We are all aware of that," said the Science Minister. "You should make diligent efforts to avoid pointless repetition of facts that we are all aware of. It is a stupid and irritating habit. Are you an eel? A squid?"

The Minister of Health and Welfare shifted uncomfortably in his chair but said nothing.

"The situation is utterly unacceptable," decided the Science Minister. "The situation must be remedied. Someone must go to Sierra Leone to gather the facts and revive our biowarfare programme."

"Someone must be sent to Sierra Leone," said the Minister of Health and Welfare.

"I've just said that. I've also just instructed you to make diligent efforts to avoid pointless repetitions. And what is your response? An immediate pointless repetition."

"I can arrange for a team to depart immediately," said the Minister for Transport, stepping in hastily. "There will be no mistakes this time."

In a pleasantly airy conservatory in Kent, overlooking rose beds and the river Shribble, the phone rang, startling birds from the dangling peanut feeder.

The man who picked it up was wearing slippers, a dressing gown, and had not yet finished his breakfast, which consisted of an obscenely large steak – black on the outside, dripping raw within. Like Campbell, who was phoning him, Doctor Philip Pleasant was a big man who ate big. Like Campbell, Dr Pleasant was also using an assumed name. Unlike Campbell, who was already attracting covertly appraising glances from passing women as he thumbed coins into the Paddington station telephone box, Doctor Pleasant was an eyesore.

Pleasant's ham-like, jowly face had thick, fat lips, and the eyes that were already narrowing in suspicious concentration were chilled; reptilian, pallid blue. Back when he'd worked as scientific advisor with South Africa's shadowy Civil Co-operation Bureau his nickname had been "The Crocodile".

"Campbell Freetown there?" asked Campbell.

"No, I'm afraid not," Dr Pleasant responded with a friendly chuckle that emerged from his impassive, sinister face with engaging sincerity. The face was a fright, but oh, ho, ho! the jolliness, the sheer amiability of the laugh. It had won him friends throughout the village where he now practised medicine. Or maybe it was the cheap fees he charged.

"I think you appear to have the wrong number, I'm sorry to say."

"Really? I was given 020 7498 6248."

"That is a London number."

The call ended.

Dr Pleasant shovelled another chunk of steak into his mouth, shrugged himself out of his dressing gown and into his tweeds, collared his spaniel and set out at a brisk stroll towards the public telephone box across the pristine green beside the Saxon church.

En route he bade a hearty "Good Morning" to Mrs Everance, previously prominent in the now-defunct Anti-Apartheid movement, the bitch. Mrs Everance had once met the evangelical kaffir Boeter, subsequently jailed for embezzling poverty relief funds, the bastard. Mrs Everance was currently an active participant in fundraising for Food For Africa and was planning to visit Prague to urge the IMF to cancel Third World debt, the gullible bloody moron.

"Another lovely day, Doctor," chirped Mrs Everance. "Do you think it will hold for the church fête?"

"Bound to, Mrs Everance," chortled Doctor Pleasant. "After all we've got God on our side."

Despite the beauty of the green, the serenity of the village, someone had scribbled graffiti in the phone box. The part of the phone box you couldn't help noticing when making a call. The part that had the 999 emergency services listed.

"Pleasant is a carp," read the graffiti. "He uses this phone too much." Someone else had added, in a different rather fussy hand, "Last call. Don't you have a phone to go to?"

This wasn't funny. Quite the reverse. It was precisely the sort of petty lawlessness that led to further trouble in Dr Pleasant's opinion. And he looked nothing like a carp.

He dialled the number Campbell had given him, frowning thunderously at the graffiti.

Campbell picked up on the first ring.

"Name?"

"Sayuri Amada."

"Occupation?"

"Solly?"

"Occupation?" Jim, the immigration official asked again with a bright and careless smile, all the while tapping passport details into his computer and wondering whether it was worth giving Valerie from the cafeteria a call. He'd got tickets for a Bach concert at the Albert Hall. Question was, would Valerie think a man who liked Bach was a proto-geriatric? Or would Valerie regard him as a cultured individual worthy of serious attention?

The computer considered the imputted data and responded with alacrity.

All thoughts of Valerie and Bach vanished.

Danger signals. Undesirable alien. Aum Shinrikyo aka Aleph. This was one Japanese citizen Britain apparently didn't need on a tourist visa taking pictures of Big Ben, Stratford-upon-Avon and Peter Rabbit's house. The computer spat out more.

"Ye gods!" thought Jim.

He looked up at the face that was trying to look politely quizzical. Simultaneously he discreetly pressed the panic button that was concealed in the booth. It was a very odd face that was confronting him. Elfinly-pointed chin, broad forehead, with a dark smudge of fine hair above the small mouth and a sort of waxy sheen about the skin. The whole thing looked misaligned, awry. Not an odd face, the immigration officer decided, a horrid face.

With an effort he kept his own expression pleasantly neutral. But his palms were sweating.

"Occupation? Job? Are you an office lady? An OL, isn't that what you call it in Japan?"

"I am a zoo-keeper," said Sayuri Amada.

"Really? How astoundingly interesting," said Jim glancing along the lines of passengers from the British Airways direct flight from Narita. Armed police were beginning to coalesce like genies at the exits.

Most of the passengers waiting in line to clear immigration were still oblivious to the fact that something was wrong. Two oriental men in the same line as Sayuri Amada, however, were clearly becoming agitated. Their faces were also inherently peculiar. Jim had seen Todd Browning's film, *Freaks*. And he hadn't enjoyed it much. If there was ever going to be a remake the two men would romp through auditions. No difficulties at all.

"Is there a probrem?" asked Sayuri Amada.

"No, not at all," said Jim, thinking that he had to keep this going, give his security people time. "You've picked the right time of year to visit, Miss Amada. The weather's set fair for at least the next ten days. Bar a bit of rain this weekend in Kent."

The computer had warned that Aum Shinrikyo aka Aleph used nerve gas. It had advised the exercise of extreme caution. Was this Amada creature packing gas? Would nerve gas show up in the normal hand luggage screenings? Jim had honestly no idea. Probably not. How, he wondered, would you train a sniffer dog to sniff out nerve gas? One successful sniff and the dog would be history. Bye bye basset. He fought a bizarre urge to laugh.

"How long are you planning to stay, Miss Amada?" he managed. The urge to laugh had now been superseded by the urge to collapse.

"One night. I fry to Sierra Leone tomorrow."

Fry? *Fry?* Why were these people always getting their ls and their rs confused? Sometimes they'd get it right. Then they'd get it wrong. No logic to it. Was it a genetic thing? Physiological? Jim's heart was thumping like a hammer. Why, he wondered, as if observing himself from somewhere else, was he worrying about something so trivial?

"Ah," Jim said. "Sierra Leone. That should be nice. Part of the world I've not got round to visiting yet. Always meant to. But there's usually a war on."

Christ, he thought, I'm babbling.

At the next desk someone from Latvia was explaining that she had come to England to enrol at a cooking college in Croydon but that the college had not sent her a letter of confirmation. Or if they had, the letter had not reached her as she had moved house recently because her father and mother were getting a divorce. The immigration official was asking whether she could supply the college's name and phone number. And saying that if she could show a return ticket it would be helpful.

Typical Heathrow immigration rubbish. Complex. Inane. Commonplace. And here, instead of an entrepreneurial Latvian prostitute trying to slip into the country pretending she wanted to learn how to cook fish and chips, was a poison gas-wielding cultmaniac. Stuck at *his* desk. While armed response units slipped off safety catches. Jim felt faint. He also felt vaguely ridiculous. A potential nerve gas attack. On his shift. Right under his nose.

"Is there a problem?" Amada repeated. Sweat was beading on her broad forehead and her body was beginning to shake. You and me both, thought Jim. Amada began fiddling, looking for something in her handbag.

"No, no problem," said Jim, thinking, no, no, *no*! The handbag!

Security guards finally – *finally!* – closed in. Smooth, easy, Amada was blanketed, walked trembling away, her hands held very tight, her handbag held very cautiously by a white-faced policeman.

Glad that's over thought Jim, collapsing onto his swivel chair.

But it wasn't.

All hell broke loose in the arrivals hall as the police swept after the two other Japanese.

CHAPTER THREE

What Happened at Lalapanzi

The village of Lalapanzi, as Rindert's convoy approached, looked wrong. Wrong in that it looked no way near right.

It was far too attractive. An old, grandiose Catholic Mission was perched on a red rock bluff overlooking a slow green river. The houses that clustered beside the river were, by Sierra Leone's standards, extra-respectable. Their walls were white-washed in the Spanish style. They resembled cakes. They showed none of the usual pockmarks of gun-fire. That in itself was peculiar.

The street, however, while rubbish-free and neat (again damn peculiar), was empty. Somebody had been watering the flowers that glowed in neat little gardens. But there was no smoke rising from cooking fires. No draped laundry drying. No wayward hogs rootling. No drunken men lounging around swigging beer out-side the chop shop. No women doing all the work.

Lalapanzi looked like it was planning on entering a "Nicest Village in the Cape Area" competition.

Pretty, very pretty.

And wrong.

Rindert's neck began to itch.

A stillness, yes, a wrongness, sat on the village like a shroud.

"We'll wait," announced Rindert, scratching at his neck. "We'll wait and watch for a while."

The militia clambered off the Bedford truck and, like the morons they were, began to squat at the road-verge and spark up further joints.

Rindert had seen British paratroops entering Freetown to secure Lungi airport earlier in the year and had felt actually, physically, sick at the sight of their discipline, their efficiency, their well-maintained equipment. If Rindert had a force like that to command, this foul little war wouldn't have got beyond day two. Rindert yearned for that sort of manpower. Immediate discipline, immediate response. Instead he had the rubbish that was smoking itself into sufficient courage to engage in action.

Benjamin Franklin, who alone had remained in the truck, said, "There's something bad here. I am thinking that it is a bad place. Abandoned by God."

Rindert took a long look at Franklin. His black sweat-beaded face reminded Rindert of a Shoveller duck. There was something about the way his nose turned up. And he needed to lose the top hat. It was frankly ridiculous. But there was something about Franklin that muttered potential.

"Benjamin," said Rindert, "if I had a real army, I'd want you in it. Take the glasses and watch the street. Anything moves, let me know. I'm off to speak to our clients."

Rindert hopped easily out of the truck and walked towards Sato and Suzuki, who sat impassive in their car, video whirring.

Franklin's words played again in his head.

Abandoned by God. Abandoned by God.

Sato's real name was Toru Fukuchi, and he'd been a member of Aum Shinrikyo since the cult's establishment in 1987.

He watched the burly mercenary as he approached, stopped, kicked one of his men in the head said something that made everybody – even the man he had just kicked in the head – laugh. It was appalling. Why couldn't he do things like that? He knew that if he tried the same thing he'd be kicked back. He *knew* it. The blacks knew it too. He could sense their contempt when they stared at him with their foul, gorilla eyes.

The mercenary was coming. Huge. Fleshy. Repulsive. Like a slab of sweating meat.

Fukuchi's heart thumped with horror at the impending confrontation. Dealing with foreigners always filled him with a sick revulsion. He was not confident with his English, could not be sure that what he said was what he meant to be understood, and loathed the loss of control.

He also hated and feared foreigners. He would actually shake with terror sometimes. His knees would wobble. Once he'd been stopped by a blonde girl in Harajuku who'd asked him how to get to Sensoji. He'd wet his pants and stumbled mutely away, flapping his hands in shame. He knew this *gaijin* complex was a dreadful weakness. He should be stronger than these hateful *gaijin*. He was weak. He knew that. He had studied under the leader Shoko Asahara to be strong. He had survived the burning baths at the cult's compound at Kamikuishiki village that the guru had said were needful for cleansing weakness. The temperatures in the baths had been hell.

He had put one doubter caught escaping from Kamikuishiki into the cult's microwave facility and had personally thrown the switch and watched her die. The power he had felt then had been electric, glorious – like a halo embracing him in its purifying holy glow.

But still he was frightened of foreigners. Especially big ones with guns. Even when he was paying them.

The white man was now at his window, tapping at it to make him wind it down. Tapping at his window, as if *he*, Fukuchi, was a traffic offender, parked in the wrong place.

Fukuchi, decided that it was time to be strong.

"We don't wait, Linda!"

"Linda?" The mercenary looked confused.

Why did the mercenary have all his hair? Fukuchi thought irrelevantly but furiously, when Fukuchi's hair was going and not going well? He'd spent a fortune on hair sprays that claimed to restore hair. No results. Fukuchi smashed at his mosquito welts, ground his teeth.

The mercenary was still tapping at the window.

"You! Linda! We enter town now! You follow! We pay for you. We will lead!"

"Wind the window down properly. We can't talk like this. I can't hear you."

" Right now!" Fukuchi shouted. The mercenary did not look perturbed, showed no reaction. No fear. No respect.

"I've killed thirteen people!" yelled Fukuchi in Japanese. This wasn't true. At least thirty wavering cultists had been killed since the founding of Aum Shinrikyo, but Fukuchi had only killed one of them. The one he had microwaved.

"I'm on an important mission." That was true. The Science Minister had stressed that he come back successful or not at all.

Fukuchi was aware that his colleague with the video camera was staring at him strangely. But still filming. *Filming his humiliation.*

"I'm here expected."

Rindert merely looked irritated, then smiled at Fukuchi; and Fukuchi, defeated, furious, floored the accelerator and the Hi-Lux roared into life and shot like a bullet into Lalapanzi.

Where it hit the biggest landmine incident Rindert had ever seen.

TELEPHONE CONVERSATION (I)

Dr Pleasant: Then what?

Campbell: No idea what they thought they were doing. They just took off. Their Hi-Lux was fine. Then – bang! – the car shot up I'd say twenty feet, then did a spin and hit another mine, bounced off that and hit another. We're talking big mines here – anti-tank stuff. We just watched the bloody bakkie bounce from one mine to another like a firecracker. It was dancing down the street.

Dr Pleasant: No?

Campbell: Yes. You just didn't know where it was going to stop banging about, the tyres flew off as if they were, hell, acrobats or something. One of the Japs went out through the door and his backside was on fire. You know what the Japs are like on hygiene; I guess it was some sort of hair spray, ant spray, freshen the air spray, whatever the hell, in his bum bag or his pockets. He made it through that whole bloody inferno and then he's out of the door with his arse on fire and these aerosols, I'd guess they were, just went off one after the other. And he's flying down the street, seriously on fire now and ...

Dr Pleasant: What happened next?

Campbell: You wouldn't believe what happened next.

Dr Pleasant: Go on.

Campbell: Well, I put the Japanese guy down.

Dr Pleasant: You shot him?

Campbell: Sure. It was a kindness. He was on fire. He was exploding. Over. The guy's aerosols were going off in his safari trousers ...

Dr Pleasant: I hear you. It's funny. But Rindert, I'm not interested in the war stories. What happened next? How can I be of help?

Campbell: I'm getting to that. Like I said, you wouldn't believe what happened next ...

CHAPTER FOUR

Father Jack

Father Jack was in the Lalapanzi Mission drinking warm Cape brandy straight from the bottle when he heard the detonations. He was a tall man with long, curly orange hair tied back in a pony-tail and acne-mottled features. Hook-nosed, stoop-shouldered, he would have made a very passable Fagin had his talents and inclinations led him to the stage.

Neither had. Instead they had led him via a circuitous and untidy route to temporary exile in this West African village, and, from the sound of explosions, further trouble.

Although he affected the robes of a catholic priest, and was known to those few that were aware of his existence as Father Jack, he was in fact an Irish biochemist, born Robert Snoade. Indeed, he was a particularly brilliant biochemist who had graduated with a double first from Oxford and then vanished from sight following police investigations into a series of random pigeon poisonings (field tests of a chemical he was developing) and animal mutilations (illegally conducted vivisections) in the London area.

The police had not found the human remains buried in the back garden of Jack's detached house in Muswell Hill, but Jack had felt instinctively that it was time to take his vision and experiments elsewhere.

Somewhere he could lay his hands on the necessary body parts to pursue his alchemical researches without attracting unwelcome official attention.

Sierra Leone was an obvious choice. He'd toyed with the idea of Colombia or the Peruvian altiplano but didn't speak Spanish. Somalia? Too Islamic. Jack was fond of his drink. And Somalia was dry. In every sense of the word. Also he hated Muslims.

Sierra Leone had put in a brief, and what he'd thought at the time, fortuitous appearance on his television screen while he'd been sifting his overseas options. The images he'd seen had immediately appealed. Anarchy, anglophone (mostly), a port that was still functioning enabling the shipment of his equipment, maiming and dismemberment on a rampant scale and no-one in the international community giving a hoot. Great beaches, too!

Sierra Leone. The more he researched, the better he liked it. Where else in the world could one get hold of so many fresh cadavers? Hook up with voodoo practitioners? Do whatever the hell you wanted? Break the laws of heaven and earth both, without the slightest whiff of police interest? Sierra Leone. Land of opportunity!

Or so he had reasoned when he'd booked passage on the Liberian-registered tramp freighter in Liverpool after forging letters of recommendation from a church in County Cork and hooking up with a missionary group via the Internet. A rather desperate-sounding group of missionaries ...

By good fortune their resident priest had just passed away at a place called Lalapanzi. Jack had rechecked the map. Lalapanzi wasn't even on it.

Established Mission. Decent facilities. Workshop. Operating theatre. Cold storage. Solar power. All mod cons.

And in the beyond of the back of the back of the fucking beyond!

"Yes!" Jack had crowed and punched air with a delighted, distinctly unclerical fist.

"Perfect."

The missionaries, while clearly delighted with their job applicant's references and enthusiasm to assume the post, had been vague about the circumstances surrounding the creation of the job vacancy. Jack subsequently learned that the priest had been machine-gunned by a drug-crazed RUF cadre while assisting at a birth.

Things hadn't gone quite as smoothly as Jack had anticipated. It had taken him almost three months to come up with an effective way to kill all his co-workers, take supreme control of the Lalapanzi Mission and organize the delivery of all the equipment he needed.

And that had been the easy bit.

Outside there was another explosion.

He could have gone anywhere, they'd told him when they'd awarded him his double first. And how right they had been, he reflected. He'd gone straight down the toilet. Ended up in this wild west cesspit But he'd be back, God willing, he'd be back. And soon. With results.

More explosions. Father Jack dropped the bottle, hurried to the window and looked down across the river at the main street.

"Ah, for the love of Mary," Father Jack squawked incredulously, "will ya just look at that turkey!"

The turkey he referred to was the blazing Fukuchi. Another aerosol detonated with a jet of flame.

" You're three days early, you dimwit!" yelled Jack, beside himself with fury. The burning Jap represented financial possibilities that went beyond grandiose and into the field of dreams. And there he was exploding, the stupid, yellow bollix. "I was expecting you in three days," Jack yelled superfluously after throwing open the windows. "If I'd known you were coming today I'd have cleared the road."

The wailing figure continued its doomed stampede.

"Your arse is on fire, man. Get in the river."

A gunshot rang out. Fukuchi fell flat. On a landmine. And shot up and over the river, out of sight.

Jack wiped sweat from his eyes, bitterly regretted dropping the brandy and sized up the scene. One ex-four-by-four, what the South Africans referred to as a bakkie; one ex-Japanese cultist, charbroiled; a bunch of blacks howling with laughter at the street entrance; one Bedford truck that looked like an unsuccessful entry in a demolition derby; one white mercenary. One sniper's rifle pointed at him.

It looked like white flag time. That and an utter fucking fiasco.

"Don't shoot," yelled Jack. "I'm coming down to you. Don't shoot. Don't enter the village. Under no circumstances enter the village. You must not alarm them."

"Alarm who?" yelled the merc.

"I'll explain. Just stay exactly where you are. It's more than your life's worth to come into the village."

"And don't shoot me," Jack added again.

He hurried for the door, exited the Mission, waded the ford and took an un-mined side street towards the visitors.

Dark eyes watched his progress from the shadows of the doorways. Chemical steam drifted in the air. They were whistling. Low piping whistles. They did that when they were getting agitated. It was an uncanny sound, and as always when he heard it, Jack felt a queasy knot of fear in his stomach. He had very much meddled with things man was meant to leave alone. And was under no illusions as to the potential consequences.

Perhaps, he thought, perhaps there are more Japs in the other truck, perhaps we can still deal, then I can make some real money and get the hell out of here.

Before the wheels really fall off.

Not a remotely religious man, despite being raised in the close bosom of the Faith by his prehistoric moron of a mother and doing full duty as an altar boy, Father Jack surprised himself by finding that he was praying as he hurried forward. Praying. Praying.

CHAPTER FIVE

The Homunculus

Rindert, like many men who have walked the darker paths of sub-Saharan Africa and lived and worked and fought and talked among the tribes, was no stranger to the supernatural. As a boy growing up on a failing cattle farm in Kwazulu, he'd heard the throb of drums at night, the pulse of a distant village's "muti", low and thrumming and potent in the sweet, dangerous dark. Muti. Literally translated into English as "medicine". But much more than that.

When he was five years old, three of the farm-hands just withered. The withering had affected only half of their faces. That was all. Half the face was young; with smooth, beautiful black skin and a swivelling, healthy eye, like the eye of a young bullock being led to the slaughter and sensing that there is terrible danger. The other halves of the labourers' faces crinkled like prunes overnight. The eyes grew milky and died. None of the men could speak. Half of their tongues resembled dried meat. Biltong, Rindert had thought sickly. The other half, pink and healthy, struggled and flapped. Eventually, all of them were taken by Oom Piet into the bush. Shots were heard. The cook was then led into the bush.

No shot was heard, but the cook never came back. Oom Piet said that she had gone to visit relatives in Mozambique. No-one said it but all knew. She had quarrelled bitterly with the three men. No-one said it, but all knew. She'd been a witch. Bad bloody muti indeed.

Just eight years old, he'd seen a zombie walking in bright day-light by the bank of a creek where he was fishing and trying to light an illicit cigarette that he'd lifted from a packet left by his faded, unhappy mother, who secretly drank and was even then becoming forgetful.

It had been a hot December day. So hot. Bright sun. The creek had been serene. Beautiful and a place of refuge. Then there'd been the crack of a branch snapping. He'd thought at first it was his uncle, drawn by the smoke, and he'd desperately thrown the cigarette into the creek and feared for a whipping.

The zombie had come out of the bush, a small thin black girl, face caked in chalky powder, eyes rolled up to the whites, wrapped in a pale shawl. He'd seen her – it – tread blind but sure-footed down to the creek. Then he'd seen the terrifying, silent fig-ure step out onto the water and cross it without sinking or even making a ripple on the surface. It crossed the creek, entered thorn scrub on the far side, and was gone. Later, after he'd fled wailing to the knees of Oom Piet – big fat, bearded, uncle Piet – later still, after he'd been beaten for telling lies and smelling of tobacco and had calmed, Oom Piet had gathered the white men from the three neighbouring farms and they'd gone off into the bush, grim-faced, armed with guns and Oom Piet's bible.

The subsequent police investigation into the burning of the hut on Witboi Kloof revealed that the victims were sixteen. One old man and fifteen girls. The police seemed satisfied that a kid-napper had been brought to justice by persons unknown. No-one thought much of a killing like that in those days and those parts. Not if was just kaffirs doing the killing and the being killed. It was their way.

Much later, Oom Piet had told Rindert that the girls had been dead for many months but had still stumbled in the flames and ignored his bullets. The old man, too, wrapped in skins and gourds and reptile skulls, had rushed about and waved his arms long after he should have stopped and died. They'd all reeled and

swayed before finally being overwhelmed by the fire and crum-
bling into final ash. Oom Piet had finished the story, so long
untold. He'd apologized for beating Rindert. Then said that it was
necessary for Rindert to know that there was a devil. For that was
proof of God.

By that time, Oom Piet had been wobbling along the plank
towards the final drop into senility, Rindert's mother dead, and
Rindert training with the Recces for special operations against the
communist enemies of the Republic. Rindert had listened to the
old dying man, stored the information away for future use, then
thrown himself into the war for the survival of his threatened
homeland. It hadn't been a dream, he hadn't been lying about the
dead girl walking, the zombie. He was glad that Oom Piet knew
that. He'd always known it himself.

He'd bumped into the supernatural repeatedly since that time,
seen things that defied science, defied nature. In Benin, there'd
been a sorcerer follower of the god Koku who slept suspended
upside-down, like a bat, from a banyan tree in a village square.
Any normal guy doing that, well his head would blow from blood
pressure. Not the Koku man. For the whole week Rindert had
been in the area the figure had dangled, its face smeared with
orange fat; two dead owls, also upside down, beside it. Once,
while setting landmines in Rhodesia with Rob's Raiders, an old
crone had ridden past on the back of a hyena. There'd been other
incidents.

Like the killing and the living rough, Rindert had adjusted to the
hidden twists of Africa. The otherworld, the witchery, simply *was*.
All the hymns and bibles and missionaries in the world couldn't
change it. Rindert had learned to take whatever his native continent
could throw at him and, when possible, put it to use.

Which is why he did not shriek, flee or go insane when he met
what the two Japanese had really been invited to see in Sierra
Leone. And which is why things turned out so badly for so many
and so well for so many more.

He met the thing in Father Jack's study. Jack called it a homunculus.

It was still the day of the exploding Hi-Lux and their arrival at Lalapanzi, but the sun was now waning.

The Kamajor militiamen, under the command of the top-hatted Baptist Benjamin Franklin, were bivouacked half a mile from the village entrance at Father Jack's suggestion.

When Rindert questioned the necessity of sending his men away when there was apparently plenty of accommodation in the village, the Irishman had loudly talked about anti-tank mines and then slyly muttered that there were things in Lalapanzi that it was best the niggers did not see. Intrigued, Rindert had shrugged and issued his orders.

Rindert had had to enforce them with a minimum of violence, the men still being in good humour after the Hi-Lux mine affair and the exploding Japanese in the safari trousers. Rindert had raised the troops' morale further by handing out a few of the less charred dollar bills that he had recovered from his late clients' top pockets.

True, "bivouacked" was just another way of saying most of his men were lying around in clouds of weed smoke, slapping bugs and reminiscing about their conquest of the late Abraham Lincoln and other excitements. But basically the militia was quiescent. The Baptists among them (and they'd started the trip with three but now had two new converts) were painting more boards for the necks of RUF "rebs". Non-Baptists were whittling stakes designed for unwitting RUF rectums. Franklin, when Rindert had left him, had his earnest Shoveller-duck face stuck against the sights of an RPG. It was one of four that Rindert currently possessed.

The road was as secure as secure could be Rindert had decided, assuming Franklin didn't forget how to pull the bloody RPG's trigger.

Now Rindert and Jack were in the Mission in the priest's office and dust motes were drifting in the red glow of the dying sun.

Immense possibilities were dancing in Rindert's head like mutant sugar plums. Possibilities that were utterly profound. That could shape the world.

They were not alone, but the third figure in the room wasn't a man. At all.

The homunculus had been partially cobbled together with human body parts (of various ethnic extractions, mostly black but quite a bit of catholic missionary white). It was bipedal, had two arms, a torso and a head but thereafter all resemblance to mankind ceased.

In place of a nose, a small copper tube jutted from the blackened leathery bladder that was its face. Just as Abraham Lincoln had said, a wisp of greenish, chemical smoke was drifting whimsically from the tube.

There were coils of wire, cogs tucked here and there, and what resembled a fan belt whirring slowly around its neck.

"Solar-powered," Jack had explained. "Small cell, keeps it going real well. You think of the global consequences of the internal combustion engine and it makes you really think."

Rindert had said, "Yes. Yes, it certainly does."

"This is eco-friendly."

Rindert had had another long hard stare at the abomination and was pretty sure that Greenpeace wouldn't be endorsing it at any time in the near future as a solution to global warming.

The thing's feet were well-oiled wheels with bone nubs for brakes. The eyes glittered and rolled and twinkled and swam in their sockets. They were very confusing eyes indeed. For reasons unknown – perhaps to prevent personal contact? – it was wrapped with several strands of barbed copper wire.

The whole thing didn't stand more than four feet tall. It looked like a nightmare.

"Are you OK with it?" That had been Father Jack's first

question. The man had led Rindert into the Mission, a small cob-web-filled chapel overseen by sorrowful gaudy statues of saints, and poured him a huge brandy. He'd hovered around, shooting nervous glances at his guest, then started to wrap his wrists with his hands and shift his weight from one leg to another. It reminded Rindert of two things. Some Jew he'd seen in a film about orphans and pickpockets. Just before the Jew had been hung. And a man queuing for a crap.

He'd finished his brandy and said, "If you want a crap, go away and do it. If not cut to the chase or I'm off."

That had decided Jack. He'd led Rindert to his study and introduced him to the horrific occupant.

"Are you OK with it?" Jack had asked again, his voice hitching with anxiety.

"Tell me about it."

"It's called a homunculus. It does what it's told. I made it. That's to say, it's a collaboration."

"You and who?"

"You wouldn't know him," Jack had said jumpily. Rindert had immediately known that Jack had regretted making the collaboration remark.

"Tell me anyway. Just for the fun of it."

Father Jack had watched the merc and decided not to tell too many lies.

"Papa Det," he'd said. "He's a porroh man."

"I know," Rindert had said flatly. Papa Det was a name to conjure with in Sierra Leone. A mad, shadowy bastard, apparently a graduate of Princetown before he'd come back to his native Sierra Leone and sailed far too far up Conrad's river and into the Heart of Darkness. Papa Det – the black hand behind one of the nastier magical secret societies that flourished in the bush. If one tenth of the things Rindert had heard about Papa Det was true, the porroh man was big bad news. It was even rumoured that he was no longer alive. Not in the conventional sense of the word.

"We ... er ... put our heads together so to speak," Jack had said. "African porroh, biochemistry, alchemy. Lateral thinking. It all came together and that, my dear sir, is the result."

"What's the point?" Rindert had asked.

Jack had explained. When he'd finished, Rindert grunted, thought and drank more brandy.

"You're sitting on a gold mine," Rindert said eventually, after deciding that the thing's head resembled a psychotic prune. "Not true," he added. "*We're* sitting on a gold mine." He moved his rifle meaningfully.

Jack nodded doubtfully. "I hear you. I was planning to soak the Japs 15,000 a unit."

Rindert could not quite believe it.

"15,000 US dollars?"

"Pounds," said Jack with a shake of his head. He winked cleverly.

"Are you a moron?" asked Rindert. The homunculus began to emit a low sibilant whistle. Rindert settled back into his chair.

"The pound's good," droned Jack. "Always will be, so long as we don't join this Euro project. If they'd called it a shilling or, I don't know, a florin or something reassuring, then investors wouldn't find the new coin so worrying."

The man, thought Rindert, *is* a moron. A twisted genius, but a go-for-broke, babe-in-the-woods, capital-M moron.

"£15,000 plus change is what I was getting for shepherding those two Japanese freaks you just blew up. It's nothing! If these units are as good as you seem to think, we're talking millions. Utter, total unthinking obedience, you said? They'll follow any orders? Just like that?"

Jack nodded.

"Water the flowers, sweep the streets, manufacture a bicycle, build landmines, kill, explode. Whatever you tell them to do they do it. And they – er – innovate. They reason. In a sort of a way."

"Unquestioning obedience," said Rindert, his eyes shining.

Rindert now was thinking aloud.

"The military applications are enormous, but it's not stopping there. You could use these – what do you call them, homunculuses? – for anything. Mining work. The diamond mines here. Theft not a problem. Twenty-four-hour-a-day labour. Cave-ins? Who gives a shit? They just dig themselves out, right? And if they can't, no-one's died. You've just lost a unit." Rindert's mind was humming. He felt that the world had become a place of intense, extraordinary opportunities and expeditious solutions.

"Assassinations. I know more than a few who'd order one right now for a hundred grand to take out Mugabe. It would be the best thing to happen to Africa since the Tanzanians kicked out Amin."

Jack gulped brandy. Perhaps things were going to work out after all. The merc sounded plausible and enthused. More to the point, he hadn't freaked when he'd seen the homunculus. Just blinked. Any normal man would have run like shite, or gone into a screaming fit. This Rindert, though, he'd just asked for another brandy and taken the thing in his stride.

Most impressive of all, though, was that it had only taken him five minutes before he was talking money.

Jack himself had never been too good with finances. Stuck largely to the creative stuff.

"You were going to sell each unit to the Japanese for £15,000?" Rindert repeated reaching for his brandy balloon. He did it without losing control of the pistol that he now held in his other hand. The rifle was tucked under the chair.

"I offered them Ebola to get them here. Then I was going to show them the units," said Jack. "Aum Shinrikyo's loaded by all accounts. Stuff like this, too, it's just up their street. They're lateral thinkers when it comes to weapons. You know they were working on an earthquake machine? The Tesla Electromagnetic Pulse? Plasma weapons, too."

Not only did Rindert not know, but he didn't care.

"What has history taught us about the Japanese?" he bore on in.

"They work hard?" said Jack, looking puzzled.

Rindert dismissed the comment. "They buy one unit of anything and then they copy it! No respect for patents, the Japanese. None. You'll have them running these units of yours off some factory floor and selling them to the Chinese and then the Chinese'll start copying them too. Do you want the whole world overrun with these units of yours?"

Rindert stood and paced.

"No, I've got a better idea. And I know just the man to help us put it together. He used to work with RSA's Civil Co-operation Bureau."

"Sounds an interesting man," said Father Jack, meaning it. Some of the results of CCB's experiments into inducing sex changes on homosexuals had been incorporated in Jack's own work.

He hesitated. "Do the same thing, then?" he suggested. "Promise him Ebola or some virus to spark his interest, get him over here then show the units?"

"I don't know why you keep harping on about Ebola. Anyway, knowing him he's already got some in his fridge. And he won't leave England if he can help it. He's paranoid about safety. He was body bombing SWAPO terrorists from aircraft over the Skeleton Coast – fly 'em out, nice little debrief, then chuck 'em out at 5,000 feet for the bronzies."

"Bronzies?" Jack was confused.

"Bronze whalers. Sharks. Skeleton Coast's lousy with them. He did some chemical stuff – muscle relaxants to induce asphyxiation, poisoned the wells at Dobra, used to hang with Eugene de Kock out at Vlaakplaas, designing exploding Sony Walkmans, all kinds of mad shit. He steps foot back on African soil and there's a couple of million people who'd stick him straight up against a wall."

Jack blinked owlishly as the setting rays of the sun caught his face turning it the colour of blood.

"If he won't come here then what's the use?"

"Well he's not what you'd call conventional, but he's well connected. Knows a lot of people who'd like your units a lot. He's always been interested in this kind of thing. Spooky stuff. He had a bunch of Inkatha witchdoctors on his team. Curses. He was researching curses for use against the ANC. And I know for a fact that some of his chemical work was pure muti. Porroh. Yes, The Croc's our man.'

Jack leered drunkenly. "That gets it said," he said.

"You on the phone here?"

"Was," said Father Jack with a suddenly dejected expression. "Had email too. That's how I rustled up the Japs. The system packed in though. Lightning strike. Blew my computer too."

Rindert pondered on this one. He'd probably have to go to England. Phone up The Croc, maybe meet him in person, buy communications gear, a satellite telephone. But the thought of leaving this red-headed Frankenstein and his potentially priceless homunculuses in the area unguarded was unsettling. General Butt Naked might decide to swing through. Anything could go wrong. He reached a decision.

Who dares wins. He would go to England, contact Dr Pleasant, sell him on the idea, pick up a sat-phone, then get out. Quick and smooth. Leave his men here to guard the road. Speed. If everything went well, he'd be back in Lalapanzi within the week.

And if the whole deal collapsed in anarchy and flames, well, it wouldn't be the first time in Rindert's experience.

He outlined his proposal to the priest who had just one objection.

"It's your niggers," said Father Jack. "Send them away. They see the homunculi and the word's out. It's why I set the mines."

Rindert disliked the word nigger. It was all-inclusive. Implied lazy thinking. Just because someone was black didn't mean they should automatically be called a nigger. It was discourteous. But the priest had a point. This thing needed keeping quiet.

"I'll have a word with my corporal. Tell him Lalapanzi's one hundred per cent mined, off limits, verboten. You'll be safe while I'm away?"

"Safe you say? Have another look at that," said Father Jack, pointing at the homunculus, the unit. It steamed away. Its ears twitched. "I've two hundred more and they are currently instructed to do just two things. Obey me. And look after myself and no other man living."

Rindert changed the subject. "So how do you make a homunculus?"

"Alchemy. Porroh. Like I said. Lateral thinking."

"And I suppose we're not going to hear much more about that? It'll be your secret?"

"It takes years, Rindert, years. And alliances. I don't think you've got the time."

TELEPHONE CONVERSATION (II)

Dr Pleasant: An auction?

Campbell: Why not?

Dr Pleasant: In Sierra Leone?

Campbell: Why not? The two Belgians are auctioning diamonds in RUF territory. No-one knows. Everyone knows. Top dollar.

Dr Pleasant: I want some field tests before I'm even taking this seriously. It sounds ... well, you must know how it sounds.

Campbell: I'm still in this bloody telephone box. There's a queue.

Dr Pleasant: Conversation takes time. We'll meet. Do you know The Fox?

Campbell: Last I heard he was in Caracas.

Dr Pleasant: Not that Fox.

After he'd received directions from Dr Pleasant, Campbell left the phone booth for a pub called The Fox. He thought that The

Crocodile was one of the most tedious men he'd ever needed. No sense of humour. Good when it came to chemistry, physics, auctions, but otherwise a man tailor-made for a dumdum bullet in the balls. Some of the stuff he'd got up to in Namibia, Angola and southern Africa was pure loony tunes. Releasing syphilitic mice in black ANC hostels. That business with the blooded feathers and the anti-apartheid mailing lists. The thing he'd done to Jones. Rindert shook his head at the memories as he exited the station.

He hoped The Fox was open and had a room free. Last time he'd been in England every damn pub had been closed and the only grub available an ailing egg sandwich off the Edgware Road, served with a Pakistani's thumb-print in it. Mind, that had been in the dark days of the 1970s. Strikes. Socialism. According to what he'd heard on the BBC World Service, Britain under New Labour was a brave new world nowadays.

CHAPTER SIX

More Bad News

More newspapers on the table in the room above the Akihabara computer warehouse.

The deaths of the two doctors had flared in the Japanese media but had not caught fire, largely because the correspondents despatched to Freetown had deemed the city too dangerous, not to mention uncomfortable, and had returned post-haste to Nairobi after various incidents.

The story had died. Along with three of the freelance journalists. They'd been young, keen, uninformed, a trifle radical, and interested in getting the RUF's side of the story.

The RUF road-block they'd met en route to Freetown had obliged. In spades. After the questions began to annoy Ronald Reagan, who had a splitting hangover (the Japanese had asked how old he was, and "what did he like – sports?"), he had rubbed his bloodshot eyes and snarled an order. The pangas had come out.

Reagan's RUF cadre now owned an enviable array of camera gear, jackets with lots of pockets for lenses, US dollars, outré pornographic *manga* comics, Sony Walkmans, mobile phones, letters from worried mothers, business cards, heroic bandannas of the sort worn by war correspondents, passports.

And testicles. These latter, when dried, would be attached to Reagan's earrings.

So, yes, much to the relief of all present in the room above the Akihabara computer warehouse, *that* story had died.

Whether the latest breaking news would follow suit struck the assembled Aleph ministers as distinctly unlikely.

Two Aleph members detained at London Heathrow for questioning. A third Japanese national in hospital after running amok in the arrivals hall, then taking a suicide capsule.

It was the last thing Aleph needed. *The last.*

"Why?" Chubachi thundered. "Why were they routed through Heathrow? Why the overnight stay? If they'd stayed in the terminal they'd not have needed to clear customs! Who is the idiot, the moron, the monkey who arranged their itinerary? Why didn't the suicide pill work? Answer me that WHY DIDN'T THE SUICIDE PILL WORK? A SIMPLE SUICIDE PILL! SIMPLE. SIMPLE. SIMPLE."

Speckles of foam were accumulating around Chubachi's lips. He stood, he raged, he walked in circles, spitting and clawing at ropes of thickened foamy saliva that hung from his mouth.

The other ministers watched nervously. They were no strangers to Chubachi's pentobarbital-fuelled frenzies.

After a minute of increasingly incoherent screaming, Chubachi fell to the floor wracked by spasms.

The ministers waited for the fit to pass. When it finally did, the Minister for Transport provided answers to the questions.

"There are no direct flights from either Osaka or Narita to Freetown. Freetown is not Guam or Hawaii."

Was this a joke, the other ministers wondered. Was the Minister of Transport making a joke?

"The flight from Heathrow to Conakry to Freetown departs from a different terminal than that which they arrived at. Customs and immigration were an inevitable risk. We selected personnel who we believed were not known life members of Aleph and were not listed on police files with the Public Security Examination Bureau. Our belief was misplaced."

"The two doctors got into Sierra Leone without difficulties following an identical itinerary. It is safe therefore to deduce that their names were not on any list."

"Do not mention those idiots again," hissed Chubachi whose face was still mottled purple and whose chin was still slick with thickened spit. "What utter sea urchins to get blown up and eaten. What monkeys."

"Even a monkey can fall from a tree," ventured the Minister for Transport.

"Your statement is meaningless," howled Chubachi. "You are a meaningless man. A sea cucumber."

He calmed abruptly.

"Email contact with the priest has resulted in no response. All our messages are returned. We must send a further team to ascertain the status of the project, the priest and the weapons that he has developed. Choose operatives who are not on any list. We have people in the Public Security Examination Agency?"

The Intelligence Minister nodded. Aleph had people in every branch of national government as well as in the Japanese Self Defence Force. Some had no idea for whom they worked and from whom they received such large salaries, others were deliberately-placed moles and believers. The majority, though, were blackmail victims or had been deceived into thinking that they were actually *assisting* Japan's intelligence service.

"They must access the computers and update our information on the lists. They must also be reprimanded for their negligence in not doing so before our last team left Japan."

The Minister of Intelligence, who had forgotten to ask them to do that, kept quiet.

"Contact the Russians for logistical support. We want proper security guards, proper protection for our people in the field. We cannot keep losing people like this."

Aleph had expended well in excess of $800 million in payments to senior Russian scientists, politicians and military officials. Oleg Lobov, a Yeltsin crony and confidant, had alone received $100 million.

The Russians could be relied upon to help. They'd do anything for money. And Aleph was not short of money.

"Our people in British detention. Will they talk?"

"Never. The British police are too soft. British police can't even beat their prisoners," said the Minister of Defence. "Our people are too strong for them. They will be eventually repatriated. That is when their police beatings will start. But who are they? Just tourists. What have they done wrong? They're tourists."

"Tourists don't take suicide tablets. Tourists don't go to Sierra Leone. Sierra Leone is not Guam and not Hawaii," said the Minister of Transport.

In the five days that Rindert had been away in England, something had shifted in the atmosphere in Freetown. In recent years, the city had always had a besieged feel to it. It had always been unsafe. Always looked sordid. But despite its gutted buildings and its leaking drains, its frequent blackouts, its reeking piles of garbage, its child prostitutes, it had had, too, a vibrant life about it; there'd been a defiant vitality. Dancing in the ruins. Laughter in the markets.

As his rented truck pulled away from Lungi airport towards the Hotel Bristol, Rindert sensed that there had been a swing in the balance of things, that something was more wrong than usual.

There was a subdued feel to the streets. People hurried. There were no loungers on the pavements. A lot of doors were closed, a lot of shutters barred. There were groups of youths here and there, aimlessly waving guns, shouting and hooting at scuttling passersby.

The truck swerved to avoid a pothole full of rank, green water and passed a gang of five boys beating a man with sticks. Not one of the boys could have been older than twelve, Rindert thought. The man who writhed on the pavement was middle-aged. Rindert noted that his shoes were bright and shiny with polish. The man clearly took pride in his shoes.

The boys with sticks thrashed. The victim writhed.

"Stop the truck," said Rindert. The desperate futility of polishing shoes in the shit-smeared streets of Freetown had touched a nerve. The victim had attempted to retain his dignity, his self-respect, his civilization. Moreover, and this was the point, he was being beaten to death in bright daylight and no-one was intervening.

"Stop the truck!" Rindert barked again. The driver floored the pedal. Not the brake. The gas.

"You are, of course, fucking kidding," said the driver, Graham McDougal. McDougal was a jowly, alcoholic Scot who ran an ailing haulage operation in the city. McDougal's fleet was reduced to just eight trucks. He used to have forty.

"Stop the bloody truck," insisted Rindert. McDougal flinched at the fury in his passenger's voice, thought about what to do and reluctantly applied the brake. Rindert snatched the keys and the truck's engine died. He got out, leaving the door open and headed towards the gang of boys who were beating the man with the shiny shoes.

Their eyes, thought Rindert, when he reached them. Their eyes. Flat, glazed, drained by drugs, intensely threatening. Bunch of bloody homunculuses. Little men, birthed and warped by war. Homunculus. Rindert had checked it in a dictionary. Latin. It meant "little man". The parallels were exact. Man-made monsters. Little ones.

The beating stopped. The boys lowered their sticks. All the cold, cold eyes were now on Rindert with the exception of the eyes of the beaten man who curled and held his bleeding head and made degraded snuffling sounds and whimpers. A squashed tomato was now on the man's left shoe. A silly detail, but Rindert noticed it.

"Fuck off, blanc," said one of the boys. He drawled the words in a slurred imitation of Bob Marley. He had the dreadlocks, too. They were shiny with oil.

It was, Rindert suddenly realized, seriously unfortunate that he didn't have a gun. The boy did. A revolver. Its grip was decorated with mother of pearl. A pimp's gun – Rindert wouldn't have been seen dead with a sidearm like that – but a gun nonetheless.

"Who is he?" asked Rindert attempting to dominate the situation.

The boy with the revolver looked momentarily off-balance.

"Who the fuck's who, blanc?" said the boy. He smelled terrible. The rusty stink of someone who had his last bath ten years ago and hadn't washed since. His T-shirt had a slogan on it. "There's No Justice. Just Us."

Too bloody right, more's the pity, thought Rindert.

"The man here. The man you are beating." Rindert was deliberately keeping his voice steady.

The boy giggled then became stone. This was now a one-on-one confrontation. Both of them sensed it. The other children were watching with hungry, anxious expressions. The boy looked around and confirmed that this was a time of testing. His crew, his gangstas, were watching for weakness. The blanc was huge but he didn't have a gun. He pushed the revolver into Rindert's stomach. It hit hard muscle and stopped.

Rindert didn't flinch. Didn't look down. Didn't back off. The boy blinked.

But Rindert was sweating. He realized bleakly that he was about to be shot in the stomach by some kill-crazy, stoned-out little thug, just because of a pair of meticulously shined shoes.

Rindert wondered whether McDougal was going to come to the rescue or do anything useful. He dismissed the possibility. McDougal was a coward and a wreck. If he hadn't taken the keys to the truck, McDougal would have already taken off faster than a Jap cultist with an arse-load of exploding aerosols.

"Who's the man?" Rindert said, his voice still strong. He knew the kid was disconcerted by his display of apparent fearlessness. Unsure. Keep some dialogue going. Let us both walk away from this alive.

"He's the man who owes me some shoes, blanc. Wouldn't give them over. No generosity in him, man." Still that appalling imitation of a laid-back Jamaican in the boy's voice. Rindert's mind raced. Inspiration came.

"They won't fit, son," he said. "They're too big."

"Whuzza?" The boy was confused now. He looked down at the man's shoes. It was the moment Rindert had been hoping for. He swung his fist, caught the boy on the side of the head, smashed his knee into his crotch and grabbed the pimpy pistol.

The boy subsided, was out cold. His comrades gaped at Rindert. They hadn't expected that. Rindert held their gaze, deliberately ground his boot on the unconscious boy's face, then crouched and flicked his Zippo into life. When the little shit's oily dreadlocks were properly alight, he began to back away towards the truck, the revolver steady in one hand. In the other hand he dragged the man with the shiny shoes.

As he climbed into the cab, he pulled the victim after him but had to lose the pistol. The boys who had been preoccupied with putting their leader's burning head out (that had been Rindert's motive for the Zippo war-crime action), spotted Rindert's sudden vulnerability. They became brave again and unleased a barrage of stones. One side-window starred then shattered. A wing mirror exploded. A plank bounced off the door. More boys were running down the street, waving pangas and clubs.

"Happy now?" asked McDougal, starting the engine with fingers that shook. There was the brittle crack of small arms fire. Someone, somewhere threw a grenade. A freak ricochet drilled a neat smoking hole in the driver's door and smashed McDougal's speedometer.

The Scot screamed.

"Jesus," Rindert muttered shakily, picking glass shards out of his lap as their truck rounded the corner and roared away from the gathering mob and across Freedom Square. "What the hell's got into everybody today?"

"RUF's in town for peace talks," said McDougal weakly. "The UN's fixed it. RUF arrived yesterday."

"What the catastrophic hell are they thinking of?" thundered Rindert. The last time the RUF had come to town there'd been a blood-bath. In fact every time the RUF had come to town there'd been a blood-bath. No-one knew exactly how many people had been raped, chopped or murdered. Twelve thousand, Rindert had heard. And from what he'd seen that had been as good an estimate as any. They'd beheaded the solicitor general, killed all the doctors, shot or chopped the human rights activists. Kidnapped people. Every bank, parastatal, business, office, shop had been looted by gunmen.

And now the RUF was back in town again. For peace talks. Swell.

"Country needs peace. UN's just doing what it can," said McDougal, slowing to avoid a legless man on crutches who was struggling to cross the road. "Country needs peace," McDougal said again. Then, "Can't believe you set fire to that guy's head. Just like that. I couldn't do that. Not someone's head. Not just like that." Then, "Where the bollocks am I going to get a new speedometer?"

Rindert couldn't have cared less.

Disaster was imminent. There'd been rumours of peace talks for months but in Rindert's opinion the RUF was in this game to win, not share power, disarm, or reach accommodation with anyone. Letting them into the city, Rindert thought, was on a par with asking the Manson family round to do the baby-sitting.

And if McDougal had any faith in the UN then the Scot was grasping at straws. All those overpaid deadbeats were good for was running up parking tickets in New York and burning out photocopy machines with brain-dead memos and reports in triplicate. Like many people who got things done in Africa, Rindert regarded the UN as a bunch of self-serving, weak-kneed, vacillating, self-righteous, out-of-touch, interfering, sonovabitching, preaching, money-grabbing, supremely incompetent parasites. Fuck them. They'd done more damage, continent-wide, than the RUF, the LRA, Colonel Gaddafi, Kabila, all the monsters. And with those UN horses'-arses bringing the RUF into Freetown, they were about to screw up again.

But Rindert kept his own council. If he started on the topic of the UN he knew he probably wouldn't finish. And in any event he was now mainly preoccupied with the injured man who was clutching him like a baby and bleeding all over his khakis.

"People are scared," said McDougal. "There's a lot of fear here right now."

He coughed wetly, fumblingly lit a Lucky Strike, and changed the subject.

"You on for drinks tonight? There's a get-together at the Sport bar. Assuming no-one's blown the bloody place up. Fats Dupree's rustled up a video of the latest Springboks game. Christ alone only knows how. Schlessinger's celebrating his forty-fifth birthday."

Schlessinger. That would be Mad Mike Schlessinger, CEO of SHEELD a thriving private security firm that had government contracts to guard those diamond fields that were not in RUF hands. Mad Mike and Rindert went back a long way together. They'd both served in Angola. And what a snarl-up that little war had been. Or more accurately, still was.

"No," said Rindert with an absent-minded shake of his head. (What was he going to do with this poor, bleeding guy? He was clearly concussed. He couldn't just be dumped on the street. Wouldn't keep his shoes for five minutes. And how the fuck was he going to get his gear clean? Blood all over his damn jacket. His shirt. His pants. Jesus! He was going to turn up at Lalapanzi looking like a slogged hog!)

"Just a shower and shave, then I'm heading in-country. I've got a job to do," was what Rindert said. Maybe he could buy fresh clothes at the Bristol. He slipped McDougal a couple of twenty dollar bills. "Drop this poor bastard at Connaught hospital, there's a pal."

McDougal looked put out.

"He's bleeding all over my damn seat cover. You're the sodding good Samaritan. *You* take him to Connaught hospital."

"Ach, man, have a heart!"

"That's rich coming from someone who just set fire to a guy's head."

More notes changed hands. McDougal began to bleat about the bullet and rock damage to his truck. About his speedometer.

His speedometer.

"You expecting a ticket from the traffic police? Get real!" Rindert was becoming increasingly annoyed.

"He's puking! Get him the hell out of my cab," Mc Dougal bleated.

Rindert briefly contemplated smashing his fist into the Scot's blotchy face but then decided: fuck it. He'd started so he'd finish. Decently. And to be fair to the Scot, there *was* a lot of blood and puke. McDougal would be needing some sort of fire hose. So would Rindert. "Here. Three hundred bucks. All I've got and I don't have time to waste. Job to do."

A job to do was right.

Rindert had eventually sold The Crocodile the auction idea, in principle, but The Croc was a cautious man.

He'd said he'd not move until there'd been a field test of the units.

That was the job to do.

CHAPTER SEVEN

RUF Stuff

It was morning. Almost. Pre-dawn, to be precise, with an eerie mauve mist flush in the east, the uncanny effect being aided by the smoke that rose from two burning villages and a UN convoy that had been neatly surrounded after it had run out of petrol. The petrol situation being what it was – the RUF had used their own petrol in Molotovs to set fire to the villages – the convoy had not been stolen. Instead it had been set on fire with torches.

In General Butt Naked's radio station, time was relative. The bright new prospects of an impending dawn were a broadcasting opportunity missed. The Midnight Hour show was still going strong. Occasional commercial breaks were allowed and these slots were largely occupied by impassioned pleas from captured Indian peacekeepers that someone release them in exchange for the immediate overthrow of the elected government President Alhaj Ahmad Tejan Kabbah and lots of money.

Shots had been heard interrupting commercial breaks when the panic-stricken UN bluehelmets had reverted to what the DJ described as speaking "Indy".

Brief speeches had been made that dwelled on the Freetown peace talks. There had been a short cookery slot. A young man named Comrade Curtiss had explained how to mix gunpowder with palm wine and marijuana. The cocktail, he assured listeners, would make them fearless and immortal.

Mainly though, the Midnight Hour was incoherently rambling talk radio interspersed with *Wait till the Midnight Hour* and two ABBA singles which were the only discs that had survived the RUF assault that had secured them the radio station in the first place.

"I'm Commander Joe," said the latest guest on the Midnight Hour. "The RUF is my father and my mother. I was young and had no chances. This is the lost generation with no housing, no schools, no education. They had stolen our schools and taken our houses to where they were living because ..."

There was a pause in broadcast voice. A long pause. Rindert, who was listening to a small transistor from bush cover only 200 metres from Radio Butt Naked, smirked then flashed Jack an evil smile. The speaker, Rindert guessed, had no idea that he had to turn the paper over to finish his talk. He'd just reached the end of the page and stopped. It was something of a miracle the little shit could read in the first place.

In the background, audible but indistinct, were the sounds of a voice shouting for beer, yammering in Hindustani and another gunshot.

"Yo! Sun's coming up," said a new voice growing louder as it approached the mike. "Sun's up. We've must stop this Midnight Hour. It's Good Morning Liberia time."

"Good Morning Sierra Leone, you idiot!" said another voice, sounding angry. "And you stop that! No-one's raping my Indy hostages. You fucking rape my Indy's I'll—"

ABBA cut in unexpectedly. "Waterloo, Waterloo ... ooo ..."

Listening to this Swedish rubbish, Rindert thought that no more appropriate field test could be devised. The timing was perfect. He switched off his set, checked left and right to see that the homunculuses were in position and then re-focused his binoculars on the radio station poisoning the airwaves.

Time to move.

"Radio Butt Naked!" he shouted through the bullhorn, "you

are about to be destroyed by the antichrist. Jesus from on high has judged your infamies. The monsters are coming now."

A little religious psych-war never hurt in Rindert's opinion. Blacks were superstitious as hell. And officially most were Christian. Even though this lot were performing like Caligula on a bad day.

"Well, get on with it." He added, turning to Jack, "Get the homunculuses going. Let's break some heads!"

"I wish you'd brought a change of clothes," said Jack, "You look awful."

"Marks & Spencers was closed and I gave my last buck to rescue some— Ach, man, I don't have time to explain. Get your homunculuses going!"

"Homunculus singular. Homunculi plural," said Jack.

"Got it," said Rindert. "Homunculi. Fine. Get them going!"

Time to kill.

"You hear something?" Commander Joe asked. No-one was listening. The two pro-RUF Liberian technical advisors were squared off in one corner, both drunk and both in-country for just a week to help set up the station. They were locked in serious combat. A third Liberian advisor had just put on *Waterloo* for the fifth successive time. He was fat, old and lordly. He too had been drinking heavily, but red eyes and sweat were the only obvious results. The young man who had handled the cooking slot was asleep. The cocktail of invulnerability he'd been recommending had pole-axed him. Two RUF officers who had been talking about peace had joined him in the brew and had also collapsed.

Commander Joe, aged twelve, was awake, sober and furious. His speech hadn't been finished. He'd been told to say nothing that was not written on the paper – on pain of branding – and then his speech had ended in the middle of a stupid sentence. Because one of these men hadn't finished writing it for him. The fat one.

"Monsters! Monsters! Monsters coming! Apocalypse RUF!" Joe could hear that noise, metallic, unemotional, through a loudspeaker. So why couldn't the Liberians? Worst of all, in Joe's opinion, was that it was a white voice. When there was a white voice saying monsters were coming, monsters were coming. That's what Joe had heard. It had happened repeatedly over recent weeks in this area.

"Monsters are coming!" shouted Commander Joe.

"You fool of a nigger," said the fat Liberian, busy trying to find the *Wait Till The Midnight Hour* single. ABBA was beginning to get on his nerves too. "There's monsters only in your simple head. Monsters don't exist. Why can't we get some more fucking records?"

"Don't call me a nigger," said Commander Joe. "You're the nigger – not finishing my speech."

The Liberian turned from his search for the disc. At first he looked surprised. Then he looked thunderous.

"What did you say?"

Joe wasn't about to back down. This radio thing had been important to him. And through no fault of his own it had been wrecked.

"I said you're the nigger for not finishing my speech. Making me look stupid."

The Liberian stepped forward and brutally slapped Joe's ear. Commander Joe brought up his AK 47 and shot him in his fat gut. Missed. Fired again and hit. The Liberian, his mouth a disbelieving O, subsided.

Joe then shot at the two fighting Liberians in the corner, missing on both counts.

ABBA had stopped. Live radio was once more paralysing the airwaves.

"You two fools, stop fighting! The monsters are coming!"

The two other Liberians disentangled slowly but appeared befuddled. They were hugely drunk. Palm wine bottles littered their table. Most were empty.

One hobbled towards the mike, shouting that he was opening a new day for Radio Sunshine. It made no sense.

"You got no minds? Monsters are coming! Alert the people on the radio!"

Inexplicably, the two Liberians began swinging punches at each other again. The Indians were hollering and weeping.

Indians everywhere, thought Joe. Naked, tied, yelling, pissing – there was barely room to move. Why hadn't someone just shot them?

"This is no way to run a radio station," Joe said, suddenly disgusted. "And you little people ..." He was now yelling at the Indians. "You aren't warriors. You can't keep peace. Look at yourselves. You're babies!"

The Indians flinched. But the AK47 moved away from their faces. Commander Joe raced out of the room and grabbed his binoculars.

At the edge of the scrub forest, just before the beginning of the tall grass, he could see a white man – Joe assumed he was one of the British soldiers who had slaughtered the West Side Boys gang or a South African mercenary. The white man was shouting into a bullhorn. The white man's khakis were totally stained with dried blood.

RUF training had emphasized that white men were weak, so weak that they were incapable of doing manual work in any form but relied instead on black slaves.

Commander Joe had believed the teachings until he'd met his first white man, a muscle-laden, red-faced giant wearing a SHEELD uniform, shouting loud and hurling grenades with terrible accuracy.

The white man with the bullhorn looked like more of the same. Only a hell of a lot more. His khakis! It looked like he'd bathed in blood. And puke.

Just behind him was another man wearing a priest's robe. It couldn't have been worse. Abraham Lincoln had told him that a priest was always with the monsters.

He scanned the bush closer with sweat clogging his eyes. Nothing obvious.

Closer to the radio station he scanned the short grasses.

Focused in on a head that looked like a swollen raisin. Its eyes twinkling. Dynamite strapped to its back. Round its neck a placard read, "Don't Join RUF. Trust Lovin Jezus."

The monsters weren't coming. *They'd come.* They were already so close you didn't need binoculars.

Commander Joe scrambled through a back window and scooped up his cadre who were gathered in a huddle around a fire behind the building, cooking a guard dog and planning the assassination of every fucking Liberian they met, every time they met one.

The cadre had not been allowed into the radio station by the Liberian technicians on the grounds that they stank. Only Joe's influence had restrained them from torching the place in response.

"Move!" Joe yelled. "Monsters coming! Run, run, run!" The cadre was quick. One lanky youth hauled the smouldering dog off the coals, slung it over his tattooed back (Joe had told them all that an army marches on its stomach), then with his free hand grabbed a bulky sack of bushweed (also a Joe-recommended essential for effective combat). Four of the older boys seized tins of palm oil, sacks of rice, flour and peanuts. Sister Sue, a breathtakingly beautiful girl of seventeen, who had been boiling a mess of greens taken from the two nearby villages she'd helped burn the previous day, hoisted the similarly looted cauldron from the fire. Commander Joe was always talking about vitamins. Sue and Joe had a thing going and she didn't want him to miss his vitamins. The cauldron was heavy. She tried to steady its swings. Scalding water slopped onto her feet and over her naked breasts and stomach.

Jolly Roger, Joe's second-in-command, lunged for the box that contained ground chilli, black pepper, other looted condiments and approximately 4,000 US dollars'-worth of uncut diamonds taken from the stomach of a thief at a local diamond mine Joe was in charge of overseeing.

"Where's the milk?"

Joe couldn't believe what he was seeing. Just couldn't believe it! Yes, he'd given everyone a lecture on armies marching on their stomachs and vitamins and anyone who didn't abide by Joe's wisdom was in serious trouble, but ... BUT ... THERE WERE MONSTERS COMING!

"Where's the milk?"

Who cared where the fucking milk was!

"Forget the food!" Joe yelled. "Drop that dog. Forget the fucking milk. Sue! Roger! Sue! Run, Sue, run!"

Joe's army stopped marching on its stomach and started running on its feet.

Joe led them at a sprint in the opposite direction from the blood-spattered white-man-murderer and the redhaired demon-priest.

What had been hiding in the grass rose to meet them. Its nose was jetting green smoke. A small chainsaw revved and snarled in its fists.

Commander Joe ordered the eleven soldiers in his cadre to run faster.

Sister Sue, thin, so fine looking – she could have been a model had circumstances been very different – couldn't keep up. Her feet were scalded. She was weeping.

"We can make it. Left. Left!" Commander Joe's cadre – and he'd built it with care, reading and discipline – followed his orders and ran to the left.

"Sister Sue. Try. Try!" Commander Joe shouted, desperation in his voice. "Drop those greens!"

Sister Sue still held a pile of parboiled greens in her hands. She didn't want to drop them.

Joe needed vitamins.

One monster rose directly ahead of them on long ostrich legs. High above the grass, it stood for a moment then waded rapidly in the direction of Sister Sue. A tape recorder strapped behind its earless head started bawling in a drunkenly vengeful Irish accent. "Find you RUF. Find you RUF." There was a hideous blast of static. "Take your teeth! Take aaaalll your teeth!"

Commander Joe watched his cadre's discipline collapse into wailing stampede-panic. Some simply fell to the ground, covering their faces. Others blundered into each other, shrieking.

The monster strode forwards on its long jointed legs, slicing at the air with hands that were not hands but sickles. Curtiss tried to intervene, then lost his head. Or most of it. The horror clawed at his corpse with its horny ostrich feet, opening him up, scattering him around, then stooped over Sister Sue. The girl closed her eyes, Joe saw her make the sign of the cross, a fluttery little gesture. In her other hand she still clutched the greens.

In a strangely long, slow moment that was actually less than a second, Joe saw them steaming. Sue's feet. Sue's body. Sue's mess of lovingly protected greens.

Joe let loose with his AK. Missed. *What the fuck was wrong with his AK? It kept missing.* The sickles flashed down.

Well, that, realized Joe, was that. Sue's game over. The death of his woman flicked a mental switch.

Commander Joe, unlike his panic-fogged cadre, immediately dropped into the peculiar state of calm that General Butt Naked had promised him would make him president. When Joe was like this, he felt no emotion. He felt distant and unconnected with what was about him. His mind was clear and clean as a diamond. No fear. No anger. No emotion.

He didn't bother watching the rest of the unequal fight. His people were mince. Instead, he fell flat and wormed through the grass towards the latrines. No-one looks for anyone in an African latrine. Butt Naked had said that, and Commander Joe respected him, never missed his advice. He fell in with a splash and pulled the lid closed, wondering as he did so whether the same rule applied to monsters.

No-one in Denmark noticed the dramatic closure of Radio Butt Naked (formerly known as Peace on the Airwaves). The Danish tax payers had built the radio station, most without noticing that either. The Danish Overseas Development people mourned the loss of the radio station (a gift from the citizens of Denmark to the citizens of Sierra Leone) in the way that most people might mourn the loss of a one-dollar bet on a three-legged horse.

Aubrey Wiley, however, took a rather closer interest.

Wiley was with British Naval Intelligence and, from a cramped, unprepossessing, box-sized office on HMS *Clam*, it fell to him to monitor both government and rebel-held radio stations broadcasting in-country.

Wiley called coming on shift "falling down the rabbit hole". Anything could occur. And routinely did.

It was Wiley, sipping a mug of sweet tea, who first learned that the peacekeeping column had been attacked and that seventeen Indian UN bluehelmets had fallen into RUF hands. Indeed it was also Wiley who had first learned of the capture of the radio station and its conversion from pro-democracy broadcasts (interspersed in Wiley's opinion with some awful music) to the entropic howl that was Radio Butt Naked.

It was also Wiley who had first learned of the deaths of two Japanese doctors. General Butt Naked made the announcement, adding that he'd eaten them himself. Wiley had heard enough from Butt Naked to recognize when the general was lying or, in this case, winging it. He was slightly more than one hundred per cent sure that Butt Naked hadn't had so much as a mouthful. Pure macho porroh, psych-war hearsay, overexcitement, whisky, dagga ... a classic Butt Naked cocktail.

That the Nips were dead. Well yes, Wiley trusted Butt Naked on that one.

The press had been having fun with that particular slaughter story until they'd seen the state of the Freetown hotels and had all run away. Apart from the ones who were still in the Connaught Hospital's morgue. Wiley now referred to this under-refrigerated, rat-infested facility as "The Press Office".

In a perverse way, Wiley found himself fascinated by his radio monitoring. It certainly beat listening to Radio Two or Voice of America.

Nothing previously recorded however was to match the surreal quality of the station's final broadcast which, as recorded by Wiley's shorthand, read thus.

> *6.02 a.m.* Juvenile voice (agitated) self-identified as *Commander Joe: "You got no minds? Monsters are coming. Alert the people on the radio."
> Sounds of scuffling.

> *6.03 a.m.* Sporadic gunfire without the building. Muted screams.

> *6.05 a.m.* Male adult voice (slurred): "They are monsters. It's the end of the world! Take a look."
> Male adult voice (slurred): "You're drunk."
> Sounds of scuffling. Muted bullhorn: "Monsters coming, RUF! God has judged you!"

> *6.06–6.30 a.m.* Loud screams from within radio station. Mechanical repetition of the phrase, "Get you RUF!" interspersed with static. Sawing noises. Sounds of struggle. Cries for help in at least three languages (presumably the Indian contingent). Screams. More screams.

> *6.30 a.m.* Unidentified male voice (Irish accent): "Thank

the devil that's over. What are all these dead Pakis doing here? I thought this was just the RUF."

Unidentified male voice (Southern African accent): "It's like an abattoir."

Unidentified male voice (Irish accent): "It *is* an abattoir. I need the body parts."

Unidentified male voice (southern African accent): "I've got to hand it to you. Your homunculuses get the job done."

Unidentified male voice (Irish accent): "Homunculus singular. Homunculi plural. Is that thing still on? Shit it is. What have they heard?"

6.31 a.m. Music. "Waterloo. Waterloo."

6.32 a.m. Transmission terminated.

* Commander Joe identified as one of the RUF cadres responsible for attack on media personnel August 9th. Wanted for numerous war crimes.

Wiley rechecked the text, sugared another mug of tea and spiked it with a shot of rum.

"Odd," he muttered. "Really, very odd." He began work on the necessary memos while HMS *Clam* lolled in the Atlantic blue and, just across the water, Sierra Leone sat in its darkness and its shadows despite the new dawn.

Commander Joe emerged at noon from the latrine with snakebite. There'd been a snake just sitting there, waiting for mice and insects, and Commander Joe hadn't noticed it for five exhausted hours.

He'd just slumped waist-deep in waste water and turds, waiting for the monsters to leave, listening to the gruesome noise from the radio station.

As the hollering grew louder he'd strained to listen, to find out what was going on. It clearly wasn't an interrogation. There appeared to be no questioning at all going on. Just the wails of tortured men.

It became increasingly awful.

He had risked all when the screaming reached its worst and fired up some strong weed. Joe was a planner. Kept his weed dry in a plastic baggie round his neck. With the weed's assistance he had then exchanged circumstances, fallen into a happy dreaming state where he was surrounded by jovial, grinning faces, all calling his name and acknowledging his part in the fight for freedom. Sister Sue was there, saucy winks, her breasts pert – she was the most beautiful thing Joe had seen – and she'd slipped in and out of Joe's dream like a giddy phantom.

"Joe," Sister Sue had whispered, "I'll love you strangely because I know that's what you want."

In his dream, she'd begun to do just that.

Joe woke with a smile. Then he realised where he was. And his loss. The Sue phantom vanished. Joe saw the snake and thrashed violently. The snake, as snakes do, moved away.

Joe, as most Africans do, did what most Africans do when they meet a snake. He tried to kill the snake. It bit him in the face.

Commander Joe left the latrine at speed. The snake, now highly aggressive, remained where it was.

The monster that was monitoring Joe's latrine was a small one. Binoculars appeared to be welded into its head.

"Wuzza. Snoal," said the homunculus, turning its back on him. "Phizzwiggs."

Joe's first thought was to jump back into the latrine, but then he paused.

With the bush-fighter's instinct, Commander Joe sensed that this monster was going wrong. Was somehow sick, or broken. Vulnerable.

What to do? Shoot the monster? If he took a monster's hand

he'd be famous. No-one had taken a monster's hand before!

Then he saw the horrid-looking, hook-nosed priest approaching with the same white death-mercenary who had been yelling all that spooky Christian stuff through the bullhorn. Simultaneously he realised that his gun was in the latrine, and in his calm fashion he ran away. The monster made no effort to follow him.

One shot cracked over his head. Very close.

A second shot. Nowhere near. Commander Joe ran and kept himself low. The general would want to know what had happened to his radio station. Joe had to stay alive to tell him.

Still calm, still running, he reached the edge of the yellow grass and was swallowed by the forest.

Rindert finished typing and pulled the sheet of paper out of the Mission's cranky typewriter.

He re-read what he had typed.

FIELD TEST RESULT

Casualties:

    17 Pakistani or Indian peacekeepers UN;

    3 Liberians;

    14 RUF;

    Homunculus: none.

All bodies taken for processing.

Note:

The Homunculus shows a cost-effective tendency to initiate and improve on mechanical repair regimes, particularly with respect to vehicle mechanics and direct human anatomical work. They are impressively adaptable and show attractively appropriate inclinations to adjust behaviour to achieve optimum results, while remaining within the boundaries of instructed orders. We have here organic robots. Good ones.

Rindert

Time to use the satellite phone he'd bought in UK. Phone The Crocodile. Tell him the glad tidings.

CHAPTER EIGHT

Peace Talks

In Freetown's UN HQ the news of the abduction of the Indian peacekeeping convoy caused mixed degrees of confusion, fury, fatalism, indifference, fear and despondency.

After close to a decade of open hostilities, agreements that collapsed, treacheries, massacres, backsliding, after *all that*, a tentative peace treaty was again being proposed. Various senior RUF officials, their families, advisors and security were openly back in Freetown, staying at the Hotel Frangipani complex.

All good on paper. The RUF people came in peace, but were dressed, by necessity, for war. Apart from the RUF politicos in from overseas, many of whom hadn't set foot on Sierra Leonean soil for years. They looked dressed for a party.

The Hotel Frangipani was now effectively an armed camp in the heart of the city, the RUF bush-fighters being under no illusions regarding the fact that they were loathed and feared by the bulk of Freetown's population. Admired by a minority. Financially important to who knew how many. The RUF controlled many of the country's diamond areas.

The UN Resident Representative, the "Res Rep", was an obese Australian called Sharon Stone. It was a name that attracted numbingly repetitive attempts at humour at social events. Stone bore these with fortitude.

Stone had organised a series of low-level meetings, then tabled higher-level meetings between RUF and government officials. At least that was her story. In fact, UN Special Envoy Ahmadou Lye had shuttled to and fro between the parties concerned. Lye was the one who had done all the work. As Res Rep she'd just signed things, forwarded copies, made lengthy phone calls to people who weren't interested, and spent a lot of her time taking sick leave – she was owed thirteen days – and fretting by her pool in her fortified and extravagantly-furnished compound. For some reason the pool was full of frogs. She kept telling her gardeners to pour more chlorine in, but chlorine was in short supply.

The talks had so far achieved nothing concrete but – and this was the Res Rep's proudest boast to New York – they had not collapsed. Yet. Both sides were behaving like children. But, so far at least, they were behaving like polite children, albeit polite children who hated each other.

Dialogue, the Res Rep had decided, was once more being achieved. And that was something to put in her reports. Once a UN highflier, she'd been shunted to Sierra Leone after an unfortunate incident in Lagos. A waitress had complained when Stone had made ... approaches. It wouldn't have gone any further in normal circumstances, but this particular conference had had as its theme, "Empowering Women Against Sexual Harassment."

Some French weasel of a journalist called Pierre Spong had met the waitress in the conference centre bar, heard her story, and *Paris Match* had splashed it over three prominent pages. In most organizations Sharon Stone would have got the sack. The UN being what it was, Sharon Stone got Sierra Leone.

Initially the posting to this homicidally-inclined West African backwater had filled Stone with despair.

And then Lye had turned up with his suggestion that peace talks might be possible. He had "contacts". He'd heard "things". It was a straw. Stone grabbed it with the desperation of an exile and had frantically attempted to enthuse her superiors over the ocean in the Big Apple. "Dear God," she'd thought, "if I pull this one off, I'm saved."

For weeks nothing had come back to Sharon Stone, or nothing useful. Then some Filipino guy had caught on to Sierra Leone as a possible "UN cause". That it was a Filipino didn't come as any surprise to Stone. There were more Filipinos working for the UN in New York than there were Filipinos working in Manila. They knew where the gravy was, they surely did.

What *had* surprised Stone was the Filipino's energy.

The guy had latched on to Sierra Leone like a terrier on a rat. He wasn't just keen, he was enthused. Almost manically enthused! Stone realized that she'd done the equivalent of win the Irish Sweepstakes. She'd found someone in her monolithically self-serving bureaucracy who actually *cared*. And not just that. Someone who *got things done*.

Miracle!

Others joined the bandwagon, the Filipino guy was transferred to Reproduction. (When Stone heard she'd assumed the office was devoted to sexual health, population, something important like that. It wasn't. It was a department full of photocopy machines to reproduce documents. The Filipino guy was never heard from again.) But the bandwagon still rolled. There had even been plans mooted to bring in big guns, perhaps even attempt to invite Nelson Mandela, should things develop in a positively positive fashion. African leaders, the Res Rep corrected herself, *some African leaders,* were beginning to cotton on to the fact that the continent was increasingly being regarded as a global embarrassment and that action was needed. Even the UN seemed marginally aware of the need for a success story.

The UN Special Envoy, Ahmadou Lye, was from neighbouring Liberia, a country that vigorously denied offering any support to the RUF, but supported it anyway – whether in an official or an unofficial capacity, it was hard for Sharon Stone to say.

Lye, a flabby man, struck the Res Rep as slick and self-important.

In her heart of hearts she sometimes wondered whether he actually *was* a UN Special Envoy. No-one in New York had notified her of his arrival. He'd just turned up, flashed business cards, occupied an office and taken it from there. Stone had been on sick leave at the time of his arrival and when she'd finally mustered the energy to turn up for work, Lye was a fait accompli. His CV still hadn't come through and there was something a trifle uncanny about the way he managed to meet and talk to people whose normal language was gunfire.

But as he had played a significant – no, significant was not the word – a *pivotal* role in bringing the RUF back to the table, he was to be afforded some respect. He didn't appear to want the glory for setting up the peace talks. Indeed he seemed more than happy for Stone to take all the credit.

And he had, in the really real sense of the word, saved her ass.

Until Lye and his scheme, the Freetown UN office had morosely been going through all the usual motions of a UN office – compiling reports, applying for non-core funding, submitting expense accounts – but all the jaded, washed out people working in the building were under no illusions.

Without peace, nothing much could be done beyond the immediate application of Band-Aids to a body corporate riddled with cancer cells.

With Lye had come momentum, ideas, ass-saving.

The Res Rep sifted papers. The Indian peacekeepers. She groaned.

This stupid pointless kidnapping. Now. Of all times!

Were things going to go to hell, Stone wondered. Again? If the peace talks collapsed, well it wouldn't look good on her CV. Jesus, she thought in sudden alarm, if they start fighting again we'll have to evacuate. Nothing triggers bloodshed more than failed peace talks.

Stone knew that all too well.

Her girlfriend! How was Stone to get her out? Jaqui was a

Sierra Leone national. And underage. The UN wouldn't author-
ize her evac. No way. And then there was the issue of Stone's
piano. How was she going to get *that* out?

"Oh Jesus!"

CHAPTER NINE

Mission Abnormal

The Mission, Rindert soon discovered, was a maze and a good deal larger than it looked from outside. There was an entire floor that someone, he presumed it was Father Jack, had walled off with wooden planking then daubed with red crosses and (presumably) warnings in a language that he could not understand. The planking put him in mind of some medieval scene: a house perhaps playing host to bubonic plague. It was unsettling.

Jack, in raucous high spirits following the compelling demonstrative field test of the morning, had applied himself with rigour to the Cape brandy, and was now dozing, draped in an unlovely, gape-mouthed sprawl over a table in what he described as his study. Rindert had sat with him for a while until he became conscious of a repellent goat-like odour. He'd looked about seeking its source.

There were enough unpleasant looking objects floating in yellowing formaldehyde to keep him guessing for several minutes. Alchemy, if Jack's version of the art was anything to go by, struck Rindert as a particularly messy pseudo-science.

The origin of the smell was not in a jar, however. Nor did it come from the dangling herbs or the old books that cluttered the walls. It was Jack. The reek was coming off him in waves.

Rindert himself did not smell particularly sweet. He planned a dip in the river later to rid himself of the cordite, blood, sweat, brandy and dust that were the scent of the morning's efforts. But they were healthy smells. Or if not healthy, at least they were excusable smells.

The odour from Jack wasn't. It hurt the nose, jangled the viscera and rang a few primeval survival-of-the-fittest instinct bells that Rindert didn't need ringing.

He thought for a while, trying to pin down which bells they were. Bad ones. Jack was ill.

But how ill? And with what?

Jack had already shown Rindert where he kept his homunculi bivouacked. Most were standing but inert in Lalapanzi's huts and houses, hidden from the sun which Jack had explained was bad for their skin.

He had then laughed. So Rindert was still unsure whether this was a joke. Or a useful fact.

A workshop in the village, sponsored by the Christian American Charitable Foundation to help in the production of handicrafts for export as Fair Trade goods, was the site of a new sort of endeavour unenvisioned by the Charitable Foundation. Eight homunculi were at busy, if robotically unenthused, work preparing the morning's human remains for the decidedly un-Christian resurrection that awaited them.

Reproduction is the meaning of life someone had told Rindert. He'd thought it might be true at the time. A bit of a bleak utilitarian view of one's role in the universe. But not without its moments. He was reminded of the comment when he watched the homunculuses – homunculi, Rindert corrected himself, plural homunculi, damn it! – working with hacksaws and other equipment. They appeared hell-bent on reproduction.

Jack was out cold. Smelling like a goat. After a while in the company of both, Rindert decided it was time for a snoop.

Whoever had built the Mission had had funding, or funds, and had built the place to last. Rindert began at the top by scaling a wall choked by bougainvillea to check the roof, which was corrugated iron, layered thick and surrounded by a rather teuton-ically prissy series of decorative battlements.

There were solar panels and someone had angled all the roof's component parts in such a way that they diverted rainfall to cor-ner collecting pipes. Very eco-friendly. Rindert glanced over the phoney battlements and was surprised by the drop.

The top floor was given over to laboratory equipment and a series of oddly-shaped copper furnaces decorated with moons and depictions of women and men representing the zodiac. There was something jarringly discordant about the images, as if they'd been rendered before artists discovered proportion.

The furnaces had jointed legs and copper chickens' feet. They looked very old, almost beyond antique. Archaeological. They also looked to Rindert as if they might just take it into their heads to waddle off. There was something about the chickens' feet that hinted at unnatural mobility.

Absurd of course.

But this was hardly Mission Normal.

Everything in the laboratory looked scrupulously clean. Bottles gleamed, alembics shone. The floor was dust-free.

This was something that could not be said of the next floor down, which was busy with the rustle of furtive rats and festooned with dirt and thickly-clinging cobwebs. Prominent features here were a dormitory, a kitchen, refectory and a larder. The latter was well-stocked, Rindert noted despondently, with cans of fish with faded Russian labels. The vilest, cheapest canned Russian fish ended up in Africa and this looked typical of the species. Bully beef fortified with hippo fat, the sort of greasy pink sludge that apparently sold well in the South Pacific islands, was also massed in cardboard boxes. Rindert shook his head. Father Jack lived off this muck? He must be madder than Rindert had given him credit for.

Further checks of Mission stores revealed a sack of withered yams, insect-damaged dried fruit, maize flour, three crates of butternut (that was better, you could do good things with butternut), uninspired coconuts, sugar, Cape brandy (a lot of Cape brandy) and, humming in the corner, a huge fridge-freezer. It was the only noise audible in the queer, thick and, Rindert realised, sudden stillness of the Mission.

Rindert was conscious of a stiffening in his neck. This sensation occasionally indicated danger. Not always, not even often, but just enough to make him pay attention. One didn't make a moderately successful career as a freelance African fighter last as long as fifteen event-filled years unless one had a little more on one's side than just superior firepower.

Rindert wasn't psychic, didn't have second sight or a third eye. But he did have a neck that would stiffen from time to time. And looking at the fridge-freezer had set it off.

"Open me," the fridge-freezer seemed to hum in the silence. "Come on, open me. Have a peek."

It was a big grey affair with large grey handles. Floor to ceiling job. Industrial size. Would hold a lot.

But a lot of what?

The silence of the Mission. The thickness of the silence. The droning, somnolent hummm of the fridge-freezer; the lethargic urge to step slowly through the canned trash.

Open the doors. And look.

"Old soldiers, bold soldiers, but no old bold soldiers," thought Rindert sluggishly, scratching at his neck. God, but this room was drowsy.

Then he thought of who had first introduced him to the cliché. Jack Stephanski, seventy-five years under his belt and more scalps dangling there than Black Jack himself could remember.

"Old soldiers, bold soldiers, but no old bold soldiers," Jack had said. Jack had then added. "But boy, if you want to make a freelance career of this thing, you be bold but don't be stupid. That way you'll get to be as old as you can handle."

The memory of Stephanski brought a smile to Rindert's lips.

Stephanski, last he'd heard of him, was stretching a beach deck-chair's carrying-capacity in Costa Rica with a wife who was in it for the money. But she was also twenty-three and had great tits. Fair deal. No fairer retirement deal for a mercenary.

The smile broke something in the clogged atmospherics. The little noises of the Mission – the creaks of boards, the pop and ting of the tin roof as it cooled, the mild sigh of the wind, the noises of life – returned.

The fridge-freezer stopped its potent hum. Became something closer to just a large grey fridge-freezer.

But Rindert didn't open the fridge-freezer. Because he sensed that it wouldn't be bold.

It would be stupid.

Next floor down housed Jack's living quarters, study, operating theatre, some sort of basic clinic with posters advocating breast feeding and AIDS awareness. Also the chapel.

And so to the ground floor.

This was the floor that was mostly boarded up. There was a dead, sweet smell. The perfume bottle would read *Odeur de Mort*.

A photo on one wall caught Rindert's attention. The faded colours spoke of poor film or poor development, the framing was lousy but the subject matter was compelling. In a grinning group were the vanished Mission staff. And squinting, slightly off to one side, was Father Jack in his robes of black. He looked shifty. The Mission staff by contrast looked confident and kind. Yes there were a lot of kind faces there. All beaming into the camera like immortals.

Utterly unaware of the twisted Irish cuckoo in their nest.

A stumbling footfall interrupted Rindert's examination.

"They all died of Ebola," said Jack affably. He was barefoot. Still drunk.

"They placed themselves in isolation. Walled themselves in to keep it controlled. How's that for primitive hive insect mentality?"

Rindert knew that in times of epidemic some African villages did the same thing. Put up road-blocks, sealed themselves off and sat the plagues out. Selfless, really. Admirable. Very brave.

Rindert then thought of Jack's smell; that ill and poisonous reek which came and went. Now, thankfully, it had went.

"Were you exposed to Ebola?" Rindert asked.

Jack face was no longer friendly. He looked touchy and insulted. "It's blood- and body-fluid-transmitted. You think that I'd mix myself up in that? Jesus, you Boers are thick-headed. I'll not do any operating unless I'm totally covered. Ordered a Racal suit from Seattle. Nothing gets through that orange fucker and I mean nothing. Mind you it's bitch to work in. Like being in a bloody spacesuit. Should have got something lighter."

Jack hiccupped.

"No, the homunculuses as you call them do the blood work."

"Homunculi plural. You taught me that." With an auction on the horizon, the last thing Rindert wanted was a temperamental mad scientist. Though Rindert thought that after the auction Jack might be in for a vigorous beating. He might even be invited to eat his Racal suit, whatever the hell that was. Rindert did not approve of being sneered at and Jack was now sneering at him.

Naughty.

"While we're on the subject. They've got Ebola. Every single mannikin among 'em. It's what makes them that little bit extra special."

Rindert wondered what that would do to the price per unit. You'd not be able to use them alongside normal troops, not if they were virus bombs. Mind, you'd never get normal troops to operate alongside the homunculi anyway. Rindert wondered suddenly whether it might not just be better to clear off and leave the rest of his C4 in tactical places that would scour Jack and his toxic creations from the face of the planet.

Ebola! What the hell did Jack think he was playing at?

Mental note: avoid *any* contact at *any* time with *any* homunculus at *any* cost.

Rindert found himself fervently wishing that The Crocodile would hurry up and make up his damned mind. Authorise the auction. Invite the punters. Get the damn thing going.

"I can read minds," said Father Jack, breaking in on Rindert's reflections. "It is a skill achieved with difficulty."

Rindert decided to call Jack's bluff. "Tell me what I'm thinking then."

"You're thinking that I spread the Ebola that killed the Mission people. Admit it."

Rindert nodded, despite the fact that he hadn't yet got round to thinking about it.

"Well, you're right. Killed them all. The, uh, the doctor had an accident. He, uh, fell off the roof. Had flu. Was delirious. So I gave the staff their vitamin injections. I was the one who walled them up. At their request, mind. I walled them up and listened to them die. It made me cry."

Jack stopped. Rindert waited. Another sunset in the Mission began its job of turning the place to blood red colour.

Jack looked at the photo of his erstwhile colleagues and farted.

"You weren't thinking that were you?" said Jack. "This mind reading, it's what alchemists call a subtlety. You need to be focused for it to work. I'm drunk. Drunk most of the time when not working. Working most of the time when not drunk. It's a weakness."

"Ahh, to hell with it all," said Jack. "Let's hope it goes well, this auction. I've a mind to spend some long years in Costa Rica on a beach. That's funny. Never heard of Costa Rica. Did you mention it?"

Jack stumbled, then fell down. Rindert helped him up, then up again – up the stairs where he found Jack's grimy bed. The brandy and excitement had got him good. Red-eyed, ginger hair a mess,

Fagin nose smeared with soot, oddly long-limbed and sprawling, Rindert poured him into his bed.

Rindert had no idea what to make of it.

"It's a mystery," muttered Jack in his sleep. "All of it. Porroh. Alchemy. Life. A fucking mystery." He then subsided into bubbles, jerky snores and silence.

And again began to exude the odour of goat.

TELEPHONE CONVERSATION (III)

Dr Pleasant: "Father Jack, I presume. We want another field test."

Jack: "Why?"

Dr Pleasant: "You say you put down some bluehats, a couple of Liberians and some kaffir RUF scum."

Jack: "We say? We *say*? You should see the internal organs here we've extracted. Processed right, they'd make boerwurst sausages for a month."

Dr Pleasant: "What's your point?"

Jack: "No more field tests. I want to get out of here. I want my money and I want to get out of here."

Dr Pleasant: "You want an auction, then we want an out-of-country test."

Jack: "How am I going to ship one of these out of the country for a field test?"

Dr Pleasant: "That's their question. The buyers are asking that question."

Jack: "Tell them that's their problem. Smuggle them I guess, same as you'd smuggle drugs or, I don't know, guns or little Albanian girls. Things people want."

Dr Pleasant: "Give me Rindert. Put Rindert on the line."

Rindert: "Rindert here."

Dr Pleasant: "Do they work?

Rindert: "So far they work. Hurt like hell. Look like hell, too."

Dr Pleasant: "I was just telling Baron Frankenstein, I want an out-of-country test. Can you sort it?"

Rindert: "I'd rather we just got on with this auction. The sooner we sell them, the better."

Dr Pleasant: "Humour me."

Rindert: "I'm not taking this thing out of country. You want another field test, OK, but it's in-country. We've done his radio. How about we do the head of broadcasting?"

Dr Pleasant: "Butt Naked? The brave general himself? Yes. Do him. Blow his butt off."

BACK ON THE HOOK, KENT

Dr Pleasant had brought liquid paper with him to the phone box. Call concluded, he carefully smothered the sentence of graffiti that accused him of looking like a carp and monopolising the box.

He used the public telephone for security purposes. He was excessively sensitive about security. The thought that the other villagers might find it odd that he, a doctor with a perfectly well-functioning phone in his surgery was constantly using the call box, had not occurred to him before. He wondered why it hadn't. It was blindingly obvious.

He hoped that the village would write it off as just an eccentricity. The hated English were meant to be fond of eccentrics.

But for the calls he was now to make, Dr Pleasant decided that it would be prudent to travel to a nearby town. Beck's Hill. Use the phone box there. It was essential that he draw no attention to himself.

LALAPANZI

Rindert broke the connection and returned the handset to the sat-phone.

"I wish we could just get this auction over with," Jack complained, pouring brandy into a glass. "Cut all this field-test fooling around."

"One more bang won't hurt," said Rindert. "It's not as if you're short of homunculi or anything."

"And," Rindert added, "I want to do Butt Naked."

"You're really going to kill Butt Naked?" Jack looked startled. "I thought you were just spinning him a yarn."

"Nope. Butt Naked's going to be riding the rocket. You've a problem with that? He's a buddy of yours or something?"

"No," Jack said hastily. "No. Not at all. Never met the man."

Methinks the priest doth protest too much, thought Rindert. Jack was lying. Rindert wondered why.

CHAPTER TEN

Field Test II

General Butt Naked was wearing thick clothes in Freetown and liking the thought of the stir it would make. The suit was pink, the silk tie decorated with a woman being whipped and loving it. A Chinese guy had painted it for him.

He'd also obtained white golf shoes and socks which had little designer crocodiles on them. The sartorial crescendo arrived in the form of a Panama hat that had been given to him by Commander Joe after the successful ambush of four internationally respected war correspondents who had been shot dead snooping around the RUF diamond field at Tongo a week earlier.

The hat from the ambush had taken some getting used to. And had needed a bit of repair.

Initially General Butt Naked had had his doubts. It rode his afro like a cowboy on a feisty mustang. Never quite here. Never quite there. A precarious sort of hat.

But then he'd seen it on his head from every angle possible. Two of his general staff had held mirrors and made efforts to ensure that they reflected every potential view. Eventually Butt Naked had decided that the hat was *him*. It was a hat that could go anywhere at anytime.

Perfectly clothed, and impeccably, if provocatively, hatted, Butt Naked sailed out of his Freetown hotel, the Frangipani, surrounded by his customary dagga and whisky fumes to meet the International community's movers and shakers. As an afterthought he clamped down on a fat, assertive cigar that had been confiscated from a Cuban military advisor months, perhaps a year ago.

"This is," he declared, with pride, and supreme self-confidence, "my day!"

Disappointingly, though, the media was not assembled. The only ones who cared about stories were out of town, covering the latest media martyrs. One of whom, via Commander Joe, had furnished Butt Naked's hat. Preliminary low-level peace talks in Freetown were not an international news priority.

A surly group of supporters, who half-believed that being naked would afford them protection from bullets, began growling. The appearance of the general fully clothed struck some as a bad omen.

He identified faces in the crowd. Not all his men. Not by any means. There were General Murder's men there too. Butt Naked and General Murder did not always see eye-to-eye. Neither did their men.

The growl spread and became a roar. The call of "Show us your butt!" became a chant.

General Butt Naked was incredulous. This one time he was invited to peace talks, *this one time* he was wearing clothes and everyone picked up on it as if he was selling out.

"You people got a problem with my suit? I can kill you any time I'm wanting," yelled the general, one hand steadying the hat, the other clenched around his AK which he had christened Gutfucker. Gutfucker had been painted with the words, "Peace Now". The paint was not yet dry. He hadn't wanted to paint over Gutfucker but in the interests of diplomacy had compromised and attached several Band-Aids to obscure the name. There hadn't been enough of them. His assault rifle's stock now read "Peace Now" and "Gut ... er".

"I'll gutfuck you all!" explained the general, whose mind was now firmly focused on crowd control.

He would have said more, but his ample lips and horsey teeth were combined in a desperate mission to support his assertive Cuban cigar at an angle appropriate to his new-found status as a diplomat.

The cigar was twelve inches long and the very devil to control.

It had already fired inflammatory shards into the curtains of the Hotel Frangipani's lobby, which were still being extinguished. The match he'd imperiously tossed over his shoulder hadn't helped. And now the cigar was making a mockery of his pink suit with gobbets of burning ash.

The general's good humour evaporated completely. What to do with the cigar? He didn't want to throw it away. Castro had a huge cigar and his clothes didn't catch fire when he was speaking. And he sometimes spoke for twelve hours. Winston Churchill had a cigar. A cigar was the thing to take to international meetings.

He stood for a moment in a mood of truculent indecision.

What to do? Throw the cigar away? Keep the cigar? Ignore the crowd? Open fire on the damn crowd?

"Show us your butt!" shouted a gaggle of scrawny grinning childen.

"Show us your butt!"

"That skinny shanks ain't got no butt!" bawled an angry and immensely fat woman who had already had one of her children mutilated in the war and wasn't about to see it happen again.

"He's just a murdering butt-less coward wearing clothes!"

"No butt! What are you saying? No butt?" The general was appalled at the impudence. His reputation was entirely built on the fact that he waded into bloody battle butt-naked. He whirled furiously. "No butt? I'll show you my butt."

He was about to do just that when the antique cigar exploded with a small crackle then a flare of fire that touched off his afro. He'd doused it in Hai Karate aftershave. It might as well have been drenched in petrol. The sudden flare ignited his hat.

Unbelievable! Butt Naked, quite simply could *not believe* how the day was turning out.

In order to quell the embers that had already claimed his eyebrows and which smouldered on his head, he reached for his whisky bottle in his suit pocket. His guards were making threatening gestures but they too were clothed and felt disoriented. One of them ran back into the lobby shouting for water.

Butt Naked tore off his smoking hat and poured whisky on his head.

While doing so he dropped the AK which discharged into the crowd and sheared a large chunk out of the fat woman's own butt, as well as the lower jaw of her infant that was slung in a bag suspended low.

A white face appeared as if by black magic. It had a camera. The press! Outrage! Here he was going to peace talks with his fucking hair on fire and he'd just been photographed shooting some bitch in the butt! How was that going to look on the front page of *The Mail and* fucking *Guardian*?

And what were his guards doing?

A UN car with tinted windows installed to conceal the identity of peacekeepers pulled up.

"Salvation!" thought the general. "Time to blow this scene and hit conference tables."

A bucket of water hit the general from behind. His guards. The idiots. His suit! Scorched then drenched!"

The camera clicked again.

"Deal with you bastards later!" howled Butt Naked at everybody. "Gutfuck the lot of you! I just don't have time now. I'm off to the UN peace talks."

The general's day continued its downhill slide as he approached the Toyota.

The UN car door was opened by a fat hand attached to a ropy, withered arm. The leathery face beneath the chauffeur's cap had a mouth that was pink and puckered as tight as a rose-bud. It had no nose. Instead, it had a child's trumpet from which smoke was curling in oily liquid ripples.

"Get you, RUF. Get you," droned the homunculus through its trumpet.

The general fell backwards.

The homunculus reached for the detonation switch on the bomb that was strapped to its chest.

The car exploded with such force that almost everybody near was killed instantly. Body parts and chunks of twisted metal from the car showered the square. Every facing window in the Frangipani shattered.

The survivors were just four. A fat woman, missing some buttock, a child without a jaw and the white man who had taken the photographs. Named Pierre Spong, he was stringer for *Paris Match* and freelanced for *Voice of Africa* and *Le Monde*.

Spared by the whimsy of ballistics, the fourth survivor was Butt Naked, who crawled unsteadily for cover back up the steps into the Hotel Frangipani.

Spong, shell-shocked, came in close to photograph the jawless kid, took some shots then ran, his stomach wailing at itself. The square was a charnel house, drenched in blood. A few minutes later, though, he returned to the scene of the inferno. His head had cleared somewhat and he was thinking that he might have a chance of getting the kid to Connaught hospital.

There was an ambulance there already. Things in green coats and wearing face masks were already collecting the body parts.

Spong frantically fired off the remaining two shots in his camera and then ran, heart thudding, in the direction of his hotel and jerry-rigged dark room.

CHAPTER ELEVEN

Bar Talk

"I have some frank reservations about these people." He meant
Africans.

The American CIA chief of station was wearing a polo shirt,
slacks, a sun hat that flopped and only upon occasion shielded his
long, peeling nose from the sun.

He looked like a caricature of a failed and exiled CIA chief.
Behaved like one too, thought his partner at the table who was
himself pretty much a caricature of a British military officer. Trim
moustache, straight back, even tan, expression of polite boredom
and conversationally addicted to the British art of understatement. Or, in this case, silence.

"Whole goddamned continent's a basket case," went on the
CIA chief, fumbling a red bandanna out of his back pocket and
wiping at the sweat on his face. Irritably he turned towards the
bar. "Where's that goddamned drink got to?"

There was no-one behind the bar of the Jardin de Sygnes. A
fan stirred lazily, the small restaurant's beer garden was a hot
green cauldron. Jewelled lizards skittered along the walls. The
tropical plants in the pots along the walls exuded a damp, hot
musk tainted with decay.

"Will you see that?" said the CIA chief, turning back to the
table. "I come in and there's five guys behind that bar wiping at
shit with towels and shit, polishing glasses, dicking around with
napkins and those cherries they try and stick in your Martini

when they're out of olives. You know how old those cherries are? I checked the jar last Thursday. Sell-by date? 1987. '87! Not '97 which would make those cherries just purely out of date. '87 – that's like some kind of toxic waste. '77 – no problem. Those cherries'd be fossils. Fossils don't hurt. They're too old. Too god-damn dead to matter. Jeezus!" The last word spoken like a sigh.

"Five guys when I order it. Not one guy now when it's time to deliver. Reminds me of Kabila. DRC. Guy's head was fat as a watermelon. Stone psycho. Never turned up to anything. Peace conferences. SADC get-togethers. Most of those African leaders, they're at conferences all the time. Makes them feel like world leaders. Hogs round a trough. This Kabila? Guy's head was fat as a watermelon. Never turned up for nothing. He was assassinated anyway. His idiot child's running the show now."

The Briton struck leisurely at a mosquito. Hit it. Quite why the Yank was blathering about Kabila was beyond him. Kabila was Democratic Republic of Congo. DRC. Nothing whatsoever to do with Sierra Leone. The barmen he guessed had gone to try and find his boorish counterpart an olive for the ordered Martini. He rated the barmen as decent men stuck in indecent times. Trying, he guessed, to do the right thing. In this case, find some olives.

They might have luck at Oliveira's, a Portuguese-owned shop a few hundred yards away that was still, incredibly, doing business. Portuguese shops always had olives. It was something of a rule.

They'd all gone, the barmen, he guessed, because at the moment walking alone through Freetown dressed in a black pen-guin jacket and barman's tie was the equivalent of strolling up the Belfast Falls Road catholic nationalist enclave solo wearing a "Fuck the Pope" T-shirt. An invitation to trouble. Not that here there were any political implications to wearing a barman's outfit in Freetown. More spiritual. The people who'd mug the solo barman would be after his tie and tails. The weirder the clothes the more powerful the porroh, the stronger the magic, the less likelihood of catching a bullet. That was the way the Freetown logic flowed.

Most modern armies dress to hide. Camouflage. Rather sensible, though it had taken the Boer War before the Brits had decided that marching around in bright red was like painting men with bullseyes.

The concept of camouflage had yet to take firm root here, though. This war was still being fought in fancy dress.

Combatants' choice of clothing, or lack of it, however, was a side issue. Peterson-Smith brought himself back to earth, censored the mental digressions. The arrival of RUF for peace talks had left the city dangerously charged. That was the point of this meeting.

"So, shall we start ..." he began, but his counterpart was still doing what the Americans call "venting".

Wasn't ready to listen to anything. Not just yet.

"You hear 'em hollerin' and yellin' about civil rights and how wonderful goddamned Africa is and Roots and all that happy horseshit," vented the CIA man. "Jesse Jackson, you know what he said about the RUF? Said they were the West African equivalent of the ANC! The way I see it is ship Jackson, Al Sharpton and the rest of 'em over for a fortnight. That'd set 'em straight about what we done for 'em."

The "'em" meant African Americans. The "we" was vaguer. Perhaps it meant white America. Or perhaps it meant what the freed African American slaves had done to their native Continent upon their glorious return to colonise West Africa. Which was bugger things up just as badly as every other colonial power.

Probably the former definition. Peterson-Smith suspected that his drinking partner had yet to take the great step forwards into the US racial and cultural melting pot.

"You know what I read? Today?" The CIA man thumped a file, then confirmed the Brit's psychological diagnosis.

"What?"

"I read that some guy was claiming Beethoven was black African. Beethoven black! You know what we'd be listening to if

Beethoven really was black? I'll tell you. The unfinished symphony that's what. With about five hundred movements all fighting over the biggest drum. And the goddamn trombones forgotten about, and no violins because they'd been stolen. Where's the goddamn drink?"

"Peace talks," said the CIA man. "Know what I think about these peace talks? I think they're just a damn ruse. Know what I think RUF's got up its sleeves? Arms! That's what. And Ahmadod Liar or whatever the UN special envoy guy's called. You know that snake? He's a liar!"

The Briton smiled. What's the RUF got up its sleeve? Arms. Very good. He'd pass that funny on to HMS *Clam*. The "unfinished symphony" line wasn't bad either. And the "movements" gag. *Ahmadou Lye?* Worth checking. Fitz sometimes got things uncannily right.

"You know what I got on my desk this morning?" the American swivelled from his latest fruitless scrutiny of the bar. "A memo about monsters. Monsters! You believe that?"

The Briton hit at a mosquito that was whining at his ear. Missed.

He kept his bored expression as politely irritating as ever, but something was tweaking uncomfortably at his gut. He'd had a memo too.

The memo had had a very peculiar, very unsettling ring of truth, mainly because it had been recorded by Wiley on HMS *Clam* from a rebel-held radio station and had come in live. The screaming had been intense. Wiley's memo indicated that something very untoward had captured the radio station. Monsters? In this fantastic disarray of a country (and the American had it right to a degree, a disarray of a continent) rules were bent and not infrequently discarded.

Monsters? If anywhere, monsters were possible here. They'd turn out to be human, of course, but monstrous. Perhaps a new battalion wearing Halloween masks.

More worrying immediately were the peace talks. What disturbed him most about the peace talks was their timing. Sierra Leone's President was not in the country at the moment. He was attending a summit conference of the Organisation of African Unity (an oxymoron *extraordinaire*) to try and resolve the ongoing crisis in the Democratic Republic of Congo (even more of an oxymoron *extraordinaire*).

When the cat's away and all that. The big question? What kind of games were the mice planning to play? War games, he guessed, played rough.

"I say," said Peterson-Smith. "Let me fix you that Martini. As we are currently abandoned, and lack of olives notwithstanding, it is for us to take the initiative."

Peterson-Smith did just that. He strolled across the beer garden into the dim shadow of the bar and made the Martini long and very strong. The American drank Martinis no other way. He resisted the temptation to add a cherry.

Thump.

The distant bomb blast shook the Jardin de Cygnes. Dust floated from the beams. Glasses rattled musically behind the bar.

"The hell was that?" the American said, looking shaken.

"Bomb. Out towards Oliveira's. Hope the bar staff didn't catch it."

"Goddamn it, Pete, you make a lousy Martian."

That's what "Fitz", *né* Herbert Selby, called Martinis. Martians. Despite his comment, Fitz sucked at the glass with genuine greed. Peterson-Smith suppressed a wince at the "Pete" familiarity.

"You want to look at my monster memo or not?" asked Fitz, finishing the glass.

CHAPTER TWELVE

Strange Developments

Rindert was sitting on a desk in the Mission building watching Jack decanting a palely phosphorescent liquid into a large glass flask. Outside, the weather had broken. Thick sheets of rain were beating against the walls and fierce gusting winds were rattling the palms. Despite the hour, just past two in the afternoon, the clouds were massed so thick that it could have been dusk.

It was a haunted light.

"What's that?" Rindert enquired. Not particularly interested. It was just something to say. He felt uneasy, had felt uneasy all day. The weird weather perhaps.

"Distilled moonlight," Jack responded. "Crucial stuff. The homunculi sleep in it. They need their sleep my little manikins do. Get no sleep and there's hell to pay. All systems break down. Psychotic episodes."

Bottled moonlight. Rindert pondered the concept for a moment. Lightning flared outside. The roar of rain off the Mission's tin roof was unsettling.

"How do you distil moonlight?"

"Same way as you catch dreams in a mirror. You need a silver sieve."

"Show me."

"No can do," said Jack absently, squinting at a retort. "There's a man in the north of England does it for me. Godfroi Mungo. Best damn alchemist in Europe. Certainly produces the best moonlight. The African stuff's too bright. It'll work at a pinch but your best stuff's from Northumberland. No idea why, but that's just the way it is."

"And the homunculi need this moonlight?"

"Like I just said." Father Jack shot Rindert a petulant glance. "I just told you they sleep in it. No moonlight. No sleep. Breakdown. Hell to pay. This retort's cracked. No bloody use to me in this state. Could you get me another one?"

"Not a problem," said Rindert sliding off the desk.

"You'll find them in the cellar. It's the same place I keep my moonlight. Don't break anything. Wouldn't want to run out of moonlight."

Rindert left to find the retort. The rain thrashed down relentlessly.

It was raining, too, in Freetown where Spong was in the murky gloom of his dark room staring at the newly-developed film. Spong was tall and thin with overlarge hands. His camera jacket had the words "Don't Shoot Me I'm Only the Piano Player" painted on its back. A nervous tic twitched by his eye as he worked.

Butt Naked's burning hair? Caught to perfection. Butt Naked with a bucket of water in the face? Very nice.

The shots of the jawless child, the littered bodies, and the burning remnants of the car were fine too. Eminently saleable, thought Spong. Grim. Disturbing.

But not remotely as disturbing as the last two photos that he'd shot.

He wiped a lock of his thin fair hair back over his sweating forehead and peered at the enlargements. Mutants. That's what the ambulance crew looked like. Mutants. Most of them, and much of their faces, were swathed in green robes or the green face masks, but the small portions of their anatomy that were visible were terribly wrong.

The figure to the left of the picture hauling a mangled body towards the back of the ambulance appeared to have one eye, centrally located in its smooth bladder-like face. There was something – Spong reached for his magnifying lens – something brutish, almost proto-hominid, about another figure's head. The skull appeared foreshortened.

A third ambulance operator caught by the camera staring straight at Spong with tiny, shadowed eyes had a scalp that was crinkled. A burn victim? Possibly. Those hurt often wish to help the hurt. Spong knew that.

But why was he so small? Why were they all so small? Not one of the ambulance crew looked to be much more than a metre in height.

Spong had not heard of pygmies in Sierra Leone. As far as he could recall, pygmies lived in central Africa. Congo. Cameroon. And if they *were* pygmies, well, who would crew an ambulance entirely with pygmies? Even by Sierra Leone standards it made no sense.

This looked, Spong decided after a close re-examination of the photos, like the ambulance crew from hell.

He decided to phone Connaught Hospital and ask a few questions.

The line, though, was dead.

And no matter how often he phoned it, it stayed that way.

Later in the day his editor phoned Spong at the Foreign Correspondents' Club informing him that the bomb photographs might be used but that the ambulance shots were surplus to requirements.

They were irrelevant, the editor said.

The editor then said she was interested in doing a feature on West African cuisine and asked Spong whether he could check out some restaurants, interview chefs, get some shots of market colour.

Spong told her that there was a war about to happen. Reminded her that he'd narrowly escaped being killed.

But people still have to eat, the editor reminded him. "There is a lot of interest here in Paris right now regarding the cuisine of the West African region. They do something clever with a kind of banana."

After Spong had slammed the phone down he shook his fists at the ceiling. When he'd calmed he went in search of a brandy, wondering who he could sell the ambulance shots to. It was lean work being a stringer. All editors were swine. Every sou mattered. He entered the bar at a fortuitous time. There was Fitz, lumbering forwards in search of Martians to conquer.

"Nothing ventured," thought Spong, "nothing gained." The CIA, as everyone knew, had fat guts and deep pockets.

"Hey Fitz, my old friend," Spong hallooed gaily as he advanced across the shabby room, nervous tic dancing frantic jigs beneath his eye. "Will you take an aperitif with me? I've something to show you that is, how do you say, curious."

"New face at the bar," said Fitz, settling fatly on a stool and waving the Frenchman over. "What's your name, buddy?"

"Hoppy Pongo," said the young man. He had a glazed expression and astigmatic eyes. "I'm the new bar manager, sir."

"Hoppy Pongo, huh?" Fitz shook his head. "Hell of a name. There's some real dirty work at the font in this part of the world. Still, guess you're stuck with it. Well, Hoppy, first things first, hop along and get me a Martini. Then tell me this. What the hell happened to Stompy whatever-the-hell-his-name-was? You know, the last bar manager."

"He's gone, Commander," said Hoppy serving the drink.

"Sonofabitch," breathed Fitz. "Goddamn barmen disappearing all over the goddamn city. Someone collecting them or something? What have you got for me then, buddy?"

Hoppy was dismissed. Fitz had his glass. Spong now had Fitz's full attention.

And after a bit of negotiation, Spong had $300 and Fitz had the photos.

Hoppy watched the transaction through his muddled eyes from the far end of the bar.

He was grinning. A slack, sick grin. Soon, Hoppy was thinking, very soon.

TELEPHONE CONVERSATION (IV)

Dr Pleasant: Did you put him down?

Rindert: No idea. Killed forty people, though, according to some frog on the BBC World Service. It's kind of a garbled report actually. A lot of body parts missing. The units do that. Take bits. Hello? You still there?

Dr Pleasant: Forty? Good result. Good enough. I'll make the calls.

Rindert: So it's auction time?

Dr Pleasant: Indeed it is. It's auction time.

CHAPTER THIRTEEN

The Buyers

Colum Muccio replaced the telephone on its ornate gilt receiver and tapped thoughtfully at the notepad on his desk with his Parker pen.

After a while he shouted, "Pepe!"

A huge man with a thick dark moustache stepped in through the open French windows. He was in green jungle fighter fatigues and wore reflective sunglasses; the Uzi that he cradled seemed toy-like in his hands.

"Bring me a world atlas and coffee. Strong. Bottle of Pisco, too. Ice." Muccio ordered curtly.

Pepe withdrew silently. Muccio continued his distracted pen-tapping.

To say that the call he'd just received had been peculiar was an understatement. He'd have written it off as crank lunacy were it not for his caller's reputation. The Crocodile, El Crocodrillo, was a man to respect and Muccio and he went back a long time.

Guns, money-laundering, fighting the commie subversivos here in Colombia, and, of course, the cocaine. The Crocodile had always been of help. Disconcerting man. But they shared the same dream. A world free of reds and a life of personal enrichment and power.

Muccio ruled a series of fincas. Coffee farms. Cattle ranches. A stud horse spread. The acreage combined was just larger than Belgium. But Muccio knew a man in his position could never have enough. It's the Red Queen race, he'd tell his eight sons. Read *Alice Through the Looking Glass*, he'd tell them.

You've got to keep moving, not to stay ahead, but just to stay in one place. Miss a step and you've the gringo DEA, the upstart Bolivians, the upstart Argentineans, the subversivos – all of them, howling at your heels. Nipping at your profits. Tearing at your world. Bringing it down.

Keep running or you don't come to a standstill. You go backwards. That's what he'd tell his eight sons.

Pepe returned with all the items Muccio had ordered plus a tray of dried sardines. That was one reason Muccio held Pepe in regard. Most of his private bodyguard army just did what they were told – if they didn't, they got the so-called Colombian necktie treatment which involved pulling the tongue out through a slash in the throat – but most were just boys with guns. Pepe was different. He'd always do just that little bit more. He had initiative. Some of the others had too. On occasion too much initiative, hence the need for neckties.

But Pepe's initiative was sensitive initiative. To date, he'd always got it right.

Like bringing the sardines. Muccio had, in the back of his mind, been wanting dried sardines. They went so well with the Pisco. He'd have ordered them if The Crocodile's call had not been so bizarre and set his mind in such turmoil.

Pepe spread the items on the desk and then wordlessly departed to resume his vigilant patrol of the flower-drenched veranda.

"Think of a robot," The Crocodile had said. "But not made of steel. Made of flesh."

"You trying to sell me the Frankenstein monster?" Muccio had asked.

"The Frankenstein monster screwed up. These won't."

Muccio wondered about that. So far his life had taught him that everybody and everything screwed up. Sooner or later. The secret of success was to screw up as late as possible. Then look good in a coffin.

He poured Pisco, sipped, chewed another sardine. Liked the way its brittle bones crunched. Wondered a little more as he flicked through the atlas. He wasn't ignorant of Africa. Indeed he was moving encouraging quantities of crack cocaine into South Africa.

But for the life of him he could not recall where Sierra Leone was.

The Spanish on the map caught his eye. He found it.

"The units have the following principal points of recommendation. You don't pay them," The Crocodile had said.

(But you have to pay *for* them, Muccio had thought.)

"They'll donkey your product, won't steal it, and if they're intercepted by DEA or anyone else there's a self-destruct facility. They'll also deliver explosives to targets."

"You can trust them."

(But can you? Muccio had thought)

More sardines. More Pisco. More thought.

This was taking Muccio longer than usual. He normally made swift decisions. An hour after The Crocodile's phone call he noticed that the Pisco bottle was empty and the sardines gone. The coffee was untouched and cool.

"Pepe!" he bawled. Muccio was curiously immune to alcohol. He just got redder and louder. Perhaps repeated himself more often than was necessary.

"Pepe!" he shouted again.

Pepe was already there.

"What happened to your face? Your lip's swelling. Makes you look like a nigger."

"I was stung by a bee," responded Pepe. "They are plentiful in the flowers now."

"Didn't hear you shout."

"I didn't shout. It is my last wish to disturb you."

"Bring fresh coffee and cups for two," said Muccio, his mind made up. "I want to send you to Africa for something that might be important. We just need to discuss some things. Just a few things, over coffee."

Ariel Scharansky put the phone down.

He had already decided to go to the Sierra Leone auction and had said so. He had also decided who to take with him. His three best comrades. With a homeland under threat, his people terrorised, his very race and religion at risk, the tables needed turning.

Total war. Any weapon permitted. Even on the Sabbath.

He just hoped these weapons would work as well as The Crocodile thought they would. If they did, then Hamas, Hezbollah, and all the other enemies would reap the whirlwind.

Eretz Israel. On the rebound!

Of the other prospective buyers only eight declined The Crocodile's invitations. In six cases the reasons given for not attending were insufficient funds and personnel. Such was the care with which Dr Pleasant had compiled his buyers list that only two people dismissed his proposal as the ravings of a diseased mind.

The Crocodile had never dealt with Aleph and Aleph did not receive a telephone call inviting representatives of the sect to the auction.

Neither did any Islamic group.

Communists were not invited.

Nor were persons of colour.

And Americans.

The Crocodile wanted the weapon used by the right people. Not unstable types. Flakes. Or Scum.

White European groups were not invited for different reasons.

Dr Pleasant was as yet unsure whether the units to be auctioned would be appropriate for European work. "They hurt like hell." Rindert had said that. "They look like hell too," he'd added. In Dr Pleasant's opinion Europe was a little too overpopulated and organised for homunculus operations to remain for long outside the public eye.

Perhaps later. When the designs had been developed upon more aesthetically pleasing lines.

Dr Pleasant dearly wished he could see one of these homunculi in the flesh.

They sounded frightful.

CHAPTER FOURTEEN

A Week Later

At the Jardin de Cygnes the beer garden tables had been dragged under cover and the drinkers, of which there were just two, were sheltered from the pelting rain in the damp, gloomy bar.

A bomb attack on the power station earlier that morning had cut electricity supplies to this part of Freetown. Not that a bomb attack was a Freetown prerequisite for a black-out or, as Fitz called them, "brown-outs". The power company was a mess; cables were rotted, power stations derelict, transformers blown.

Everyone was used to being suddenly plunged into darkness. Everyone who could afford to took precautions.

As Fitz and Peterson-Smith approached the bar, two storm lanterns hissed and flared throwing weary pools of light on the counter. Management needed to light a few more. The light from the two lanterns merely served to accentuate the shadows in the room.

The five bar-staff were still missing and there was a new man behind the bar. He had an earnest, monkey-like face and a syco-phantic bow. He introduced himself as Welshman Ngadi.

"Your mum called you Welshman, huh?"

"That is correct, sir."

"What the hell she call you Welshman for? What kind of a goddamn name is that to saddle a kid with?" Fitz shook his head bemused at the ways of the West African world.

"Welshman! Jeez."

The barman looked polite.

"The hell's going on with this weather," Fitz said. "We'll be building arks soon. 'Bout the only way there's gonna be to get out of the country, Welshman."

"Shall we skip the small talk?" Peterson-Smith suggested, moving his beer from the bar and sitting at a table near the scarred billiard table. "There's a lot to discuss."

"Welshman, old buddy, I'm asking you, is this some serious rain?" Fitz went on, ignoring the Brit. Damn man. Acted like he'd got a stick up his ass. Brits!

Welshman nodded solemnly.

There was the muted thud of a distant explosion.

"Another bomb," Fitz said unnecessarily. They'd been going off all morning.

"Oh, for heaven's sake, come and sit down, old chap. There's a lot to discuss."

Fitz lumbered over to the table, stared at his counterpart balefully for a moment, then lowered himself into a chair.

"Know what I think, Pete? I think this place is going to blow sky diddley high diddley high. We're getting reports of a lot of weird-looking characters out by the airport. State Department's gonna advise every non-essential American citizen to leave ASAP. That's on my advice. All the others to gather in at the Sofitel Mammy Yoko until the cards fall. I'm telling you this shit's getting really out of control here."

Peterson-Smith thought the same. He remembered a conversation that he'd had with an Irish Guards officer during the West Side Boys militia kidnap fiasco.

"We just don't get it," the officer had said. "We look at these irregular forces. We look at these kids and young women fighting in trainers and T-shirts. We laugh at the way they wear charms to ward off bullets. We look at their drunken and doped-up leaders and we cannot take them seriously. But these kids have grown up fighting and killing and committing atrocities."

Peterson-Smith was taking the RUF threat very seriously.

He'd not been in Freetown last time the RUF had come to town. But he'd heard the stories. They'd infiltrated thousands of their people into the city dressed as civilians. By all accounts they'd nearly taken the country. If it hadn't been for Nigerian intervention there would have been hell to pay. Or more accurately, more hell to pay. Thousands of people had been killed, maimed or raped. Or raped, maimed, then killed.

Yes, he'd heard the stories. But Peterson-Smith hadn't seen it first hand.

He had, however, been in Angola in '92 just before UNITA and the MPLA got into serious headbutting. There was exactly the same haunted, clogging atmosphere of impending doom in the capital. The same desperate rush to get seats on planes, the same sudden lack of planes and chaos queues at the airport, the oddly empty streets and shop shelves, the same influx of what he called "war filth".

It was the war filth – the profiteers, the arms suppliers, the hard cases – that worried him most. These people had the devil's own instinct for impending anarchy. They knew when. How they knew was a mystery.

But they knew.

War filth was gathering in droves – Lebanese businessmen, South Africans, Israelis, even Colombians had all been logged arriving at Lungi airport over the last couple of days.

In a perverse way Peterson-Smith held a grudging respect for some forms of war filth. It went wrong for so many of them. But still they did it.

There was a New Zealander who'd had renegade gurkhas working for him in Mogadishu during the carnage of Somalia's collapse. Cold champagne, stolen UN radios, lobsters – anything you'd wanted, he'd get it. Went breezing about, in his fortified "technical" – Somali-speak for the Mad Max-style vehicles that prowled the streets – not a hair out of place, knew every market in that dying city, was even – and this had really made Peterson-Smith's eyebrows rise – coordinating the continued export of Somali fruit while the bodies clogged the harbour and the lights went out.

He'd been killed eventually.

But he'd had that romantic flair that in earlier centuries would have earned knighthoods; that merchant adventurer dash.

Most war filth lacked it. Some were just flat-out desperate. Some, particularly the Lebanese, were silky businessmen. They'd murmur low over coffee. Ships would arrive or leave with guns. Diamonds would be traded. Fortunes would be made.

Other war filth were psychos. Quite why, he was not sure, but African soil seemed to nurture criminally insane whites in the same way that it threw up completely barmy blacks. Take the Belgian who'd just been sent down by the International War Crimes Tribunal for running Hate Radio in Rwanda. He'd actually met the man. A little plump. Wore a straw hat. You'd think he was a Left Bank artist.

But he wasn't. And with a little nudging from Hate Radio, the imbecilic tantrums and prejudices of an overpopulated land had erupted into full-blown genocide. No-one knew how many had died in Rwanda. Not for sure. Some estimates went as high as a million.

"Penny for 'em, Pete," said Fitz.

Peterson-Smith looked up from his untouched drink, stared at Fitz for a moment then said, "Yes. I agree. The RUF's going to pull something major league. These peace talks are all wrong. I mean really. These bombs going off, it's like Mogadishu, and yet the peace talks are still ongoing. Lunacy. And I've done a backgrounder on our UN Special Envoy Ahmadou Lye. On paper the slick bastard doesn't exist. No-one's asked why."

"You a religious man, Pete?"

Peterson-Smith blinked. This was the first time that Fitz, whose conversation could go anywhere, had broached the issue of God.

"C of E," he said giving the standard response that had decorated every job application form he'd ever filled in.

"Never heard of 'em," said Fitz. "Me, I don't give a shit. You know? Mormons, the Antioch Baptist Church, Christ on a Crutch Ascendant, the way I look at it is the same way Marx did. It's about the only thing me and he see eye to eye on. Religion's the opium of the people."

"Opiate."

"Opium, Pete. It's a drug. Opiate's stuff you put in your eye. But anyway, who gives a shit? I want you to take a look at these shots. You being a religious man will be put in mind of John's Book of Revelation. A froggy journalist shot them. He couldn't sell them to his magazine. Nervous guy. I bought them. I'd have shown you them earlier but I've been kinda busy. By any kind of standard I think you'll agree it's a startling little ambulance crew."

Peterson-Smith looked at the photos. His skin crawled.

"Fakes," he said after a while.

"Ah, gimme a break! Are you stupid?"

"Am I stupid?" thought Peterson-Smith suddenly incensed. "Am I stupid? Here I am putting up with the stupidest man ever employed by Intelligence and he's asking me if I'm stupid?"

"How many drinks have you had today?" Peterson-Smith asked voice cold.

"Ten, Pete. Ten long ones. And I'm aiming to have ten more. Then I'm looking at ways to get out of this crazy country ASAP. These (he tapped the photos) aren't fakes. These are monsters. Monsters, Pete. And I'm telling you straight, this country's going straight to Christian C of E hell! Shut down. Pull down the flag, pull down the blinds, get the hell out of it. And then for me? I'm gonna order myself up a whore, a fishing rod and a cabin in Where-the-Fuck Montana. Somewhere where nobody goes!"

"Hey, Welshman!" Fitz didn't even turn in his chair. Just bellowed to be heard over the numbing roar of the rain. There was water slopping over the floor. "Fill me up! No cherries!"

"Yes, I'll fill you up," said Welshman. He too was shouting. "Fill you up with lead!"

Instead of a long Martini, Welshman produced an AK47. He steadied it on the bar and pulled the trigger. The burst of fire tore holes through every plant pot on the west-facing wall of the beer garden. Shards flew, ricochets whined skywards.

"RUF!" screamed Welshman, spraying bullets. "RUF!"

The clip emptied, the three men stared at one another dazed. Welshman seemed astonished to have missed. His mouth gaped. His eyes bulged.

"Sorry," he said. Presumably he had no other magazine for he made no attempt to reload. "Sorry," Welshman said again.

"Sonofa ..." said Fitz ponderously hauling out a pistol. He pointed it at the RUF gunman.

"Don't shoot him!" shouted Peterson-Smith.

Fitz ignored the Limey pussy. He opened fire. Two shots and the clip was empty. Bottles shattered behind the bar. There was the sudden sweet reek of a fruit cocktail mix.

Welshman was untouched.

" ... bitch," Fitz finished lamely. He looked foolishly at his weapon.

"Will you knock that off?" Peterson-Smith was on his feet, his own pistol out. Holding it on Welshman, he moved swiftly to the door to the street and turned the key. It was a stout door reinforced with old iron bands. If there were more RUF outside he wanted them to stay that way. Outside. His legs felt weak, as if they might collapse from under him, but with tremendous effort he kept his expression indifferent.

"Fitz, old chap," he drawled, childishly pleased to hear no wobble in his voice. "I think this explains the mystery of the missing barmen. The establishment is under new and unfriendly management. Let's ask Welshman why, shall we?"

* * *

The assassination attempt on the heads of UK and US Ground Intelligence was not an isolated incident. Nor was its failure unique. RUF gunmen were involved in a total of eighteen attacks that day in Freetown. Their targets were all influential figures in the expatriate community or just simply foreigners.

Two French air traffic controllers were shot dead driving to work. The Swedish ambassador who had ignored recall orders was killed when a mortar fell on the greenhouse where he was watering his beloved collection of African orchids.

Eight flight staff, seven of them Italian hostesses and one an Australian pilot, were severely injured when their hotel minibus was raked with machine-gun fire by a roof-top sniper.

The Foreign Correspondents' Club was blown up by its recently appointed bar manager, Hoppy Pongo, whose real name, though Fitz would never learn it, was Brigadier Mamba RUF. Killed in the explosion were stringers for Reuters, AP, Jiji and South Africa's *Mail* and *Guardian* newspapers.

Spong's luck held. The concussion flung him out of the window of the FCC lavatory, but beyond scratches and a nose-bleed he was undamaged. Only his dignity was badly hurt. But he was used to that.

Spong tried to report the atrocity to his editor, though he was determined that the world would never learn that he owed his life to a stomach problem. Spong, however, failed to spread the word. The FCC's phones weren't down. Courtesy of Hoppy, they were out. Permanently.

The only foreign media personnel to get the day's mayhem out to international eyes were employees of CNN. And they did it inadvertently. Given the choice they wouldn't have done it at all.

The CNN TV crew, led by an overbearing blonde with prominent teeth, were en route to an evacuation flight, when they were taken hostage by their own newly hired bodyguards. Pleas to let CNN let the rebels "tell their side of the story to the American people" fell on deaf ears. Ronald Reagan wasn't interested in telling stories to anybody, least of all the American people. He *was* interested in aquiring more camera gear.

At Reagan's urging, the cadre put worn-out Firestone tyres round the journos' necks. Then set the tyres on fire with paraffin

The grisly execution was filmed on CNN's own equipment by Reagan (after the blonde woman had tearfully shown him which buttons to press and begged him to spare her life). The film was subsequently delivered to the airport by a young female RUF courier who posed as a CNN employee.

It was then sent back to Washington where it was to thrill, appall and revolt America.

Eleven other people died. Ten were Nigerian and Indian officers with the UN peacekeeping force. The eleventh was a Palestinian businessman who was in Freetown attempting to resuscitate the once thriving Sierra Leone export of rutile, a mineral form of titanium dioxide used in paint pigment.

The most significant RUF failure occurred in the Hotel Bristol. Here a four-woman team stormed the lobby throwing grenades. There had been a logistics snarl up. Instead of discharging shrapnel, they turned out to be smoke grenades. Swirling green fog engulfed reception but there were no casualties among either hotel staff or guests.

Esther Speeks, a South African mercenary in town to attend Dr Pleasant's auction, shot all four RUF women dead from the covered sandbagged balcony of his second floor room as they fled in confusion back into the street and scrambled for their getaway truck. His pulse did not change as he shot them. Nor did his expression, which remained relaxed. When he had satisfied himself that they would all die – he'd deliberately gone for gut shots to prolong their misery – he then shot the truck tyres flat and returned to his placid contemplation of the square.

During the Rhodesian campaign gut shooting had been a logically-applied technique. The victims were known as "warblers" and their screaming and wailing played hell with the opposition's morale. In some cases, Speeks' warblers warbled for as long as an hour before the music stilled.

No-one ventured on to the street to attend them. No-one dared.

Despite the Hotel Bristol fiasco, the RUF terror campaign largely succeeded in its objective. The residents were cowed, the foreigners panicked, overseas media totally disrupted, the crowds at the airport ever more desperate in their efforts to leave. The first columns of refugees were packing their most important belongings and beginning to flee the city. At the office of UNHCR, the United Nations High Commissioner for Refugees, emergency evacuation plans were being put into motion.

Not for the refugees. For the UNHCR staff.

Only one UNHCR staffer remained aloof from the panic. But she would not tell her colleagues what work it was that so absorbed her. It was Eileen Holden's secret.

At three o'clock on that wet and bloody afternoon, RUF loudspeaker vans careered into Freetown blaring that Liberia had invaded to support the RUF in its campaign for democratic power. Government soldiers or Kamajor militia destroyed twelve of the vans. Three became bogged in mud and their occupants were butchered by mobs of terrified and angry citizens. Speeks, still on his balcony, destroyed a creaky Volkswagen van painted black and red that clanked rheumatically into the square below. He shot the driver, blew the radiator, front tyres and then made warblers of the two crew who emerged from the crash. But overall there was little coordinated resistance.

It was rumoured that those members of the Kabbah government who were not at the Organisation of African Unity summit in Namibia were planning to seek safety on a Royal Navy vessel. It was rumoured that the RUF was offering amnesty to soldiers who joined them. It was rumoured that the RUF would execute every man, woman and child. It was rumoured that units of the

Kamajor pro-government militia group believed to possess supernatural powers were preparing to take over the defence of Freetown. And the government. It was rumoured that members of the hated former military junta the Armed Forces Ruling Council (AFRC) were in league with the RUF ... It was rumoured, it was rumoured, it was rumoured ... Rumours flitted like bats.

At dusk, Speeks and some thirty other South African mercenaries there for the auction gathered in the Hotel Bristol Bar for a sundowner. There was no sun in evidence, just sheets of rain. Buckets pinged and plopped as leaks in the ceiling dripped relentlessly.

They called it a raindowner, all carried weapons and they made no pretence of hiding what they thought as they drank heavily.

This was one stupid place and one bloody silly time to be holding an auction.

CHAPTER FIFTEEN

Chatting to *Clam*

"Peterson-Smith for you, sir." The rating handed the phone respectfully to Colonel Dalziel, a grey-eyed man in the SAS. Rain was still thundering down and HMS *Clam* wallowed in queasy troughs.

"Dalziel," Dalziel said. "What's the verdict?"

Peterson-Smith was still with Fitz and was still in the Jardin de Cygnes. Welshman was hanging inverted from the ceiling, his face swollen and blackened with the blood that was still running to his head. Peterson-Smith hadn't wanted to do that.

Fitz had.

Fitz had assumed complete responsibility for the debrief. The Briton had demurred.

Peterson-Smith put down the ferocity of the debrief to the fact that Fitz, while under fire from the wretchedly inaccurate Welshman, had soiled his trousers. Neither Fitz nor Peterson-Smith had mentioned it. But the fact was a truth that was self-evident.

Although it blatantly flouted the terms of the Geneva Convention the debrief had been extremely enlightening. Welshman had told them a lot more than his name, rank and serial number.

"Not rosy," Peterson-Smith said into the Jardin de Cygnes phone. That the phone worked in a city suddenly and largely phoneless was not a miracle. On the Fitz expense account the establishment had been presented with a bulky, obsolete but still functional sat-phone. That's why they met there.

"I'm thinking of that line of Blake's. 'What RUF beast, its time come round at last slouches towards Freetown to be born.' That line."

"Who's Blake? One of your people?"

"No. Blake the poet."

"Blake wrote a poem about Freetown?" Dalziel sounded perplexed

"No, Bethlehem."

"Yes, well that would be more understandable." Dalziel still sounded perplexed.

"RUF ascendant," Peterson-Smith continued, moving the topic hurriedly away from Blake, who had not been a conversational success. "These peace talks were just a ruse to get their people into Freetown. A lot of city movement. Mortars. Ambushes. Light arms. Telephone wires down. Still no electricity. We've a source hanging here from the ceiling says the RUF are planning more of the same tomorrow and that Liberia is coming in on the RUF side. Can you confirm?"

"Negative to the Liberians as of yet. Officially they're denying any involvement. No sign of Lib gov soldiers hopping borders. They've been sheltering Sierra Leone RUF cadres though. They're coming back home."

"Super," said Peterson-Smith.

"Getting a lot of nonsense in about monsters," said Dalziel, his voice suddenly distorted by a screech of static.

"Look at it carefully is my advice, Colonel."

"Do we stay or do we go?" asked Dalziel. He wanted to stay. He wanted to do more than that. He wanted to become what current political jargon described as "proactive". Land British troops in force and restore order. The Nigerian and Indian peacekeeping forces were doing a piss-poor job of it.

"Stay. For the time being. Things change fast here. Could look up."

"Your call," Dalziel was gruff but pleased. "Stay in contact.

Good luck. Oh, and your man hanging from the ceiling? I assume that was a figure of speech?"

"Figure of speech," Peterson-Smith realised that Dalziel was tactfully reminding him that the call could be monitored. "We're actually just talking things over in a bar."

"Cheers," said Dalziel breaking the connection.

Dalziel left the communications room and walked up on to the rolling deck. The sea was mildly phosphorescent. Plankton, agitated by the wave-surge and HMS *Clam*'s lurching presence, were bioluminescing. Thousands, millions of tiny, shiny stars seemed to flash upon the surface.

Over the slopping waves the lights of Freetown went on, went off, as the power supply wavered. Light was a temporary thing, Dalziel thought. The darkness was more reliable. Not to be welcomed, something to be fought and postponed, but ultimately it was something that was reliable.

Something wet hit him in the face. The shock, the cold slap was completely unexpected. It scattered his gloomy thoughts.

On the deck lay a flying fish, gasping. How had it flown so high? Perhaps a wave had fired it at a perfect angle like a rocket.

Dalziel smiled. Picked up the fish and launched it over the gunwale, back into its element. Peterson-Smith was right, he reflected, anything could happen here.

CHAPTER SIXTEEN

Collision Course

Commander, or rather the former Commander Joe – now just plain Joe – was deeply unhappy. As he followed his new Commander, a brutal and dissipated-looking man called General Cain, Joe seethed with impotent fury. His backside hurt dreadfully and was still bleeding.

He'd been beaten by General Butt Naked's field officer, General Murder. He'd been held responsible for the radio station's destruction. His report of the monsters had been ridiculed. He'd also been criticised for his radio speech. About the only thing they'd listened to was his statement that the radio wreckers came from Lalapanzi.

Added to this was demotion. General Cain was now in charge. General Cain, who'd been hiding in Liberia, used perfume that made him smell like a woman and had a huge gut that hung over his belt and made him wheeze as they pushed along the road towards Lalapanzi to exact, on General Murder's orders, revenge.

Commander Cain's cadre was rubbish, Joe thought. They were arrogant with the confidence of their drugs and their soon-to-be victory. Their over-confidence, Joe thought, was the result of their ignorance and their hiding in the safety of Liberia during the RUF's time of fighting retreats.

When Commander Joe had suggested that Lalapanzi be bypassed on account of its monsters, General Murder had flown into a rage. Three of the older, larger men had been ordered to

publicly rape Commander Joe. In front of his comrades. They had
done it and everybody had jeered. He'd been bent over a concrete
mixing machine, his eyes shut, teeth grinding. He had refused to
scream or whimper as the men had reared and plunged, playing
up to the whoops and boos of the assembled crowd.

Rape was not an uncommon punishment in the RUF – it had
happened to Joe before, to most of the young boys and girls in
fact, and Joe himself had sometimes raped his own subordinates
– but this rape had been unfair. Degrading, painful, he'd felt as if
his entrails were on fire, but most important the punishment had
been totally, totally, totally unfair.

There were monsters, dammit! *He'd seen them.* Why wouldn't
anybody listen?

Joe fingered his RPG. He fumed. He hated the noise the new
men were making, blundering along in the bush. Anyone could
hear them coming. They were complete amateurs.

He yearned to tell General Butt Naked of the stupidities of
General Murder and of the indignities he had forced on him. Of
the idiot incompetence of these people. But the general was in
Freetown on important diplomatic business and it was Murder
who was temporarily in charge. Murder and Butt-Naked were
notorious rivals. Hated each other.

Behind him there were men from Liberia who had witnessed
the rape. They were giggling and making crude jokes.

"Joey," one cooed, "how's your hole?"

There was an explosion of laughter.

"Joey won't be farting now, not after they stretched his hole so
wide."

More laughter.

Joe said nothing back. They were nearing Lalapanzi and Joe
had stopped his rage, had swallowed it. He was now in that
strange flat state of calm that enveloped him at times of crisis.

He dropped behind the men from Liberia on the pretext of
tying a loose lace.

"He bending down for more of the same," said one soldier. "He develop a taste for it. Maybe I've got one for him after we take Lalapanzi!"

Let them laugh, Joe thought. Laugh away. They'd soon find out the truth.

Monsters were not funny.

Benjamin Franklin was worried. Five of his men had deserted. They'd ignored his orders to stay by the road and had slipped away to the village to loot. They'd not come back, not been seen since.

Rindert had been emphatically explicit in his orders. Franklin and the squad were *not* to enter the village, but were to guard the road. If there was any sign of RUF movement he was to fire a purple flare, but he was *not* to fall back on the village. Rindert would come.

In the ten long days they had waited by the road, the men had become increasingly bored and difficult to control. Even the Baptists were surly and prone to indiscipline. Each day since his return from Freetown, Rindert had arrived with a sack of canned fish and maize flour. The fish, Franklin thought (but did not say) was disgusting. He yearned for beef, egusi soup, groundnut stew. Real food. This foul Soviet fish diet was getting him down.

He was also becoming increasingly disturbed by the village. At night, odd lights glowed and floated and moved about and there were occasional sounds. Once a high, thin keening had risen. It put Franklin, and his men, in mind of ghosts and haunts.

Porroh. Papa Det.

In an attempt to thwart the haunts, Franklin had led the men in the only hymn he could remember all the words to – *My cup is full of running over!* – and the music had warmed them for a while. But the nights were long and the eerie lights and noises continued.

Then there had been the rain. Seven solid days of it. He'd huddled, dripping and morose, watching the road dissolve into gluey mud that was plagued by mosquitoes that whined about his ears, wishing that this mission would be over.

The Mission, too. It was, he was now sure of it, abandoned by God. It was the Red Priest's place now. His and Papa Dets. Papa Det. The Cold Man.

The men had spent most of the first days arguing, smoking weed and grousing about the food. Now they were mainly silent. Despondent and dull. Thoroughly drugged. Depressed.

Shorty Balingwe, the youngest member of the squad, had developed a hacking cough that brought up flecks of blood and several others were suffering from diarrhoea.

Franklin wondered how to explain the five missing men.

Rindert would be angry. Franklin admired Rindert. He didn't want him angry.

Noises ahead interrupted his dispirited chain of thought.

Soldiers were coming. He could hear bushes being pushed aside, the metallic rattle of weapons. Someone called "Joey, Joey, how your hole?" The enigmatic question was followed by sniggering laughter. Whoever was coming was very close and not afraid of making noise.

Forehead wrinkled in concentration, Franklin glanced at his men. Three were asleep but the others had heard and were looking at him uncertainly.

Franklin's heart was racing. Men coming. RUF. Bound to be RUF. What should he do? What would Rindert do? What would Rindert want him to do?

Franklin put down his RPG. He hadn't told Rindert because he had been embarrassed by his ignorance, but he had no idea how to use it. His AK he did know how to use. But where was it? He'd left it somewhere. And where was his purple flare and the flare gun?

"Precious Jesus, guide me with your light," he prayed as the noises got louder and the RUF men got nearer. "My cup is full of running over."

While Franklin floundered and Commander Cain's RUF cadre sloppily advanced, Rindert fiddled with the sat-phone. He was good with appliances, engines, mechanics in general, but no matter what he tried he could not get the sat-phone to perform with consistency. Sometimes it worked, sometimes it didn't.

At the moment it was not working. Rindert could not understand why. It was infuriating. He needed news from Freetown. The last call he'd had told him the city was going to hell, with RUF squads doing all kinds of damage. That had been just after lunch and Eugene Smuts, his caller, had had all sorts of whinging to do. How was he to get the men out to the auction? Were the roads safe? Was there an air strip? Why wasn't there an air strip? Was there RUF activity at Lalapanzi? Could he provide vegetarian food?

"What do you think I'm running here? A bloody beach resort? Bring your own lettuce and use your own bloody initiative," Rindert had snapped at Smuts. The Crocodile had told him that everyone had been instructed to arrive at the auction self-sufficient. Now here was Smuts with his gourmet requests.

Then the phone had stopped. Just stopped.

The time was now five o'clock. The rain had ceased, but low cloud threatened more. Jack was drunk again and asleep in his study.

Rindert abandoned his investigation of the sat-phone and wondered whether he should check up on Franklin. Morale out there on the road wasn't the highest and was declining by the day. He wasn't surprised. Hanging around in the bush in the rain was dull and uncomfortable. He knew the men resented not being housed in the village, didn't understand why they were not housed in the village and wanted to go home. He wanted to go home too.

Yes, he decided, now was as good a time as any to check on Benjamin Franklin and his men. Rindert hoisted a sack of cans onto his shoulder. Not fish this time but the corned beef with hippo fat. He added two bottles of brandy too. Jack wouldn't miss them. There was enough brandy in the Mission to float a super-tanker.

Rindert descended the stairs and was past the wooden planks and daubed warnings that sealed off most of the ground floor and the Ebola death cells. That's when he heard the first shots.

Rindert dropped the sack of food and broke into a run back upstairs to where Jack slept on, his body twitching as he dreamed.

"I've about had it with this thing," Smuts growled. The thing Smuts had about had it with was his phone.

It wasn't working again.

As dusk gathered in Freetown and smoke from burning build-ings swirled muddily skywards, Smuts and five other South Africans were assembled in the lobby of the Hotel Bristol.

Smuts was a lantern-jawed, morose-looking man in his early fifties, a veteran of Angola, DRC and guerrilla war in Mozambique. His companions and he had flown in by private aircraft the previ-ous day from Monrovia and were beginning to contemplate flying out again pronto. Auction be blowed. This wasn't Sotheby's. This was a war zone.

Others in the hotel, also here for the auction, were, by contrast, in buoyant exuberant spirits. Most were already preparing to leave for the bush. In the car park at the rear of the Bristol an assortment of Unimogs, trucks, Land Rovers and Land Cruisers fortified with sheets of steel were revving, reversing, manoeuvring for position while their drivers laughed and called out good-natured insults.

A fool's carnival, Smuts thought it. Horsing around, drinking beer, swapping war stories. Where do they think they are for Pete's sake?

Part of Smuts' ill-humour was fuelled by the lack of success the day had so far brought him.

Smuts, who was secretly terrified of landmines, had initially hoped to fly into Lalapanzi, but that bad-tempered, inconsiderate shit, Rindert, had failed to clear an airstrip.

He'd then tried to borrow a helicopter off Mad Mike Schlessinger the SHEELD boss. Schlessinger had laughed at him. Asked him how much he proposed to pay, then deemed the offer inadequate. Money had always been more important to Mad Mike than the bonds of comradeship forged by mutual service in the Angolan war.

The mercenary bastard!

Now Smuts and his colleagues were undecided. Not being able to communicate further with Lalapanzi was one factor contributing to their state of indecision. The turbulent state of Freetown was another.

All day there had been the sharp staccato crack and slap of small arms, the rattling metallic bark of AKs. World Service broadcasts had detailed a picture of entropic uncertainty with reports of haphazard fighting in the suburbs and in the vicinity of the airport. There were debates in various capitals about whether to send in more peacekeepers. No-one sounded keen.

A number of other big news stories had also broken. A 747 had crashed in Florida and Russian premier Vladimir Putin had had a heart attack. These stories were largely eclipsing the collapse of order in Sierra Leone which, after all, was not exactly new.

From the perspective of the Hotel Bristol, Freetown did not look encouraging. The square outside was deserted. No-one had brought in any of the bodies that sprawled or curled on the rain drenched asphalt. Some staff from the hotel had tried – eventually – but there had been gunfire and they'd retreated to the safety of the lobby.

The gunfire had come from the hotel itself. From the second floor. Someone up there was wrong in the head Smuts thought.

"It'll be better out of the city," one of Smuts' colleagues said. It was Herbert Dufresne, crew-cut, solidly built, Dufresne looked like the archetypal Boer. He was also wanted for a number of crimes in his native country, including terrorism, ivory smuggling and murder.

"What makes you say that?" Smuts muttered. The hotel was emptying. Men were bustling past with bags, weapons, radios. Smuts' feelings of confusion were increasing. He felt left out of the excitement. Oddly forlorn. There had been a time when he'd found war invigorating, exciting. That time was past. He wondered if he was getting old.

"What makes you say it'll be better out of the city?" Smuts repeated.

"Nothing," admitted Dufresne.

"I say we clear off," said Smuts reaching a decision. "Skip out. I've got a bad feeling about all this. If we could fly in to this Lalapanzi place I'd say we do it. But I'm not keen on a night drive. I mean why the hell convoy out at night?"

"Security?" guessed Dufresne.

"Herbert, tell me one thing that's secure about driving through a bush war, along roads that'll be mined, and doing it at night."

"Rain will have turned the road to slurry," said Dufresne bleakly.

There was more glum debate. Finally the five other men agreed. Smuts was known as a man who had good instincts. If Smuts said that things were going to go very badly wrong, then things, in all likelihood, would go very badly wrong.

"Everyone agreed? OK then, let's beat it."

Smuts' vehicle, however, was the only one that left the Bristol for the airport and out.

All the others, in convoy, departed for Lalapanzi as darkness fell.

* * *

It was Shorty who kept his head and fired first. While Franklin was searching for his AK, three men still slept, and the others stared uncertainly at each other, Shorty saw the first of the RUF party push their way past a mass of thorn bush less than thirty yards away.

He remembered to flick off safety and opened fire.

Luck was on Shorty's side. The first three RUF men were knocked off their feet and back into the thorns, where they hung motionless, heads slumped, bright red blood pumping from their necks in little jets. These were the first people Shorty had ever killed.

He felt thrilled. Felt like Jean-Claude Van Damme. Robocop. That guy, Bruce Willis, who took out all those terrorists in that skyscraper movie.

Shorty let out a crazed whoop.

The other militiamen, inspired by this success opened fire too. Bullets zipped and whined, thumped into the ground, kicking up gouts of mud, but none of their first salvo caused further damage.

The RUF began to return fire.

Shorty loosed off another clip. Man, he was on a roll! This time he got two Liberians. He also blew Commander Cain's head off. Shorty didn't see it, he had his eyes virtually closed as his weapon discharged, but that's what happened. One moment Commander Cain was standing intact, about to unsling his AK. The next, his head was knocked off his neck with such force that it broke the jaw of the man behind him.

But the abruptly leaderless RUF had numbers on their side. There were nearly a hundred men and women in their unit and as the shock of the encounter wore off they began to fan out. Grenades were thrown. The RUF grenades killed five RUF soldiers and injured two more. RUF flankers, thinking they'd been ambushed, began shooting into the bush.

A savage and well-aimed burst of bullets from the rear of the RUF cut down four Liberians. Former Commander Joe then went on to shoot two other comrades by mistake. One was a sister of Sister Sue.

In the chaos Joe didn't notice.

He was after Comander Cain. He was going to shoot that fucker. Shoot his balls off! Joe screamed, he commanded, he led the RUF into a run.

At Benjamin Franklin's command the militia turned and scattered. Fled.

All except Shorty, who just stood there yipping and firing from the hip. Just like Bruce Willis. Just like him.

"Wake up!" yelled Rindert.

Jack did. His eyes were red, his hair one godawful tangle, his cheeks puffed with brandy and sleep. Rindert thought that he'd never seen an uglier sight.

"Get your units going! We're under attack."

"Hell's bells," said Jack blearily. "Who's attacking?"

"Well its not Jews for Jesus and we can pretty much rule out the Salvation Army. Now will you get your units moving. Please!"

Jack stood, reeled and steadied himself with one hand on the table. He looked as if he was about to faint. "So drunk," he said. "So damned drunk. Can't think straight. It's my weakness. I should get Papa Det out of the freezer. No I shouldn't. Where's my Christ-forsaken kelp horn?"

"Your what?" Rindert had moved to the window from which he could see the advance of figures. There was a characteristic loping shamble to an RUF attack. They looked like apes, bent-kneed, loping, shambling apes. This lot also looked a thoroughbred rabble. Not just confused. Totally erratic. They were shooting each other.

"Bloody morlocks," Rindert said unlimbering his sniper's rifle. "We're in deep shit. Get your units moving!"

"My kelp horn. It's a horn made of dried kelp," Jack said. "I'll need it to blow it. It's the signal."

The first RUF fighters were entering the village. Rindert kept his head low. There were bullets anywhere and everywhere.

Jack began to rummage in a chest by his cluttered table. He emerged with a black and curling horn. He puckered his lips, blew.

"Nearly got it," he said, red in the face. "Nearly there."

He put his lips back to the horn. Blew again.

There was a barely audible farting noise. Then a muted pheep. Jack lost his balance, wobbled and fell over. Passed out.

"Great," said Rindert.

Rindert picked up the horn and after several fruitless attempts was rewarded by a startling metallic bray that echoed through the Mission and out into the damp, hot air of Lalapanzi.

The response was immediate.

The monsters came. Commander Joe had known they would. And they did. From out of every house and hut the homunculi swarmed.

Some moved slowly, others with a startling jerky speed as if they were puppets. Green smoke jetted from their nose pipes, many of them keened and whistled in their agitation. It was a hellish noise that set one's teeth on edge. Like nails scratching on a blackboard or biting into tin foil.

"Get you RUF! Get you RUF!" intoned a shrill, crackling, static-ridden tape recorder.

The first RUF soldiers loping towards the Mission building stared at what was emerging about them in horrified, incredulous shock. None thought to employ their weapons.

They screamed. They ran. Porroh! Monsters! They were pursued, overwhelmed and brought down. Then butchered.

On the fringe of Lalapanzi, most RUF soldiers simply turned, dropped weapons and stampeded back down the road. A few attempted to shoot. One threw a grenade which landed at the feet of a particularly bloated homunculus.

The explosion showered the street with cogs, Ebola-infested blood and shredded body fragments.

This brief resistance was overwhelmed. Only one of the RUF attackers kept his head.

Joe, who had known what was coming, had slipped to the rear of the assault party. He raised his RPG and through the sights saw, briefly, the bloated face of Sister Sue. Her features were swollen, grotesque, like the skin of a black, rotting melon and the neck which supported her head was thin as a broomstick. Sister Sue's mouth was opened in a fixed, gaping O that showed razor blades as teeth.

It, the Sue abomination, was staring straight at him as it ran, windmilling its arms, short legs pumping. It moved absurdly quickly, like a video image on fast forward. Staring straight at Joe as it closed the distance. A hundred yards. Ninety yards. Eighty. Windmilling arms. Pumping legs. The fixed O. The razor blade teeth. Seventy yards. Sixty.

Joe fired his missile, not at the Sue-monster but at the Mission building that loomed darkly behind her. The Mission was the source of these fiends, Joe was sure of it. The Mission was the central hive. The poisoned heart.

The missile flared and wobbled off. Joe dropped the launcher, turned and ran as if the devil himself were on his heels. He was under no illusions that he was in a race for more than his life as he sprinted away into the gathering dusk.

Watching from the window Rindert saw Joe's missile fly in the sluggish slow motion of a nightmare or a car sliding towards a crash. It rose up and away from the boy soldier who had fired it, seemed to float dreamily towards him, dropped suddenly and vanished through a small ground floor window and into the basement. Where it detonated.

Everything went white for Rindert. Blinding, blindingly white.

CHAPTER SEVENTEEN

Moonshine

The simultaneous release of 1,000 litres of distilled moonlight that was triggered by the detonation of Joe's RPG missile produced a flare which was momentarily visible from space.

Most experts worldwide who monitored the satellite imagery dismissed the phenomenon as a mechanical aberration, a fault in the film or a quirk in atmospherics. Several made enquiries as to whether a nuclear test had been conducted. Or if a meteorite had struck.

The mainstream media, still engrossed with the health of Vladimir Putin and the Miami plane crash, did not pick up on the story, or if they did, they did so lightly. Additional catastrophes – the bombing of a Loyalist pub in Londonderry by the Real IRA, the drug overdose of Oasis star Liam Gallagher and a 6.6 Richter scale earthquake in Guatemala City further served to eclipse the incident. It was not, by any standards, a slow news day.

The garish tabloids that adorn supermarket shelves by cash registers in north and south America, by contrast, liked the story a lot.

Editors ran headlines such as "Hand of God Touches Africa" and "The Angels Have Landed!" and faked photos of glowing, celestial beings (the satellite photos showed a small white smear on a black background and were deemed insufficiently compelling to boost circulation).

Certain religious groups in the American Mid-West ran with

the tabloid ball, attributing the moonlight flare to Almighty God or the appearance of the archangel Gabriel. Apocalypse was mentioned in a few pulpits. There was weeping, speaking in tongues, snake handling and a marked surge in church donations.

Several sects, convinced that it signified the Second Coming, attempted to book flights to Sierra Leone in the face of unequivocal advice from the US State Department that travel to Sierra Leone was not advisable.

The moonlight flare was also visible in Freetown but most people missed it. Few people had their eyes on the skies. What was going on on the ground was more than enough to keep them busy.

CHAPTER EIGHTEEN

Brave as a Lion

The RUF peace initiative was now accepted by all but the terminally optimistic as a cynical ploy to get sufficient numbers of their radical fighters into central parts of Freetown in an attempt to shut the city down.

Freetown was in freefall.

The RUF lacked sufficient fighters to win, but had too many within city limits to lose. At least within the next few days. The result was a violently ongoing stalemate.

With most combatants lacking recognizable uniforms and with other breakaway units, bandit groups and vigilante bands also in Freetown, no-one who knew what was going on had any idea of what was going to happen.

Or, in all honesty, what was going on.

In a conversation with Dalziel during which he recommended the evacuation of all foreign nationals, Peterson-Smith described the situation on the ground as "badly confused".

Fitz preferred the phrase "fucked up". He announced his intention of leaving by the 18:00 flight to London. And never coming back. Not to Sierra Leone, not to Africa. Never again, Fitz said, never again. "Montana for me, a whore and a fishing rod!"

At 13.30 while Fitz was packing his belongings to the background hum of his document shredder he received a call from one of his five men informing him that the airport had fallen into RUF hands.

At 14:50 while Fitz was unpacking his belongings he received another call informing him that the airport was in pro-government hands.

"Will you make up your goddamned mind?" Fitz had bellowed into the phone.

"I will when they do," his informant had said dryly. "Anyway there's no chance of a flight. No planes going anywhere today. Not from here. A kamikaze wouldn't attempt a landing here right now. The runway's like the moon. Fuel depot's on fire. So is the ammo dump. I'll never understand why Africans always have ammo dumps in their airports. Are the Brits going to take people out by boat?"

Fitz said he sure as hell hoped so and then the phone went dead. Pack? Unpack? Risk another trip to the Jardin de Cygnes? Ah, to hell with it. He reached for his hip flask.

It was empty.

Ah, to hell with it all!

General Butt Naked was lying in a bath tub full of cold, rust-brown water. He was more naked than usual having lost not just his eyebrows, his eye lashes but also all of his once magnificent afro. What the cigar had begun, the car bomb had finished. He was as hairless as an egg.

While the general soothed the scorch marks on his face and body, plaster dust and small chunks of concrete rained in spasmodic bursts down from the ceiling.

The Hotel Frangipani, the entire building, was bucking and quivering as mortars fired by pro-government militia thumped down and RUF teams returned fire from sandbagged positions on the roof.

Boom. Thud. Spang. Ratter-tatter. Bang. Crash. It was the percussion backing the howling opera of the latest incompetently initiated urban West African war. Vocals supplied by the hollering of the crossfire victims.

Many of the junior RUF delegates caught in the frank, unequivocal violence of the Hotel Frangipani siege had no idea that the RUF high command was preparing to use the peace talks as an opportunity to resume full-scale war and seize the capital. They had actually thought the war would be over.

Idiots!

They had brought their women and children with them. They'd expected rounds of UN-sponsored banquets, UN-organised speeches in conference halls, shopping opportunities and days at Lumley or the beautiful River No. 2 beach.

At the end of the talks and feasts and speeches they'd expected that an agreement would be hammered out. They'd also expected that there might be something waiting for them there in Freetown that was to their advantage.

Instead they had flown or driven into Freetown from the bush, from RUF-held towns, and in many cases from their overseas diamond-subsidized homes in London, Brussels, New York and Monrovia, only to find that they had been deceived.

Particularly confusing for the besieged politicos was the absence of the RUF's ruling council, the top command. For reasons unknown they had yet to put in an appearance. No-one seemed to have the slightest idea why or where they were.

The howls of anguish and fear from the trapped family members added to the bedlam.

The children squalled.

But despite the commotion, General Butt Naked's thoughts were not on the immediate fighting but on the monstrous chauffeur that had triggered the explosion that had terminated his diplomatic career.

He'd recognized the chauffeur.

Not recognized all of it. Just the head. But there was no question in his mind that he knew it. Even though the head he had recognized was not in what could be described as peak condition.

The head, he was sure, had belonged to Colonel Brave As A Lion.

The interesting thing about Colonel Brave As A Lion was that he was dead. Butt Naked had seen him die. Brave As A Lion had trodden on one of his own landmines. He'd laid them drunk and had confused their locations. One he'd forgotten about had blown both his legs off below the knee while he was delivering a lecture to kidnapped village children (inducted involuntarily as RUF recruits). The lecture had been titled, "Why We Are Invincible".

Brave As A Lion had been brave as a lion, as far as Butt Naked could recall. He'd also been as Stupid As A Donkey.

What remained of the colonel, *and this was the point*, had died shortly after the mine accident and had then been sold to the filthy drunken priest at Lalapanzi Mission.

Sold by Butt Naked himself. Back when the priest was paying high, high prices for body parts of any sort.

So what was Colonel Brave As A Lion's head doing driving around in a UN vehicle attached to who knew what and detonating bombs?

It was a puzzle.

General Butt Naked had assumed that the Brandy Priest was using the body parts for medical research. He'd not considered the possibility of witchcraft or voodoo.

There was voodoo aplenty in Sierra Leone. The general himself was a keen practitioner. But he'd not thought white men did it.

He'd certainly never seen voodoo work as well as it had in the UN car. Brave As a Lion blowing smoke out of his nose trumpet. Obviously dead. But still capable of stealing a UN car – the general assumed he had stolen it, not even the UN would be gullible enough to lend one of their cars to a rotting zombie packing sticks of dynamite – then driving the car; then blowing up the car; killing all those jeering scumbags who'd been giving him such a hard time over his pink suit. That was serious power. Wow, yes, the general thought, serious power indeed. That was major league. Worthy of Papa Det!

He decided that this voodoo required some follow-up and resolved that as soon as there was a lull in the Hotel Frangipani siege he'd take some of his men out of Freetown and check out Lalapanzi. The yelling and screaming was getting on his nerves and he'd known this Freetown takeover was going to be a dud as soon as he'd heard of the plan.

The UNITA had tried the same thing in Luanda, marching in for peace while planning war, and 10,000 of the UNITA had been massacred.

This wasn't the same thing, not exactly the same. UNITA had left it too late. They'd not even got round to starting their massacre. They'd been massacred first by the MPLA. Here and today the RUF were pre-empting that sort of government massacre by trying one of their own massacres before the government troops got organised to get their massacre in first.

Butt Naked, a thwarted and hairless diplomat in a bath, wanted his massacre, when it came, to be a proper massacre.

Leave these fools to their half-arsed massacres.

The key to success he felt keenly was in the voodoo that made a dead man's head blow up a car. That was the stuff.

A tracer round cut through the general's window, hit his bath and shot upwards through the ceiling dislodging the light which fell in a dangling tangle of wires.

This was the wrong way to go. This city warfare was stupid. Butt Naked was decided.

Wait for a lull. Force a break out attack by the fighters in the Frangipani. Whatever the method, but get out of the hotel siege with good men, seize vehicles and get to Lalapanzi soon as soon could be.

Find out exactly what Jack was doing in the Mission.

CHAPTER NINETEEN

Aftermath

What Jack was doing in the Mission while the RUF general made his plans in the bath was simple.

Jack was sitting gape-mouthed and stunned. There were tears on his cheeks. He was stinking like a goat.

It was now fully dark outside and Jack's room was itself only dimly illuminated. A fire burned in the grate (the moonlight flare had left the Mission unnaturally cold). A storm lantern glowed weakly on the table.

"Of all the rotten, lousy bits of luck," Jack said, snorting and wiping at his face with his grimy sleeve. "Of all the dismal, blasted, unfair, rotten, lousy, lousy, lousy bits of luck ..."

He looked like a ghost. With a hangover.

"Crappy," Rindert agreed. "Thoroughly crappy."

Rindert rose and walked to the open window. Outside in the night he could see pale glows as homunculi patrolled with gas torches in case the RUF came back for more.

He didn't think they would though. Not after an ambush straight out of a Hieronymous Bosch painting followed by the explosion of moonlight.

Not even the RUF were that deranged.

He wondered what had happened to Franklin and his men. Whether it was worth going out to see if he could find them or, more probably, what was left of them.

Even if they'd survived the RUF rush he doubted very much that any of them would hang around. Who would?

If they hadn't survived, the homunculi were no doubt busy with their hacksaws. The thought of encountering Franklin's earnest Shoveller-duck head mounted on a new unit made Rindert feel queasy. Why did the homunculi have to be so gut-revoltingly hideous?

Was that Jack's madness showing its true colours? Or was it the homunculi themselves asserting their own twisted creative skills?

Behind him there was a gurgle as Jack poured more brandy. The Jack litany of complaint then resumed. "Of all the lousy, pig-arsed—"

"Can you make more moonlight?" Rindert interrupted. Jack had every reason to whine – that RPG hit through the tiny window had been a black-hearted miracle – but the man's bleating was getting on his nerves.

Jack laughed raggedly. "It takes ages here. There's no way on God's green earth I'd be able to make enough to supply the units we've got now. Not with African moonlight. I told you, didn't I, that the African stuff's sub-standard?"

"You told me. Like everything else made here. How about the English stuff from Northumberland. The alchemist you mentioned, Mango, has he got more?"

"Mungo," Jack sounded pettish, sulky.

"OK," said Rindert trying to keep Jack calm. "OK, this Mungo. Has he got more moonlight? Can he make more?"

Jack nodded. "He can make it quickly enough if there's a full moon."

Suddenly animated, Jack reared up and left the room with the storm lantern.

Rindert heard his unsteady but hurried footsteps mount the stairs and enter the room with the chicken-footed furnaces. The boards creaked above Rindert's head as furniture was moved.

More footsteps, and then Jack returned with charts which he unscrolled and studied intently. It wasn't that the charts were particularly finely drawn, but that the brandy was interfering with Jack's vision.

"Of all the lousy, rotten, stinking—"

"Please don't start all that again, Jack, I'm very tired. When's the nearest full moon?"

"Three days ago," said Jack. "They had a beauty over there in Northumberland. Shame then there'll not be another lousy moon until the twenty-first. We're doomed."

Bit of a poser, thought Rindert. Then an idea struck him.

"I bet he'll have it stored," Rindert said. "If that moon was as good as you say it was, I'll bet he was out there on the moors in his robes with his silver net or his mirror or pipettes or whatever the hell this Mango character uses. I'll bet he's got some of the freshest distilled moonlight you could hope to see."

"Hope's right. It's our only hope."

"So it's down to whether Mango has some moonlight, whether he'll sell it to us, whether I can get it shipped to Freetown and across country back to you. Before your homunculi ... um ..."

"Begin to experience psychotic episodes." Jack finished the sentence for him. "In a nutshell, yes."

Rindert stared back out of the window into the dark. The glow of the patrol gaslights continued. A low keening rose on the night air. The view, limited though it was, was pregnant with difficulties.

From the sparks flying in the Christian American Charitable Foundation's fair trade goods workshop Rindert guessed that something was busy at work with a welding torch. There was the sound of a drill, sawing and hammering. Considerable industry out there in the night. Making more potentially psychotic homunculi hungry for moonlight.

It reminded Rindert of the Walt Disney cartoon where Mickey Mouse had got all the brooms and buckets going but hadn't been able to stop them.

For Mickey Mouse read Father Jack.

Rindert spoke again. "Now our only problem is, what do we do about this auction?"

Jack eyes flashed with panic. In his anguish he'd forgotten about the auction.

"Of all the rotten, bloody, lousy—" Jack stopped suddenly. He smacked the palm of his hand against his forehead.

And a broad lupine grin spread across his face.

"Rindert, old man, we're saved! We'll auction off all the units. Discount prices if necessary. Three for two. Hell, four for the price of two. Six! The buyers will take them away and the units can go berserk back at their place. We get the cash. They get the psychotic episodes! We clear off and its beach time Costa Rica, wherever the hell that is. No more lousy canned fish and hippo grease."

Rindert thought this suggestion over.

He reached for a plate of fish, illuminated in the steady but rather futile glow of the storm lantern.

It *was* disgusting fish.

"Where the hell are you getting this fish from?"

"The Mission staff were given it by the World Food Programme. Their food's always the worst because it has been donated. Bleeding heart liberal types empty their shelves of stuff they don't want. Because it's past the sell-by date. Companies too. Dump the lot."

Rindert left the silence long enough to get just that little bit more. When it came it wasn't convincing.

"I've just been too busy to go shopping," finished the man who made monsters but who had lost all his crucial moonlight.

Jack had said he could read minds.

Rindert's mental jury was still out on that one.

But Rindert could read voices.

Jack was lying. Not about the World Food Programme. Their food was, upon occasion, appalling. They'd even overseen the distribution of donated low-to-no calories foods during the Somali famine. Go-Slim "To Lose Weight" Chocolate, Go-Slim Super

Soup, and then there had been all those electric blankets ...

Jack must therefore be lying about the fish.

Why lie about a can of fish? Rindert turned and spoke with the voice of authority. He didn't wave the gun and didn't need to. Jack was no longer a success story.

"We postpone the auction," said Rindert.

"Aw, come on, Rindert, have a heart," whined Jack.

"I said, we postpone the auction," said Rindert implacably.

He took the storm lantern and walked through the Mission for the room with the sat-phone hoping that the buyers were still in Freetown. It was bad enough postponing an auction to which one had invited some of the world's most dangerous men. It would be a lot worse if they had already started on the final leg of their journey from the Hotel Bristol into the bush for Lalapanzi.

But Rindert was not about to be stupid. Selling unstable, psychotic homunculi to men who would take it *very* personally (if they survived) and who relied on violence for their daily bread was, unquestionably, stupid.

He'd have to inform The Crocodile too.

Rindert just hoped the sat-phone was working.

Jack stared at Rindert's departing back with furious, befuddled eyes. The storm lantern's glow withdrew, Rindert's footsteps creaked away and Jack was left with just the silence of the Mission, the drip of the rain and the light of the fire. Jack curled up into a foetal position and drifted off.

"Lousy, bloody ... bloody, loussss, fisswiggs." Jack was asleep, his brandy bottle clutched against his chest like a teddy bear.

CHAPTER TWENTY

Monsters Again!

On HMS *Clam*, Dalziel was in conference with Wiley who monitored the mainland radio stations from his 'Rabbit Hole' below decks. Together Dalziel and Wiley were trying to put the pieces of the day's demented jigsaw together. It was not easy.

Government radio stations in a position to give news had been effectively targeted by RUF assaults and there had been very little that was coherent broadcast over rebel stations.

Radio Butt Naked had resumed transmission under the new name of Radio Murder.

"Out with the old boss, in with the new boss," Wiley sighed as he presented Dalziel with the transcription of the latest programming. "But the song, very unfortunately, remains the same."

"I'm not reading all that rubbish," said Dalziel tersely. "If you could be kind enough to summarize?"

Wiley explained that in between broadcasts of ABBA's *Waterloo*, Radio Murder had accused the government of using voodoo in its efforts to destabilise the peace process. The RUF was complaining that the use of monsters violated the laws of Christ and the United Nations. It promised that RUF units would stamp out persons engaging in voodoo who were also engaged in creating counter-revolutionary, recidivist, lickspittle zombies. The radio said it was going to hire in the best porroh witchdoctors in the country to stamp out the zombie scourge."

"Lot of long words for the RUF. Reckon they've probably got a pet Cuban," Wiley concluded.

"That lickspittle stuff's North Korean," said a junior officer. "Or Chinese. Cubans go on about swamp geese. Apparently that's insulting in Cuba. Hang on, no. That was Nicaragua. Sandino. Always going on about Americans being swamp geese, Sandino was. A real bee in his bonnet about Americans and swamp geese."

"Monsters again," muttered Dalziel, ignoring the swamp geese rubbish.

Radio Murder could rant about zombies and witchcraft to its heart's content but Dalziel had had reports of monsters from other unlikely sources that threw the issue into stranger fields of respectability.

Some days earlier the UN car pool had filed a report in pidgin English stating that "persons disguised as monsters" had launched a dawn assault on the premises killing two local personnel. The attackers had then stolen a UN vehicle that was subsequently used in a car bomb attack on General Butt Naked, RUF-affiliated, in Freetown for "peace discussions aimed at achieving synergy".

That had been the summary. The report itself had been pure gobbledygook. Like many a UN communique. And of course in triplicate; ccs to everyone imaginable.

Complaints about monsters had also come in from Connaught Hospital. Here they had apparently stolen an ambulance. The incident had occurred on the same day as the UN vehicle theft.

"These monsters setting themselves up for a derby of some sort, sir?" one of Dalziel's junior officers had suggested. "Should we advise guard on the Freetown fire station? They've got some shiny red engines there. Nice big bells."

"Funny at first, Jones," Dalziel had explained. "The success of a joke is for you to stop the joke before it stops being a joke all by its own little self."

The officer had stiffened to respectful attention and had fallen silent.

Dalziel had continued reading the report even as he had issued the reprimand.

One monster the hospital's report stated had been shot by a doctor with an AK47.

Shot by a doctor? With an AK47?

What kind of hospital were they running over there? Dalziel had wondered.

The body of the monster had been taken to the morgue. Here Dalziel's interest had been piqued. Physical evidence.

The morgue had then been hit by mortars, subsequent reports stated. Dalziel's interest had dwindled.

The last bit of monster-related business was a recorded message from Peterson-Smith. "Fitz", one of the Cousins (which meant Americans), had actually managed to obtain photos of the monsters. Fitz was promising to show them once he was safe aboard HMS *Clam*. Peterson-Smith suggested that Fitz was not the man he once had been.

Neither were the ambulance crew, Peterson-Smith had added, not if the photos were genuine. Nothing firm on the monster front Peterson-Smith had said. Just watch this space.

Dalziel vowed privately to do just that.

Moving on from the enigmatic monster front, Dalziel was confronted with a weird bit of news from the Hotel Bristol.

Just over a hundred men, all white or Hispanic, but predominantly white, had left the Hotel Bristol in convoy, heavily armed, pre-dusk. Peterson-Smith had logically assumed they'd deploy around State House or storm the Hotel Frangipani on behalf of the government and in return for diamonds. That was SOP for the South African contingent and had been for years.

Instead, though, they'd shot their way through several RUF road-blocks, destroyed a government-loyal police barracks that had initiated contact (which meant opening fire first) and had then left the Freetown city limits. (Not that Freetown had any precisely defined city limits. It just went on for as long as it had the energy and then petered out.)

Their destination remained unclear. Motives unreadable.

More peculiar still was a report that the convoy had re-appeared at the Hotel Bristol's car park five hours after its abrupt departure. All men resuming their rooms and forcibly evicting refugees who had occupied them. The source reported that the refugees consisted largely of RUF women, children and diplomats who had been relocated by RUF fighters from the besieged Hotel Frangipani.

"I wish the Whitehall drones would stop their vacillation," Dalziel thought. The British government had still failed to come up with a coherent response to the ongoing crisis.

He sensed that something very untoward indeed was occurring in Sierra Leone and wanted his men, not on a ship, but on the ground. Why Whitehall had withdrawn the paratroops and the Irish Guards he would never know.

Not true. He did know.

One youthfully indignant BBC camera crew at the wrong place at the wrong time. One bit of telly showing the paras kicking floored RUF suspects then throwing them out of a window – a ground floor window! – and the whole military intervention had been suspended. Ground staff withdrawn. Sierra Leone citizen groups comprised of mothers had attempted to launch a one million citizen signature petition urging the British army to upscale its involvement. Not run away.

But the British government had panicked and withdrawn. They'd thought this country was a tar baby. Were terrified of looking like colonialists. Lacked the will to do what was right.

Dalziel thought the British government was morally puny.

The Lord only knew what the Boers in the Bristol thought. Nothing at all probably. Talking about rugby while they waited to do what they had tried to do today. Boers were like that. Thick-skinned, thick-headed.

It was frustrating.

"Enough excitement for one day," Dalziel told Wiley, mentally abandoning the jigsaw with a sigh. He reached for a mug of tea, wasn't sure whether it was his, but drank at it anyway. "Good work in difficult circumstances, Mr Wiley. Very good work. Going back down the rabbit hole tonight?"

"Yes. Wouldn't miss my radio monitoring," said Wiley. "Better than shore leave at the moment. No chance of you rustling me up an Alice is there, sir? Gets a tad lonely monitoring the mad."

Dalziel nodded but wasn't listening. He sipped the heavily sugared tea and thought.

It was now time to consider the logistics for evacuating all foreign nationals from the city.

All of them. UN first. Some creature called Sharon Stone had been sending frankly hysterical help-us-get-the-hell-out-of-here messages all day. The Nigerians had promised an evac. ship but it wasn't likely to arrive for days. The UN would inevitably bring Sierra Leone nationals who also wanted to leave but didn't have passports. There'd be government people, blustering but afraid. They'd have huge numbers of cardboard boxes full of televisions and bedsteads and salted fish stuffed with diamonds and gold rings. Extraordinary the amount of stuff rich Africans thought they could hide in food.

Then, too, he'd have to evacuate the Dutch, Belgians, Indians. Effectively anyone and everyone who'd wanted to come here now or in times past. And who, prompted by the slings and arrows of outrageous crossfire, now wanted to leave and were yammering desperately for a farewell to Sierra Leone, land of opportunity.

Peterson-Smith had urged the evacuation, but would himself be remaining. Dalziel was glad. Dalziel would be relying on the man's staying power and ground intelligence.

The evacuation would be tricky, very tricky. Not because of lack of planning. There were plans upon plans. It would be tricky because of the variables.

Then the other questions. Why hadn't the mercenaries secured the airport? It was incomprehensible. Why were they haring about in Unimog convoys? It looked like a coup, but it wasn't behaving like any coup yet seen in West Africa.

Nothing going on over the water made sense. The airport loss in particular was grating.

Clam had choppers, but it was so much easier to just shovel everybody into the back of a Jumbo. Fly them away. He knew *Clam*'s captain hated having civilians – particularly refugees – on the ship.

"Back to the maps," said Dalziel. His juniors obeyed. The captain turned up looking wet and flustered.

"Fish hit me. Three actually. Sea's throwing them out at the moment. But that's by the by. The BBC want permission to film us making the evacuation plans," the captain said.

"Perhaps that would be silly," suggested Dalziel. There was a dull thud and an eruption of fire from Freetown as another variable was added to the equation.

"My thoughts exactly," said the captain. "If our brave boys from the Fourth Estate want pictures we've a jolly boat will take them to where the action is."

"Ground floor windows," the captain added savagely. "Stupid do-gooding bastards!"

"More strong tea!" shouted Dalziel. He was surprised to discover that he was enjoying himself.

CHAPTER TWENTY-ONE

Screwing Up

The Crocodile was not. Rindert was screwing up. Pleasant had got a call on his home phone just as he was settling down to watch the All Blacks destroy France. He had a plate of steak on his lap and a can of Windhoek lager on the coffee table. It hadn't been much of a day. Foul weather. Five trips to a phone booth in Beck's Hill to monitor the buyers' departure – Freetown sounded like it was going to hell in a hand-basket – and then finally the convoy had left. He'd got back home, dripping, cold and tired; chucked his clothes, got into his dressing gown and slippers, lit the fire, fixed his drink, fixed his steak.

Then his phone had rung.

And what was on the other end?

Rindert. *Screwing up.*

"Freetown Campbell," the voice had said.

"Sorry you've got the wrong number," Dr Pleasant had said back. And then Rindert had interrupted curtly and said he didn't have time for all that. That he was in a call box ...

A call box?

... and that he didn't have much more change.

Change? What the hell was the man blathering about?

"Can you postpone the party?" Rindert had continued. "I can't raise the party-goers. This phone's on the Fritz. Bit of a crisis. Nothing permanent. But it's absolutely essential, repeat absolutely essential that we postpone. The presents and the balloons aren't ready for the children yet. We just need a few more days, a week, and it's imperative that you go to Northumberland."

Go to Northumberland? Why in God's name did Rindert want him to go to Northumberland? Where was Northumberland? Dr Pleasant had never even heard of the place.

"Ach! For Christ's sakes man! Just postpone the auction."

Then the line had gone dead.

And Dr Pleasant, who was morbidly convinced that his phone was tapped, had to get dressed, miss the game, miss the steak and drive all the way back to Beck's Hill for the sixth time that day.

He was on the point of leaving the house – just fooling around with the keys – when the phone rang again.

It was Mrs Everance. Sorry to disturb so late but her husband's haemorrhoids were flaring up again. Was there an ointment? Did Dr Pleasant have an ointment? Any suggestion perhaps?

"Kiss them better you commie bitch!" was Dr Pleasant's prescription as he thumped the phone down and, snorting, made once again for the door.

CHAPTER TWENTY-TWO

Postponed

"Ah, you vicious piece of junk!" Rindert stepped back from the sat-phone which had just cut out and aimed a violent steel-shod kick at a chair which sailed across the room and bounced off the wall.

"Gone again?" asked Jack bleakly.

"I spent a fortune on the thing, hauled it all the way here from England and it's as much use as a ..." Rindert couldn't think of what it was as much use as and stopped.

"What was all that about call boxes and change?" asked Jack.

"The stupid bastard's convinced MI5 are bugging him. He might even be right. It was a sort of a code off the top of my head. Phone box is this thing," Rindert gestured disgustedly at the mute sat-phone. "No change means not much call time. He'll work it out. I just hope he gets through to the buyers before they come all the way here."

The prospect of greeting a hundred and twenty mercenaries, drug runners, assassins and right-wing psychos with a "Hi, guys, thanks for driving through a bush war. Slight delay. Just hang on here for a week while I get some moonlight," was just appalling.

"Will he stop them coming?" whined Jack.

"You're the one who's supposed to be bloody psychic," Rindert snapped. "Why don't you get drunk again? Do something useful?"

* * *

Dr Pleasant returned from the public phone box in Beck's Hill in even worse humour than when he'd begun the expedition.

He'd managed to get through to the convoy and had spoken to Gert Schindler. Schindler was Dr Pleasant's Mr Fixit man in Freetown, contracted to get the buyers into Lalapanzi.

The news that the auction was to be postponed had prompted a burst of foul expletives from Schindler. When he'd calmed, he was still ranting. The line was crackly and faint. There was a time-lag. But what Schindler was shouting into his mobile was still painfully audible.

"We've been driving for three hours man! The worst roads I've seen since DRC. Rain pouring down. We've hit three road-blocks, shot up a police station, one of the bakkies hit a mine. No-one hurt. The Afs are going wild. I'm telling you its war here. War!"

"Just get everybody back to Freetown," Pleasant had said. "Persuade everyone to go back to Freetown. Take it easy there. Have a beer. Swim in the hotel pool. I'll let you know when I know what the hang-up is. Just take it easy. Room service."

"Are we talking about the same Freetown here?"

"Listen, I'm on top of it. Just get back there and wait."

"You going to be much longer, mate? It's raining you know?" A ratty-looking skinhead with an over-painted blonde shivering and clinging to his elbow had chosen that moment to bang on the telephone box window. Dr Pleasant had turned his bulbous eyes on the couple. They'd wilted.

"Well, tell them to go back." Pleasant yelled. "Keep them sweet. Buy them drinks. Just keep them in Freetown!"

Schindler had answered. "Yes, well, I'll do that. I'll tell them. But they're not going to be pleased."

Dr Pleasant had terminated the call, left the box, driven a fist into the skinhead's eye, knocking the *rooinek* bastard flat, driven his car home and there it was again. The telephone. Ringing.

He picked up hoping it was Rindert. It wasn't. It was Mr Everance.

"How dare you insult my wife!" Mr Everance roared at Dr Pleasant by way of a beginning.

It took Dr Pleasant twenty minutes to calm the man, assuring him that he had received no such call, said no such things, perhaps she had made a mistake and dialled the wrong number, blah blah. Ho ho. Chortle chortle. More blah blah. By God, thought Dr Pleasant as Everance went on, there is no more pompous a creature alive than a retired headmaster.

Eventually Mr Everance subsided, became apologetic, then became effusively apologetic, wouldn't get off the phone, started complaining about the weather, how the church fête's cancellation due to rain would mean an extra amount of effort at the harvest festival, and then in a furtive roundabout way – like a man buying dirty pictures – asked if Dr Pleasant could oblige by delivering some piles ointment.

"For my wife, you understand, she's having a bit of a rough time of it," Everance had said. "Delicate matter."

Dr Pleasant said he'd be over immediately and after a search in his surgery for ointment stepped back once more out into the rainy night.

He was half-way across the green when his phone once again rang. There was thunder above now. He didn't hear the phone. He missed Rindert's call.

CHAPTER TWENTY-THREE

Back at the Bristol

The convoy's return to the Hotel Bristol took everybody, but particularly the management and new guests, by surprise.

The convoy had left in good spirits, it might even be said in unnaturally good spirits. It returned surly, insistent in its demands to reoccupy all the hotel rooms and, when both management and new guests complained, the convoy produced its weapons.

There followed an ugly procedure. It involved the room-to-room clearance of the suites by convoy members who wanted suites, clearance of double rooms with bath by convoy members who wanted double rooms with bath, clearance of single rooms with bath by convoy members who wanted single rooms with bath and finally a fierce fist-fight between a fat American man who was found hiding in the only single room that had a shower.

The American, who had begun the fight, was eventually subdued by a wild-eyed, mud-bespattered Schindler wielding a small television. Schindler then pulled him out of the room by his hair and threw his suitcase out of the window where it burst spilling his possessions into the rain.

Such was the departure of Fitz from the Hotel Bristol.

The other guests were bundled out of their rooms with various degrees of politeness and violence. Some, if they were humble, were even allowed to stay on the corridor or the floor in the lobby.

Most, though, were thrown out into the street and huddled in the square, unsure what to do.

An RUF sniper opened fire on the Hotel Bristol. Fire was returned from several windows. RUF fire stopped. A Panhard armoured vehicle nosed briefly around the corner of the far street. It withdrew after an RPG, discharged from the second floor of the Bristol by Esther Speeks, blew its two front tyres off.

"They're RUF families evacuated from the Hotel Frangipani," Schindler told anyone who was interested in the pedigree of the evicted hotel guests. The bell boy had told him that. The manager had confirmed it.

"It's their bed. They made it. Let them lie in it," one buyer had said. "Throw 'em all out into the street!"

Schindler had laughed at that, clapped shoulders, moved from room to room making sure that everyone had beer or wine or whatever else they wanted. He'd visited the hotel manager and had a short but useful talk about what was required. Money no object, Schindler had said, but I want these people waited on hand and foot. Do that and I'll make you a rich man.

He'd gone to the kitchens and at gunpoint had ordered the testy French chef to roast every chicken he had, microwave any pizza and keep the hotel guests in good humour.

Girls. Schindler knew every hotel had girls or knew how to get them.

He ordered the manager to order up the girls.

The Lebanese manager, who now knew where the wind was blowing and was hoping to leave Freetown with more than just the shirt on his back (plus a shitload of swallowed RUF-mined diamonds), did just that. The girls came out of a building that resembled a cattle shed at the rear of the premises.

"Girls!" said Schindler," Get upstairs and have fun. Make money. These aren't bad guys here. Keep them busy. If they want to go to sleep, don't bother them. This is important. They've had a long day."

"Do you understand?"

The girls were giggling nervously or looking mystified. There was the reek of cheap perfume.

"Repeat it after me."

"Help them relax! But don't disturb them if they're asleep."

The girls dutifully repeated the instructions.

Schindler felt like Superpimp.

"Tell them it's on the house. No pouting on special requests. If you don't want to do what they want you to do, then leave the room politely and maybe some other girl can do that thing for them. If she wants to. No-one here has to do anything they don't want to do."

"If there's violence call room service. I'll sort the trouble out."

The girls began to look pleased and excited. There was that peculiar danger-related energy in the air that prompted human reproduction and got the pheromones afloat.

"Think about AIDS and take condoms," said Schindler rather pettishly. "Stay safe, girls, and do your job."

The girls cheered Schindler when he'd finished his speech. They were relieved. Excited. Schindler guessed that the paramilitary control now governing prostitution at the Hotel Bristol was something better than had been offered before. The girls, like many of Sierra Leone's wretchedly brutalized civilians, equated white mercenaries with safety and security. Normally that was true.

In this particular case it was *mainly* true.

"Don't go anywhere near room 202." Esther Speeks was in 202.

"My womanly place is so soft," said a girl. "You can do anything that you want." She leaned closer and added, "In any of my holes."

"Yes," said Schindler, flushing with embarrassment. "Thanks."

He pushed the child-woman away.

"Girls," yelled Schindler, who was happily married and a puritan and had had about as much as he could take of everything. "Girls! Upstairs. Get up there!"

The girls rushed upstairs in a flurry of laughter.

As midnight wore on to morning the party atmosphere returned to much of the Hotel Bristol. The people who were sleeping were not disturbed.

The Colombian team leader wasted most of Schindler's time in the early hours. Pepe wasn't interested in whether the people outside in the rain (now sheltering beneath a tarpaulin that Schindler had sent out to them) were RUF or not. Pepe had never heard of the RUF. He didn't get Schindler's jokes. He said he did not need women. He expressed no interest in the Freetown situation. He couldn't sleep. He looked frightened, threatening, out of place and angry. Mainly, though, frightened. The scenes of carnage he'd witnessed as the convoy left Freetown had rattled Pepe badly. He'd seen nothing like it before.

"This is unfamiliar for me," Pepe had admitted.

"You'll get the hang of it soon," Schindler had told him. "Do you want some cocaine?"

Schindler didn't have any cocaine but suspected he could probably rustle some up. The hotel manager was, after all, Lebanese. The Lebs could get anything for a price. It was their way.

"I do not take cocaine," Pepe had said with pride. He'd then launched into a rambling speech about cocaine being a tool to be used for the freedom of southern America. Not a tool to be used by South Americans for their own enslavement.

Schindler had heard him out, eyes glazing.

"Sleep well," he had said when Pepe had finally finished. Schindler had closed the door on the Colombians. It was then 5 a.m. and Schindler had gone to sit beside the radio.

Thinking that it was high bloody time The Crocodile told him what, just precisely, the heck was going on.

In the Jardin de Cygnes Peterson-Smith was once again in communication with Dalziel.

It was dark outside, but the night was shot through with flames from burning buildings.

Things were, very literally, heating up.

The two men had discussed the current status of the civilian population. As soon as the weather broke, all evacuees were to assemble at the two beach hotels, the Hotel Sleep Tight and the Sofitel Mammy Yoko. Dalziel had finally had plans approved by Whitehall to secure the Lumley Beach Hotel Road with British troops. It was a matter of waiting for a break in the foul weather. Then choppers.

The topic of conversation turned to the clientele of the Hotel Bristol.

Dalziel's news was not bad precisely, but puzzling.

"We've had people in touch with EO," (Dalziel meant Executive Outcomes) "and Sandline in Jo'burg. The people at the Bristol aren't theirs."

Executive Outcomes and Sandline were not what Peterson-Smith referred to as war filth but they were mercenary outfits, effectively privatised armies staffed by South African Defence Force veterans. Along with a local outfit, SHEELD, both companies had been in Sierra Leone under contract to the government and both had done an extremely professional job in securing the capital and recapturing rebel-held diamond mines. The mercenaries had been immensely popular with the non-RUF affiliated population.

But despite their successes the government had been compelled by international and UN pressure to concede to rebel demands that EO's contract be revoked.

EO had been asked to leave in '97. In the interest of furthering the peace talks. With their departure had come, collapse both of civilian and military morale in Sierra Leone. Also the collapse of peace talks and an RUF recovery. Then, spectacular mayhem.

All rather predictable, thought Peterson-Smith.

Various opinion pieces in both local and international newspapers had in recent months been urging their return to Freetown, particularly after the withdrawal of the British ground troops and the recall of most UN Indian peacekeepers following rancorous disagreements with Nigerian peacekeepers. The two peacekeeping bodies had actually opened fire on one another. Fiasco!

"Sandline and EO have people in the country but not at the Bristol," Dalziel said. "They're at State House and the docks. A few out at the mines. Too few to do much good was what the EO CEO said, apparently."

"So we don't know who the hell these people are. Can you find out what's going on? How is it on the ground there? It looks like hell from the ship."

"There've been a lot of 'choppings,'" said Peterson-Smith. "Situation is basically confused. Nigerian UN peacekeeper desertions are big news. Seems several hundred beat up their officers, took off with lorries, said they were going home. They've not been paid for five months."

"Your intel's first rate. How do you manage it?"

"Same principle as Sherlock Holmes' Baker Street irregulars. Got thirty/forty children out there. They can get anywhere. Overhear all sorts ..."

"Conan Doyle. Now there was a man with understanding. And a sense of justice."

The literary conversation was interrupted by an explosion of noise as heavy machine-gun rounds tore through the roof of the Jardin de Cygnes. Reed thatch on the roof danced but mostly stayed in place. Tiles shattered. And a plaster duck that had annoyed Peterson-Smith ever since he'd begun frequenting the place fell from its place on the wall. It failed to break.

"Hang on!" shouted Peterson-Smith.

"I've been hit," said one of Fitz's guards in a squeaky unbelieving voice. "I didn't think I'd get hit. I've been hit."

Peterson-Smith scaled the ladder to the sandbagged observation post on the thatched roof. In the street below, clanking and belching out clouds of exhaust was a Panhard armoured vehicle.

Painted on the front of the Panhard were the words, "Ah! The World Today!"

The armoured vehicle didn't seem to be targeting the Jardin de Cygnes with any extreme prejudice. As Peterson-Smith watched, the RUF gunner traversed his turret-mounted .50 cal. weapon and the vehicle trundled away to rake the buildings on the other side of the street.

Singing was absurdly audible from within the six-wheeled vehicle. It sounded drunk.

"Blessing and peace be ever thine own/Land that we love, our Sierra Leone!"

The national anthem.

All rise.

On the back of the turret were written the words "The More You Hate The More God Bless". Now what the blazes does that mean, thought Peterson-Smith. Gibberish. Also written were the words, "Na King Rat Again".

Peterson-Smith descended the ladder wishing he'd had a grenade.

"All well?" asked Dalziel over the phone to nobody listening, as the wounded guard continued to repeat, "Hit. I never thought I'd get hit." Two other guards were holding him steady. The new barman helped. He was a withered old man, face furrowed by the strain of recent days. Oliveira, the Portuguese shop owner. His family were in a room that had formerly been occupied by the gardener. They were sheltering there, huddled together like baby rabbits, curled into each other for warmth and comfort.

"Blessing and peace be ever thine own/Land that we love, our Sierra Leone!"

The music was now coming from a second Panhard vehicle via a loud speaker

The singing suffered from the acoustics of the armoured car and was abrasively metallic. It sounded like a Dalek choir.

"Do not fire at those vehicles!" Peterson-Smith urged his guards in a shouted whisper. The Panhards were capable of driving through the Jardin de Cygnes wall if their anthem-singing crews felt so inclined. "Repeat, do not fire upon those vehicles. Get back down that ladder! Stay quiet!"

"Why?" asked one guard who was ascending the ladder. The guard was called Boris. He was a Russian, blond, lanky – attractive if your taste ran to tall blond Russians who were eighteen-years-old and had taken ears from Chechen rebels before deserting and finding wet work with a fat CIA degenerate like Fitz. All the guards here were Fitz's men. Fitz himself was who-knew-where.

"If nothing happens the vehicles will get bored and go away," said Peterson-Smith. "That would be a good thing."

"I never thought I'd get hit," said the injured guard again, but this time quietly. "Do you think I've caught AIDS?"

"All well?" repeated Dalziel sounding excited but also demanding and urgent.

"Very minor wound. Bit of an ear gone. The man's disorientated. RUF's got at least two units of light armour outside."

"Light armour. Is that confirmed?"

There was more fire from the Panhard but further away. The music was close but also receding. More fire coming closer. Same weapon as the first. Engine noise identical. Another Panhard.

"Confirmed. Everyone here get your heads down and keep quiet!" Peterson-Smith was talking to his men, not Dalziel.

"Find out what's what at the Bristol," Dalziel sounded suddenly distracted as if other developments had just arrived at his elbow in sheaves of paper brought by a humble naval rating. "More radio stuff?" Peterson-Smith heard Dalziel say. "Very alarming stuff too, sir," Peterson-Smith heard another voice say. The voice was indistinct. But the words were audible.

Very alarming stuff.

"First-class work in adverse circumstances," said Dalziel, then his voice was drowned in the indistinct but definite shriek of powerful motors. A helicopter was turning its engines over on *Clam*, Peterson-Smith guessed. Whether Dalziel's last comment was for him or the radio man who had brought the "very alarming stuff" was unclear.

"Did you hear me there?" Dalziel barked.

The comment was for him, Peterson-Smith realised.

"Thank you, yes."

"Stiff upper lip. Keep in touch. Out."

Dalziel was gone. "Stiff upper lip" was an expression Peterson-Smith had never quite understood. It was the lower lip that wobbled when a man was about to cry. Perhaps the idea was that you stiffened your upper lip to cover your lower lip and hold its wobbling in check. He'd look into that when the need arose. Perhaps he'd practise it in a mirror beforehand if he was given a moment's lull.

Peterson-Smith wondered then whether Dalziel was enjoying this. Probably yes, he concluded. A lot more was happening here than on a drizzly, fist-fight, Orange-Order-march type of day in Northern Ireland. And there were less restraints on the hands of law and order and military power. Here you could shoot people and never file one single piece of paper explaining the necessity of the act. Not like the poor buggers patrolling the dank, hate-filled streets of an inbred, infighting, western democracy.

Here a soldier could do what he pleased. If he had the guts and resolution.

Shame both were in such short supply.

CHAPTER TWENTY-FOUR

Captain Rat RUF

More rain. Appalling roads that were too thick to drink, too thin to plough, and definitely too shittily quagmired for any one to negotiate with a normal car (not that many people in Freetown owned cars that could be described as normal). The ruts were dissolving into one another. Desperate trucks and buses bogged, floundered, lost their gears and burnt their clutches as drivers fought in fruitless escape. Some trucks beat the odds and pulled out, hauled on through, engines howling and snarling as the angles always changed and wheels slid against the deep grooves.

Others fought but settled like mammoths mired in tar-pits. Extinct, immovable, they began to accumulate, blocking secondary roads out of Freetown.

Their occupants attempted to push them free. The alternative being a long, long walk, burdened by possessions, to the rumoured refugee camps that were in fact not being established in the neighbouring state of Guinea.

A not-unusual sight during that day of civilian exodus from Freetown was every passenger, everybody – man, woman, tiny child – covered in churning mud as the rear wheels slipped, everybody pushing, pushing, pushing.

It was at this time a new name began to be heard and feared along the tropically exuberant vegetation that lined the verges of Sierra Leone's rain-drenched roads.

Captain Rat RUF.

Rat as in an abbreviation of rat-at-at-tat, the noise of his SMG. Captain as in captain.

RUF as in RUF. Very, very rough.

Captain Rat RUF's first sweep was a UNHCR convoy. It was to establish a brutal pattern that was to be repeated over subsequent days.

The lorries in the UNHCR convoy numbered eighteen. Leading the convoy was a fortified Bedford manned by Nigerians loyal to their UN mandate but tired and frightened. In the cab with the driver was a member of UNHCR's international staff, a determined humanitarian named Eileen Holden.

UNHCR's official policy was to ignore Sierra Leone refugees for as long as they were within Sierra Leone. This rule wasn't restricted to this particular country. Worldwide, until refugees had made it over a foreign border they weren't technically refugees, they were technically "internally displaced persons". And as such they didn't fall under the remit of UNHCR.

Holden considered the distinction both fatuous and hypocritical and, while the other two UNHCR staff in Freetown made plans for fleeing the country and Sharon Stone had yelled about her piano to some haulage firm owned by a very drunk Scotsman, Holden had made plans to put the convoy together. It was in direct defiance of orders, rules and regs, and Holden knew that she was risking her job.

Well, screw her job, screw the regs, and screw that fat dyke Stone. And her precious piano. If some RUF deadhead riddled the Grand with lead, all to the good. And if the guy torched Stone's extensive collection of expensive ethnic artifacts, her his-'n-hers bedside table, her skis – Stone's generous UN shipping subsidies had enabled her to bring tons of stuff with her, indeed UN advisories had *recommended* bringing tons of stuff with her, including skis – then fine. Fine and fragging fantastic!

Pinned to a cork board above Holden's desk in her office was a picture of St Peter's Church, Monrovia, capital city of Liberia, a nation forged and founded by freed African-American slaves.

St Peter's Church had been a Red Cross refugee station, until crazed government soldiers had stormed it, in the process shooting, hacking or bludgeoning eight hundred people to death. Eight hundred people who were not "refugees" but "internally displaced persons".

Never again, Holden thought when she looked at the picture, which she always did, first thing each day, when she entered her office.

Never again.

It had taken a huge effort to organize the convoy – and to keep the organization of the convoy a secret from her feckless colleagues and the Stone monster – but she'd succeeded. The trucks she'd found in a freighter, impounded God-knows-when-and-why, and settled neatly in a silted Freetown dock. There was no-one on the freighter, no-one appeared to know about the trucks, and she'd simply misappropriated a large amount of the UN Freetown office's budget devoted to "staff capacity building" and hired mechanics, a barge and drivers to steal the damn things. Capacity building, Holden had learned, involved flying overpaid consultants into Sierra Leone to conduct team-building exercises such as throwing eggs from staff member to staff member (and catching them, then applauding each other), watching video games devoted to mine-clearance-awareness building, and lengthy seminars on subjects such as the importance of building synergies.

An utter waste of time, Holden thought.

That morning she'd turned up to work to find the office empty save for an anxious-looking security guard. She'd sent him to speak to her only real friend in Freetown: Dr Khan. Dr Khan had risen to the occasion, as she knew he would.

Now, nearly eight hundred people, mainly amputees, orphans and patients from the Connaught Hospital, clung like glue to the lurching trucks.

The convoy cleared Freetown and hit Rat's blockade after

hours of getting out, pushing, getting out again and pushing, getting out again and pushing. Always in the ears of the Nigerians was the yammer and bleat of the frightened people in the lorries behind. The incessant drum of the rain was debilitating.

Rat's blockade was manned by silent men, women and children dressed in green fatigues and plastic rain-capes.

There were fifty at least, perhaps several hundred of them on the road, standing immobile and stiff as the guards at Buckingham Palace. They appeared indifferent to the hammering rain; just stood there illuminated in the headlights of the Bedford while the wipers fought the water that beat against the windscreen.

The men at the front of the blockade flashed torches at the driver's eyes. There was a single solitary call of," Stop! Hot soups!"

It came again as the nearest soldier with a torch approached the cab.

"Hot soups. Hot soups?"

The figure with the torch was now at the window.

"Hot soups?" said the figure again, playing the torch through the cab and illuminating each of its inhabitants in a slow deliberate fashion. Torch-glow in each eye until they blinked, flinched, turned their heads down. If they didn't turn their heads down at once then the torch stayed on them. Waiting till they did.

"Can we reverse?" As Holden said it, she knew it was something that she shouldn't have said. The Nigerians were looking to her for advice and her advice had been ludicrous.

Can we reverse? Certainly. No problem. We'll just back eighteen lorry-loads of terrified refugees along a road that looks like the Somme with knobs on, and then we'll spin merrily away and try for another route. Maybe drop in at a Denny's for burgers and shakes before trying for the border. Any border ...

The RUF trooper with the torch dropped away from the lead vehicle and out of Holden's sight. After the torch in the eyes, the darkness was filled with flashing, flaring retinal images. As their eyes adjusted the people in the cab became once again aware of the lights ahead, rain-blurred and glittering on the road, and of the sinisterly immobile figures in their flapping rain-capes.

The first torch-waver had gone.

Perhaps he had moved to the next vehicle, Eileen thought. She realised suddenly that she hoped that was true. It was a dreadful admission, but it was true. This was potentially a very violent road-block. Perhaps they would just chop the civilians. Perhaps they'd let her go because she was white. She felt ashamed, wretched and ashamed. But the thought would not go away.

Perhaps she'd make it. *Because she was white.*

"I'm killing those men!" said the Nigerian driver. But he made no move for his pistol.

He was trembling.

Eileen realized that she was trembling too. Everyone in the cab was trembling. They looked at each other.

"I'm killing them," said the driver but he wasn't going to do it. Eileen wondered whether this was it. She hoped it wouldn't hurt too much.

Then he came back. The RUF cadre with the torch. This time the number of torches flashing behind him was terrifying. There appeared to be hundreds weaving through the darkness.

Fireflies from hell.

The torch beams played about the cab, flashed off the mirrors into their eyes.

"Hot soups?" said the RUF soldier. He was up on the running board and pointing a gun into the cab. He was suffering from Pink Eye, an eye infection that resulted from insanitary living conditions. He looked no older than fifteen.

"Yes, thank you, soups sounds very hot and good," Holden managed, her voice cracking. "Would you like some cigarettes and money?"

The teenager giggled, a moronic half-witted giggle, then he stuck out his tongue, winked one of his pink, inflamed eyes and dropped from view. Holden realized that he probably couldn't speak English. Just the words "hot soups". And what that meant who could say?

There was a waiting time. Holden sat there and hoped for a miracle, trying not to think of St Peter's Church. The rain drummed on the cab roof. The Nigerians shifted in their seats but weren't about to initiate combat.

Sometimes the silliest things, such as cigarettes and money, could turn things around. Eileen wished that she had more of both.

The torches began once again to rush and wobble past their truck.

The door was pulled open. A man hauled himself crab-like into the Bedford's cab. He looked wild. He wasn't a child soldier. He was in his twenties, perhaps early thirties. He wore a necklace of ears. Eileen Holden had never seen anyone more terrifying.

He flashed the torch across the faces of the people in the cab.

"Cigarettes?" tried Eileen, thanking God she hadn't managed to quit.

The man said something unintelligible then slipped from the cab with the cigarettes.

Torches waved. They waited in their cab and heard cries, shouts and gunfire from the vehicles behind. A lot of gunfire.

Rat-at-at-tat. Rat-at-at-tat. Getting nearer. Rat-at-at-tat.

"No, please, no," Eileen breathed. "They're killing them all." She clutched at her remaining cigarettes, shrunk small against the seat, and knew that this was it: the end. A squalid place for it. A terrible night for it. She hung her head, tears streaming from her eyes. "The children. The poor dear children. God help us."

Shrieks. Laughter. "Hot soups!"

Rat-at-at-tat. Rat-at-at-tat.

CHAPTER TWENTY-FIVE

Night Among the Ruins

Fitz decided that spending the night in the square under a tarpaulin with a hundred weeping RUF nigger women was no kind of plan. Come dawn, he reckoned the loony on the second floor would resume his turkey shoot. If he didn't, someone else would. RUF wasn't flavour of the month in the Freetown vicinity and the people under the tarpaulin looked like victims.

Fitz decided to try and make it to the Jardin de Cygnes.

He began a furtive crawl through the dark, flooding Freetown streets. His eye was swelling, there were contusions on his scalp where the German had broken the television over his head, his leg hurt, he was wearing pink silk pyjamas and he had never been more wretchedly fearful in his life.

Twice he hid from the hellish outlines of prowling Panhards. Once he spent what felt like hours waiting for an extremely intoxicated RUF patrol to pass – the men were falling-down drunk and kept inadvertently discharging their weapons. He made huge detours to avoid light cast by burning buildings and cut his hands to shreds on broken glass when rubble shifted beneath him and sledged him into a basement. The basement was flooded with water and sewage. Fitz splashed his way out, gagging.

His worst moment, though, came when he rounded a corner and saw a column of armed men filing quietly out of the rear of the Hotel Frangipani.

Their silent appearance on the street – while clearly designed to raise no alarms – immediately triggered intense gunfire from nearby buildings where gunmen were obviously alert.

Over drinks in former days Fitz had often accused blacks of lacking courage.

None of the street-fighters appeared to lack courage at all.

Fitz, if he'd scuttled out of the Hotel Frangipani and met the sort of firepower that descended on the RUF fighters, would have scuttled straight back into the Frangipani again and started bellowing into a phone for air support.

"They don't understand the rules," a British soldier had said after the rescue of the Irish Guards hostages from the West Side Boys militia. "No-one has ever told them that war is not like a Rambo video, about how soldiers should behave, when to be scared, so they just stand there and blast away."

Fitz at the time had dismissed the comments as Limey wimpiness. No longer. The scene was just like a Rambo movie. With one key difference. Instead of one Rambo blazing away from the hip, there were fifty Rambos, a hundred, who knew how many Rambos. Some so young they could barely cope with the recoil as they blazed away.

Tracer rounds whipped past Fitz. He was huddling beside the corpse of a very fat woman, cut down while returning from an emergency shopping expedition. A bag of dried goods, mainly noodles, was currently augmenting the obese woman's role as Fitz's sandbag. The noodles had burst and there was the absurdly motherly smell of chicken soup mix in the muddied puddles. Fitz lay beside the corpse, praying that the fighting would not surge his way.

It looked touch and go as to whether it would or not. Then it did.

"We'll kill every one of you RUF fucks!" a voice yelled

"Break right!" A voice shouted back. And suddenly Fitz was

surrounded by running men. They were everywhere. He could hear their ragged breathing. Smell the wet of their clothes. One actually trod on his arm. Another's booted foot sloshed mud in his eyes.

A third tripped over him and fell, losing his weapon. For one terrible moment the fallen RUF fighter was pulling at Fitz's belt, presumably under the misapprehension that it was his AK47 strap. Then the man found his weapon, let go of Fitz's belt and was off.

Bullets were kicking up mud and water all over the street. Windows were smashing. Dogs were barking. There were yells and howls and screamed abuse.

It still wasn't over.

"Kill you!" yelled voices. "Kill you! Kill you!"

"Kiss my butt!" One of the running men had stopped right by Fitz. He was bald. He was naked. He looked like nothing Fitz had seen before and like nothing Fitz ever wanted to see again. The man was using his weapon from the hip and was firing burst after burst back the way he had come. Spent cartridges rained down on Fitz.

When the man exhausted his ammunition he didn't run. He started yelling. "I'll be back for your butts with voodoo. You hear me? I'm gonna voodoo your butts, voodoo them to hell!"

"RUF pigs!" yelled a chorus of voices in response. Figures began to pour out of buildings facing the rear of the Frangipani.

"Come on, General!" Another man was tugging urgently at the bald psychotic's arm. "Time's wasting. We've got to steal the vehicles. We must move, General!"

"It's true though. Their butts are gonna be voodooed to hell by the time I'm done. You hear me? Voodooed to hell and back!"

Fire intensified from the buildings and from the men on the street. It was a miracle that neither of the RUF fighters had been hit yet. A miracle that Fitz had not been hit. The head of the fat female body, with its noodles that was offering him shelter, cracked as it was struck by a projectile. Stuff sprayed over Fitz who reared back involuntarily in shock.

"A blanc!" The bald man was looking down at Fitz in amazement. "Look at that! All this time and there's a blanc just here by my feet, in pink pyjamas, wearing some brains."

"You in the wrong place, blanc."

"I know," Fitz croaked. "Tell me about it."

"You should leave soon, blanc. Think this is bad?" The bald man waved his arm at the scenery and the flashing tracer fire as if he was some sort of tour guide or travel show presenter. He then crouched low and put his face straight into Fitz's. The other soldier was simultaneously hit by gunfire and flew – quite literally, flew – several yards down the street, bits flying everywhere.

The bald man either didn't notice or didn't care.

"Think this is some kind of bad?" He continued. His breath stank of whisky. "You probably do, don't you? You probably think that this looks like some kind of hell, don't you?"

Fitz nodded vigorously. Eager to please.

"Well, blanc, you ain't seen *nothing* yet! Tell them you got that from Butt Naked. That's General Butt Naked to you, white boy. Butt Naked, Voodoo King-to-be!" The man then pointed his weapon at Fitz and pulled the trigger. But the weapon was empty.

"You in luck!" The man said and left him. The gunfire petered out. Fitz waited, reversed, detoured, terrified that the sun would rise and expose him to the eager guns.

Dawn. The prospect was dreadful. Caught in the sun, in his pink pyjamas, Fitz knew he'd be lucky to last five minutes.

Dawn, Fitz thought, as he scrambled and clawed through rubble. That was the enemy. The dawn. Got to beat the dawn.

Fitz beat dawn to the Jardin de Cygnes by thirteen minutes, but it was beginning to nudge at the sky and some precocious birds were already singing its praises.

Fitz pounded the door, and at his pounding the door was opened by Peterson-Smith, flanked by two of the guards. Peterson-

Smith looked haggard but still pulled out that lousy Limey humour.

"Fitz, old chap! Had a night out on the town I see."

"Gimme a Martian," Fitz managed bravely. "No cherries."

He was hauled in.

CHAPTER TWENTY-SIX

Dreaming Safaris

The Aleph team cleared customs and immigration at Heathrow without incident, then took a plane, not to Freetown (which was noticeably absent from all international airline destination lists) but to Liberia (not itself particularly prominent on Heathrow's departure/arrivals notice boards).

They arrived at Robertsfield airport near Monrovia, the Liberian capital, on time. They were immediately collected by two Liberian officials who hurried them through the formalities and out of the airport to a discreet tarmac behind a bonded goods warehouse.

There the Aleph people met their escorts.

The two Liberian fixers retained by Aleph's Russian escort leader Vladimir Koransky had, as a matter of course, told the CIA team in Monrovia about the meet. Koransky was a CIA stringer and wet-work operative as well as a freelancer.

The CIA had two other freelance contributors on top of the bonded warehouse taking photographs. The photos thus taken were to prompt bemused snorts of wonder back in Langley, Virginia.

The scene caught by camera was bizarre.

There were five Aleph members – three men and two women if the Liberian informants and the exposed knees in the images were anything to go by – all wearing identical baggy shorts, green socks, brown safari boots and zebra-striped safari jackets. Their heads were concealed in mosquito hats of the sort popularly on sale during high summer in the Florida Everglades. Broad-brimmed and with netting draped from them. Every Japanese was wearing one.

The CIA roof-top observers noted that, while of questionable efficiency from a mosquito prevention perspective, the headgear clearly impeded its wearer's vision. Several of the Japanese contingent exhibited signs of visual disruption and impairment. Two actually fell over. One had then gone wandering off and had been collected by a colleague. Both had then fallen over again.

Meeting them were twenty-five Russians wearing clothing that boasted similarly discordant safari themes. The Russians were not wearing mosquito-proof hats, though. Their hats were all military and practical for a country where temperatures could routinely exceed 30C.

The Russians, like their hats, looked uncivilian. Large, fit, straight-backed and all with the same cropped haircuts. Koransky ran a tough crew.

Ridiculously, the ex-Spetsnaz mercs all had cameras around their necks – every single man had a camera and every single camera was the same model. Many ostentatiously clutched birding guides, copies of books written by Laurens Van der Post and reptile tick-lists.

Reviewing the photos two days later, the Langley West Africa expert, had murmured, "What in the name of God do they think they look like?"

"There's more," his underdog had said.

"Check this batch."

The new roll of film lovingly dwelled on the transport.

There were four vehicles assembled (a bus, a minibus and two long-wheelbased jeeps). All boasted the prominent slogan, "Dreaming Safaris".

Under "Dreaming Safaris" was painted an abstract of a bird.

Then the message, "We take you to safari heav'n." Beside that was a weeping panda hugging some sort of rabbit – the species was unclear, the drawing either inept or deliberately primitive – and a map of the world with a pink heart in its middle wearing a smile.

"Good vehicles, but, my Christ, that design's an eyesore!" The Langley man had said. "What kind of warped mind put that together?"

The answer was simple, though Langley was destined never to get to the bottom of the mystery.

The logo had been designed by the Aleph Transport Minister's daughter, a student at Tokyo's less-than-prestigious Tamabi Arts College.

It was the Aleph Transport Minister who had put the whole expedition together, clothing design, vehicle design, cameras, bird books, reptile checklists, the lot. Helped to a considerable extent by his twenty year old daughter whom he dreamed of grooming for his job. He also dreamed that her artistic abilities would blossom and believed that the bud needed as much of the nourishing water of practical experience as possible. The minister and his daughter had been meticulous in their planning. Nothing had not been planned. The type of toothbrushes to be taken, the horn signals to call the column to halt, the headgear, the make of camera ...

Although neither the Aleph Transport Minister nor his beloved daughter had ever actually *been* to Africa, they had seen films and together had developed very definite ideas as to what the Dark Continent was like.

Vladimir Koransky had, at first, attempted to set them straight, but the Transport Minister was insistent.

Koransky was never to find out why his ten years experience in Africa, not to mention *all* his suggestions – every single one! – went ignored.

Again the answer was simple. Aleph's Transport Minister had shown Koransky's suggestions to his daughter and she didn't like them. Not at all. When the Transport Minister had attempted to explain that Koransky was a professional, ex-Spetsnaz assassin and old Africa hand, she had stamped about and pouted and, on several occasions, hidden in the toilet refusing to come out while screaming that he didn't love her.

The Transport Minister did love her, overindulged her and was thoroughly daunted by her tantrums.

Considerable delays in the Aleph team's expedition departure had been experienced while Koransky faxed information such as:

"Suggest JICA expert/oil company/NGO disguise not safari disguise. Safari is popular in Kenya, Tanzania, Namibia etc. If we were there I would congratulate you on your artful safari disguise concept."

Koransky, as he sent such faxes from his temporary office in Monrovia, was aware that Aleph was paying not just large fees, but huge fees. Hence the repeated attempts to be as diplomatic as possible.

Aleph's expert, determined to placate his daughter, was unwavering in his design for the expedition. He insisted that the Russians be disguised as safari-goers. Sketches of clothing design had uncurled from Koransky's fax machine.

"Make a safari company," the Aleph Minister had ordered.

"I have here a Rough Guides guidebook to West Africa," Koransky had faxed back. "Two countries are complete blanks. Sierra Leone where we are going and Liberia where we are starting. This is effectively a warning that even entrepid safari-goers are not advised, etc., etc."

"Make a safari company," the Aleph Minister had ordered.

Koransky had created one. Creating a company in Monrovia took no time at all if you had the wherewithal to cover the necessary bribes.

"Call it Dreaming Safaris."

Koransky, who had called the safari company he had created "Wild West Safaris", had then had to bribe everybody again to get the name changed. But he'd done it.

"This is the logo."

Koransky had looked at the logo and winced. Enough, he'd thought, was enough.

One of the peculiarities of registering a company in Monrovia at that time was that one had to register the corporate logo at the same time.

Koransky had drawn up a stylized logo of an elephant and a lion. Been rather pleased with it actually. Had registered it.

And then this fucked-up bunny rabbit or whatever it was with a panda (a panda!) had arrived.

He had then faxed back a suggestion that while this sort of Aleph logo would do very well in another country, it might not be appropriate to Monrovia, the city, or Liberia, the country. Perhaps an elephant? Or a lion? (Not that Liberia had either). Or, he'd added hopefully, perhaps both? He'd faxed his logo.

"This is the logo," the next fax stated obstinately. And there it was again. The fucked-up bunny rabbit, the panda, the rest of it.

It was just a different aesthetic, thought Vladimir Koransky surrendering graciously to the power of the yen, as he set out to bribe everybody at corporate registration for a third time. A different aesthetic? No, not right, a *very* different aesthetic.

Koransky, had been taking the cult's money for years. Faced with this insane insistence on ignoring advice, and this vile logo, he remembered the Aum Shinrikyo political campaign back in 1989 when Aum had made its bid for official, democratically-elected, government power. Aum had established the Shinrito party and put up twenty-five candidates for election. Koransky, along with some other non-Japanese Russian and Korean notables, had been invited over by cult guru Shoko Asahara to be shown how well the campaign would work.

Koransky had gone – hell, who wouldn't if offered a first class Aeroflot seat and expenses? Flying Aeroflot's "working class" might have been like taking a Czarist cattle truck to a Siberian death camp, but they did pretty well up in first class. Ice-cold vodka, blinis, smoked duck. Quite a show, as long as the pilot wasn't drunk or had brought his kid along to have a go with the joystick.

Upon arrival Koransky had then been driven through car-clogged streets and been deposited with a flourish (and a can of caviar and a bottle of vodka) in front of Tokyo's Ebisu subway station, near the fashionable international pleasure district of Roppongi.

Koransky had looked around for the election rally, awkwardly holding his caviar and his vodka, wondering what to do with both, feeling like an encumbered idiot as indifferent commuters swept past him. Where was it? The rally?

Eventually the car driver had reappeared – Koransky presumed he'd had trouble finding a parking space – and had pointed out a bus. The bus had dominated the immediate view from Ebisu station simply because it was parked so close. But Koransky had ignored the bus. It had looked so fucking silly.

The driver had pointed blank-faced up at the bus. That, Koransky, had then realised *was* the rally!

Aum's Shinrito candidates and supporters had been dancing around on the roof of the bus handing out Asahara-head-shaped balloons (with Asahara's face on them Koransky had realised suddenly) and singing. Several were wearing pink elephant costumes.

Not a design that Koransky would have gone for. No Russians he knew would vote for people who dressed up as pink elephants.

"We Japanese," the cult guru had explained in an audience subsequent to Koransky's viewing of Aum's Shinrito party debut, "we Japanese, like cute things. Pink is a cute colour that appeals to cute girls and women who statistically are dominant in our electorate."

"Is that so?" Koransky had answered. "You are obviously very wise in these matters."

"I am," the guru had confirmed. "What Japan values now is a

word you as a foreigner won't know. It's *kowaie* (pronounced cow-eye-ee). Its a word that means cute!"

Aum's spiritual leader, Shoko Asahara, was at that moment of divine explanation, one of the more hideous sights that Koransky had been confronted with in a life that had routinely thrown the hideous in his direction: drifting, long tousled hair, a repellent semi-blind squint, and a face that floated above robes and had nothing to recommend it. Marx had once said, "I never forget a face, but in your case I'll be happy to make an exception."

Not Karl Marx. Groucho.

That's how he'd felt about Asahara's face. Closeted with the Aum leader, Koransky had wondered whether this was a mutated reincarnation of Rasputin.

Shoko Asahara had concluded the interview and then levitated away from Koransky with the help of obviously visible ropes attached to his tatami mat.

Koransky had decided, at that sight, that Rasputin hadn't come back. Just a complete weirdo.

Weirder still was the comment from an Aum member beside Koransky. "See! He flies!" the woman had said with reverence. "He's on strings!" Koransky had thought. "Can't you see them? Are you mad?"

What'd he'd said though was, "Yes, he flies like a godly bird."

When the Aum political initiative had failed – none of the people wearing pink elephant costumes had been elected – the cult had evinced increasing signs of paranoia, had begun digging nuclear shelters, developing earthquake rays and sending expeditions overseas to collect biological weapons.

Utterly barmy.

Still, Koransky had done what he could to help them because they paid: they always paid well, and paid promptly. But the people Aum, then Aleph, sent on their expeditions were always ridiculous.

Their ideas were warped. Impractical. They'd even sent a group into a gang-infested suburb of Vladivostok in search of a Hind helicopter gun-ship. That team (and its money) had never been heard from again. It had subsequently fallen to Koransky to get Asahara his Hind.

As Koransky picked up the latest loons from Aleph at the Monrovia airport bonded warehouse, noted their head gear, their clothes, the way they were already reeling in the heat (or were they having problems looking through their hats?) he thought that this expedition was going to be an obviously predictable disaster.

"Don't piss them off," Koransky had hurriedly whispered to his men as soon as the Aleph people arrived. "If they want to go around looking like the bee-keepers from Mars – fine. Remember, they're paying for the privilege."

Sergei Kutuzov, Koransky's number two, had nodded glumly. He hated Japs.

The Dreaming Safari-goers clambered into the minibus. The Aleph team were given a small airline-style tray of cod roe, sake, pickles and chopsticks to help them relax and feel at home.

All of the Aleph members ate their cod roe and kept their eyes down as the convoy left Monrovia at speed and bounced along increasingly uncertain roads towards bandit country and the border. They fed their food up towards their mouths through the folded mosquito mesh of their hats with difficulty, dropped a lot of the cod roe, and a lot of the cod roe that they dropped got caught in their mosquito nets. They talked discordantly to one another

Koransky in the second jeep – only a moron would command from the front in the mined roads he was expecting – drank occasional slugs of tepid vodka and listened to the bug that he'd placed in the Aleph seats through headphones.

The Aleph people began by complaining about the cod roe which they stated was inferior to that produced in Japan.

"It's *from* Japan, you morons," muttered Koransky who had

been ordered to fly it in on the previous day at ludicrous cost by the Aleph Transport Minister, whose daughter, unbeknownst to Koransky, was very partial to cod roe.

Talk then shifted to hygiene standards in the minibus. Some moaned about the temperature. Most began humming holy tunes, and while they did the leader explained that Russians were brute beasts and animals and were used to living in squalid minibuses. They were also criminal deviants, the Aleph leader said, only tolerated because they were helping in the preparation for the Final War. He then said that no-one should mention the emergency funds sown into their zebra jackets.

Koransky, after his years with the cult, had learned proficient Japanese.

Why, he wondered, after years being cult members with the cult, had cult members not learned to be even slightly clever? Why this mad xenophobia? Why this chauvinistic belief that no-one not born in Japan could speak Japanese or clean a minibus? Why were they so terminally unrealistic? General MacArthur had once described Japan as a nation of twelve-year-olds. In Aleph's case this description struck Koransky as overly generous.

Stalin, after a vodka debauch, had made the officers, politicians and flunkies who attended, dance to recordings of dogs barking. He'd then suggested that every catholic in Russia be crucified. Someone had hinted that it would offend the Pope.

"Fuck the Pope!" Stalin had apparently responded. "How many divisions does he have?"

What exasperated Koransky about Aleph was that even if they wanted to kill all the catholics of Russia (and it had been suggested – Asahara had wanted to fund Muslim militants to trigger Final War), they couldn't! Whether Stalin had said what he was said to have said, Stalin at least had had the divisions. Aleph's people were always hell-bent on Final War. *Saishu Sen*. Designing earthquake machines. Prompting apocalypse.

But Aleph didn't have any divisions to speak of.

Aleph to the best of Koransky's knowledge currently had him. Koransky. That was it.

And from the conversation in the minibus they didn't seem to appreciate him at all.

"We must get the weapons for Final War!" The Aleph leader was saying now, his voice boringly self-assured and very distinct in Koransky's head-set. "Mr X", as the Aleph team leader had insisted on being called, was becoming increasingly noisy, assertive and confident but monumentally repetitious. The sake probably.

"Do not remove your hat!" Mr X snapped. "The risk of malaria and mosquito-borne AIDS is considerable."

Koransky guffawed. Mosquito-borne AIDS, fa chrissakes! You could no more catch AIDS from mosquitoes than you could from sitting on toilet seats or reading a second-hand copy of *Pravda*. And these gibbering clowns were the bioweapons unit?

"What is it, sir?" Kutuzov asked.

"The bee-keepers! They're unbelievable! You know that they ran an election campaign dressed up as pink elephants?"

"How did they get on?"

"Take a wild guess."

Through his headphones Koransky then heard the Aleph team leader returning to the subject of Russians and hygiene.

Koransky, who was not the slavish serf that Aleph clearly thought he was, began to wonder whether he'd end up having to shoot his clients.

That's what had happened the last time. Koransky had chaperoned the earlier Aleph expedition into Liberia in search of Ebola. He'd told Tokyo that there wasn't any Ebola in Liberia. Tokyo had persuaded itself there was and had sent the team anyway. They'd taken some drugs – drug use was rampant among Aleph members – gone off their heads, and Koransky had eventually run out of patience and shot them.

He'd told Tokyo they'd died of fever.

Tokyo had believed him.

Hopeless!

"Kutuzov?"

"Yes, sir?"

"If anything bad happens to me, they've got emergency funds sewn into their jackets. My guess is rather a lot of emergency funds. Remember that."

CHAPTER TWENTY-SEVEN

Dalziel

To defeat the irregular, one needs the irregular, Dalziel was thinking. Reports indicated that the guests at the Hotel Bristol were extremely irregular. He ordered his communications man to raise the hotel.

The Hotel Bristol picked up immediately.

"Pleasant?" asked the German-accented voice. It sounded desperately eager.

"Not at all pleasant," Dalziel drawled confidently. "This is, shall we say, an unofficial call from Her Majesty's Ship *Clam*. I've an idea that a conference might be to our mutual benefit."

"You're not Pleasant?"

"I'm not pleasant? What do you mean? Who is this?"

"Are you Pleasant? Listen, man, I've had a fucked-up night and if you're not Pleasant I'm telling you right now that I don't want to know."

" I can be as pleasant as you like. Perhaps we should start again ..." But Dalziel was now talking to no-one.

The call had been broken by whoever the Teutonic moron it was that was manning the Hotel Bristol's switchboard. Dalziel sighed and wondered whether in a former life he had been a bad man. A really bad man. Beria maybe. Or Bluebeard. Someone really despicable. And they'd sent him back to walk the planet in a new life, not as a cockroach but as an SAS colonel with a Sierra Leone to deal with.

Karmic backlash continued in the form of a telex from London's weather people.

More rain forecast. All day. It was a quirk of meteorology that virtually all the hurricanes that played hell with holiday makers in the Caribbean, white-trash trailer parks in Florida and crooked coastal real estate development in Louisiana and the Carolinas began life as heavy weather in West Africa, particularly in Liberia and Sierra Leone. Both countries that had been settled and colonised by freed slaves. The storms then drifted off across the Atlantic, getting angrier and angrier as they went.

Dalziel had heard various jokes on the subject from one of his junior officers. "Even the hurricanes don't like it here." That had been the least irritating. And the most funny.

If the current climate was anything to go by, Dalziel decided that he'd be giving his mother-in-law a complimentary ticket to Antigua or Dade County. She could take Dalziel's feckless son Derek with her. The latest news on Dalziel's home front was that Derek had joined a troupe of New Age jugglers and was touring Brittany on something called a "sacred run".

The sacred run, Dalziel's wife had written fretfully (the newly faxed letter was folded neatly in Dalziel's top pocket), was about saving the planet. "I tried to give him money," she had written. "But Derek said that the point of the sacred run was to seek voluntary donations of food from the communities through which the runners passed. Derek said that he was aiming to live his life without ever touching money again."

Dalziel was all in favour of saving the planet. It needed as much saving as it could get in his opinion, and then quite a bit more. He was also a man who appreciated thrift. Quite how poncing around juggling and begging was to achieve Derek's objectives though, was beyond him.

"It's like the Children's Crusade," his wife had written before delivering the final body-blow. "Mother is staying here again. She's such a comfort. I know sometimes she's a bit of a trial to you but she's looking so young. She and I pray daily for Derek's safety and for yours!!!"

"Derek's safety? The little twerp's in Brittany!" Dalziel thought savagely. "Not waltzing around waving a cross at Saracens or trying to part the Mediterranean.

As for Children's Crusades, there were more than enough children crusading just over the water. The bangs and booms were, at times, audible over the pelting of the weather.

"Sir?"

Dalziel roused himself from his self-pity.

The verdict of *Clam*'s chopper pilots had arrived. They'd checked the weather reports and confirmed what Dalziel had expected them to confirm.

No-one was getting out of Freetown today. Not by air.

"Raise PS," Dalziel said. By PS, Dalziel meant Peterson-Smith.

"I want to know what is going on in that hotel," Dalziel said. "We need those mercenaries or whoever the hell they are to secure our nationals, secure foreign nationals, assert control, ignore the Geneva Convention and break heads like they should be doing ..."

Clam hit a trough, then a wave, then a trough. Everybody present clung to anything that offered support. The sea was thumping at *Clam*'s hull like a boxer at a punch-bag.

There were more flying fish.

"*HMS Clam* can weather the storm. She's made of steel. There's a lot of flesh and blood over there, over the water, that is hurting! Our people!" Dalziel was shouting to make himself heard.

"Raise PS!"

CHAPTER TWENTY-EIGHT

Just the Sat-phone

Rindert was morbidly bored as he fiddled with the treacherous sat-phone. There were flies in the Mission, lots of them. Sluggish, fat, very stupid, they just droned around asking to be bashed. It helped pass the time, but not very much.

Damned sat-phone. Useless sat-phone. But what, just what, was the problem?

"Still not working?" Jack asked for perhaps the tenth time since the last interrupted conversation with The Crocodile.

No buyers had turned up at Lalapanzi so Rindert assumed The Crocodile had got through to them in time to prevent them leaving Freetown.

That, or their vehicles had got bogged down in the flooded roads. Or had been ambushed by RUF. Or abducted by aliens. Or hit by a flash flood. Whatever. All seemed currently possible in this weirdest of all possible worlds.

Less than hour ago a civet cat had come pattering through the room. Totally unafraid. With the skeletal remains of a hand in its mouth. Just pattered in through the door, pattered across the room, and when Jack had seen it and started screaming, it had turned around, dropped the hand and pattered off. Back through the door. Calm as you please.

"Ahh get it away!" Jack had squalled, cowering in a corner. "It's got Ebola! Ahh! Ahh!"

"The civet?"

"Not the civet. The hand! The hand!"

Rindert had wondered whether Jack was suffering from DTs. He'd found a cloth, wrapped it round the civet's leavings then chucked the hand, or what was left of it, out of the window.

With the hand gone, Jack had calmed. Fifteen minutes later he was back with the "Still not working?" routine.

Odd the way life went.

Rindert walked off and away from Jack, remembering the fateful day – was it just two weeks ago? No, it was less – that he'd bought the blasted sat-phone.

Pleasant, the blundering, bloated, goggle-eyed idiot, had given him the address of a firm called White Ink Inc. The premises, when Rindert finally found them, had been an agricultural warehouse on a farm in Essex. A printing press had been churning out newspapers in several European languages, manned by a reserved looking man in a British farmer's flat tweed cap. A glance at all the lightning flashes and flags that adorned the headers, the colour of the print, had told Rindert what was being printed.

Nationalist magazines, newsletters and papers. Howl-at-the-moon stuff. A typical Crocodile contact.

"Do you mind?" Rindert had asked, plucking a newly-born copy of *Skorpion Reborn* from its rack in the machine.

"I don't mind at all," the man in the flat cap had said, wiping his hands on a cloth, although his hands weren't dirty. "More is printed than is ever read."

"It's not popular?" Rindert had asked.

"Popular enough for 2,000 twice-yearly printings," the man had said. "Plus another 500 if they anticipate a surge in sales."

"Most stuff in this modern world that's printed isn't read," the man in the flat cap had continued. "There's too much printed that is rubbish. Weigh your next Sunday newspaper. It's close to a kilogram of Zionist capitalist rubbish. They can't even get them through the letterbox. A postman told me that."

"You're probably right," Rindert had said.

"Yes, I probably am," the man had said back, still working his hands with the cloth and advancing.

He had, Rindert remembered, a very pleasant face. Pleasantly weather-beaten, engagingly stoic, a salt-of-the-earth sort of man.

"You a Red?" the salt-of-the-earth man had asked, as his seditious print presses rolled. "If you are Red, I'll not print a thing you have to say."

"No printing. I'm here for a sat-phone," Rindert had answered. "Dr Pleasant referred me to you. He's a doctor."

"Well he would be, wouldn't he? If you say his name's Doctor Pleasant. The doctor bit at the beginning rather gives the game away, now, doesn't it?"

Rindert had nodded, wondering whether it was time to swing fists.

"Sat-phone," the man had gnawed his lip thoughtfully. "That buggers me. I don't know why your doctor chum sent you here for a sat-phone. I've got one. But he's the one who sold it to me. It's not much good. It works. But it's not much good."

"I'll take it. I'm in a hurry."

"Will you be wanting any printing done? Newsletters? Magazines? Generally speaking, I offer subsidies if the content's good. Quality of writing is always of concern."

Rindert had had a look at the magazine he was holding. The quality of printing was lousy. The headline read, "Keep Britain White With Dynamite."

Not exactly practical but at least it rhymed, Rindert had thought. Sort of.

"No, no magazines. Just the sat-phone."

Three words. Just the sat-phone. Three little words.

Why did the auction fail?

Just the sat-phone.

Why couldn't you get moonlight?

Just the sat-phone.

Why were you stuck in Mission Twilight Zone infested with

flies and a redheaded lunatic terrified of civets that delivered skeletal hands?

Just the sat-phone.

Why did the Ebola-virus-bomb homunculi go berserk?

Just the ...

"Hey! Rindert! Come here man!" It was Jack, yelling excitedly. "The sat-phone's ringing!"

CHAPTER TWENTY-NINE

Tea Time

"What the bloody hell's going on?" raged Dr Pleasant from his Beck's Hill call box. It was his twenty-third visit there that day. And he'd drunk what felt like about as many cups of tea in Beck's Hills China Tea Rooms just over the road.

He'd laired there sipping Darjeeling and nipping discreetly off to the phone box every now and then. Both Schindler's and Rindert's numbers had been constantly engaged.

The tweeds and dignity of his medical calling had helped him blend in at first. No-one in the Beck's Hill China Tea Rooms had batted an eyelid until cup number four and the eighth discrete expedition out into the storm and to the phone box.

By cup of tea number five, he had begun to attract quizzical glances and stares from the staff. And the China Tea Room's pensioner clientele, who generally spent a lot of their day there but only drank a couple of pots, were shooting covert glances that soon stopped being covert and became obviously inquisitive.

"My wife's pregnant," Dr Pleasant had eventually had to explain. Then he'd added, "She's on a small boat in the Bristol Channel."

Why had he said that? He'd cursed inwardly. Some vile Freudian concoction born of the Hotel Bristol and wavelengths and channel frequencies and screwing up.

"Ach, shite," is what he'd thought.

"It's touch and go," is what he'd said. Then with a hint of cunning he'd added (in a shy, troubled voice), "Just phoning. Waiting. Need to be alone."

The announcement had reassured everybody in the China Tea Rooms.

But it had had the unfortunate side-effect of precipitating a slow but then increasingly solicitous rush of concern from pensioners, staff and every other damn person who came dripping through the door. The cunning, need-to-be-alone ploy had been a bust. The Bristol Channel birth had eclipsed it. Hardly fucking surprising. Ach, shite.

Drama was normally in short supply in the Beck's Hill China Tea Rooms. The repeated departures and reappearances of the huge and obviously increasingly-distressed man promised a lot more of interest, conversation-wise, than normal. The new Beck's Hill vicar at the church of St Lawrence had stood on a table in the Falcon Inn and then sung hymns in an obvious state of intoxication and overexcitement. But that thrill had occurred more than six weeks ago. At the meeting of the Beck's Hill Choral Society.

Six weeks of chewing it over had rendered the incident of use in future discussions should he ever do it again. But it was not what anyone in the China Tea Room would call hot news.

This was.

The next cup of tea had arrived courtesy of Dorothy Waddleside, active in the Beck's Hill Bowls club and the Mother's Union. She'd intercepted Dr Pleasant's order, had made rather a lot of obvious fuss about how she would pay the thirty-five pence bill herself. And then, when the waitress had attempted to deliver the tea cup, had made more of a fuss as she removed it from the waitress and then brought the drink over personally.

"Oh, don't fret now," Dorothy had said, settling into the chair beside Dr Pleasant and patting his ham-like hand. "I've had five and one of those took its time, I can tell you. In the Blitz too. In Piccadilly tube station it was. I'll never forget it. The man who delivered her was a coalman from Swansea. He said he'd never seen a prettier little girl. Normally, he said, and I always laugh to think of it, he delivered coal. Delivered coal! Not smiling, lovely little baby girls!"

"Ho, ho, ho," chortled Dr Pleasant.

"Well it helps to laugh, doesn't it?"

"The best medicine," said Dr Pleasant. "I'd better have another go at a call."

"Give the poor dear our love! Tell her it's all in the breathing," chorused Dorothy. "Let us know the news!"

This time the call had worked. He'd got through to Schindler, who'd pissed and moaned and said that the violence was ongoing. But at least it sounded to Pleasant as if he'd got the Hotel Bristol crowd in hand. Ordered up whores, lots of food and booze.

There'd been some shootings and a bit of Panhard action. Schindler explained that there was a psycho called Speeks who had discouraged the RUF light armour. With a rocket-propelled grenade.

At the mention of Speeks and his RPG activity, Pleasant had actually smiled. Speeks was a total monster. A kaffir killer par extraordinaire! The amusing thing was that he looked like Father Christmas. The jolliest-looking man you'd ever meet coming at you at a run out of a mangrove swamp with a frag mine in his hand and a vacant smile on his chubby red-cheeked face.

"What's with this auction?" Schindler had interrupted The Crocodile's reminiscences.

"Back to you momentarily on that. I'm just clearing things up with Rindert. Nothing serious. No serious problems. I'll get back to you soon. You still got a fax? Or has some kaffir shot it to shit? Give me the fax number."

Schindler had given it to him.

"Right, I'll get back to you."

"Please do," Schindler had said icily.

But try, try and try again, that slab of rancid baboon dung, Rindert, had been constantly engaged.

For hours, days, months, years, going on centuries, going on aeons. Empires had risen and fallen, stars had been born, died, shot madly from their spheres – or so it felt to Dr Pleasant – but all he'd got in his eternity of calling was an engaged signal from Rindert's sat-phone number. That or very strange telephonic snorts, crackles, beep-beep-beeps and zings.

After each failure he'd stomped back through the rain to the Beck's Hill China Tea Rooms. For another cup of tea.

He'd have gone somewhere else to break the increasingly embarrassing pattern but the only other refuge close to the phone box was an Indian restaurant. And it was closed.

As the long day wore on the English pensioners had become increasingly persistent in their sympathy and, by cup of tea number ten, with their questions. Dr Pleasant fielded them with increasing desperation.

What was his wife doing in the Bristol Channel? Good fucking question. Dr Pleasant remembered a radio news report he'd heard on the drive to Beck's Hill.

His wife was a marine biologist, a squid analyst.

"Well, who'd have thought it."

Why was she analysing squid?

To gauge ocean pollution. Mercury accumulates in squid livers.

"Well, you learn something new every day."

His wife's name?

Agnes.

"Lovely name. I had an aunt called Agnes. Lovely woman."

Was he a local man? No. Where did he live? Um, London. What had brought him to Beck's Hill? Nothing. Just passing through. Going where?

Mad. Going mad! That's where I'm going, you withered English aardvark turd. What the hell was going on in Lalapanzi? Curse the RUF to hell! Curse all kaffirs! Curse the damned English!

"I'm going to Bristol. No, I don't need another cup of tea."

What was the latest on his wife? Had her contractions begun?

Was there a doctor in attendance? How big was the boat? What was the boat called? Did he think it was wise to keep phoning? Wasn't he disturbing her when she needed to keep her mind focused on the job in hand?

By cup of tea fifteen Dr Pleasant felt that his head was about to explode. His head and bladder both.

And if he heard another word about giving birth in the Blitz and what the coalman from Swansea had said he was going to bring out his Heckler and Koch and blow these blue-hairs to kingdom fucking come.

It was at that moment the local press had turned up. A thin, balding man of about twenty-five, with a wet mackintosh and a notebook had approached Dr Pleasant flapping an equally wet umbrella and introduced himself as Basil Rudge of the *Beck's Hill Courier*. "It's a freesheet but very well-read locally," he'd said. "Hear there's a bit of a drama ongoing," he'd then said. "Your good lady giving birth on a squid boat in a storm, right?"

The pensioners had fluttered and quacked with excitement. The newspaper! The drama!

"Back in a minute," Dr Pleasant had chortled, hurrying over the street to the phone box.

Where miracle of miracles he had got through.

"What the bloody hell is going on?" he raged

"The sat-phone your Nazi bonehead in Essex sold me is malfunctioning!" Rindert raged back. "I'd have been better off buying carrier pigeons!"

"Why the hell did you postpone the auction?" yelled Dr Pleasant, privately vowing to firebomb White Ink Inc. as soon as the opportunity presented itself.

"There was an RUF attack. One of the little shits lobbed an RPG into the cellar and blew up our moonlight!"

"Talk sense!"

Rindert calmed himself with effort and informed his caller of the particulars. There were occasional strangled grunts on the other end of the line as he did so. Rindert wondered whether The Crocodile was going to have a stroke or a heart attack.

When he'd finished describing what had occurred, Rindert ventured to make a suggestion.

There were more gagging noises at the Beck's Hill end as Rindert spoke. Then a despairing groan. Then a pause.

"You want me to buy moonlight from a man called Mango?" Dr Pleasant finally managed. "Fly it out to Sierra Leone. Deliver it to you."

"Well, it'd be a lot quicker than me going all the way there. And it's not my reputation that's on the line here. It's yours."

All that Rindert heard was a gurgle.

Then "Urrrghnnnh!" said Dr Pleasant.

He wandered from the Beck's Hill phone box looking green.

"You all right, dearie?" enquired an elderly woman who had been waiting for the call to conclude. "You look a bit poorly, my love. Is it good news? Has the birth been without complications? How is the dear child?"

Dr Pleasant goggled at her.

"Urrghnnnnh ..." said Dr Pleasant again and reeled off in the direction of his car and the Beck's Hill parking warden who was grimly attaching a ticket to the windscreen.

A ticket! Coming on top of Christ-only-knew-how-many cups of tea, it was intolerable!

The next morning saw the Beck's Hill China Tea Rooms with more to discuss than the drama of a squid analyst giving birth in the midst of the storm-tossed Bristol Channel.

There'd been violence. Just outside the Tea Rooms. By the parking meters.

Everyone had seen it happen. The huge, fish-faced man from London had actually made the traffic warden – nice lady, just doing her job – eat the ticket she'd just pasted on his car. After she'd eaten the ticket, he'd headbutted her – knocked her cold – then thrown her away. She'd gone through the Bluebell Book

Shop's plate-glass window. Just like in an action film. The man hadn't paid for his teas. And he'd had so many teas! Not paid for one of them. Just clambered into his car and roared off.

"Oh, but he was overwrought, the poor love," said Dorothy Waddleside. "Having babies does that to a man."

Like everyone else in the Beck's Hill China Tea Rooms she just couldn't wait to see the story in the *Courier*. That young lad, Rudge, had caught the whole encounter on his natty new camera. Only trouble was the *Courier* was a weekly paper. She'd have to wait till Friday.

CHAPTER THIRTY

Chaos Coming

"The people at the Bristol are attending an auction," said Peterson-Smith to Dalziel.

"Blood diamonds?" Dalziel asked. Blood diamonds was the newly-coined phrase for stones sold illegally by rebel forces in Sierra Leone, Angola and elsewhere. The annual diamond trade was worth in excess of $US5 billion. Depending on who you spoke to, blood diamonds went to make up from two to fourteen per cent of that figure.

"It would seem logical but it's not confirmed."

Peterson-Smith then went on to summarise what Fitz had heard during his rudely interrupted stay at the Hotel Bristol.

"I've not heard diamonds being called units before," Dalziel mused. "Is that normal? Calling them units?"

"No, it's not. And our source says that it's possible that weapons may also be involved. I'm quoting here: 'If these units work like The Crocodile says they'll work, Mugabe will be looking for his arsehole in Angola and his moustache in Mozambique.' That quote from either a South African or Zimbabwe national. Either way, it would indicate weapons at the auction. Frankly, I'm mystified."

"Is your source still at the Bristol?"

"No, a gentleman of German extraction broke a TV over his head and asked him rather bluntly to vacate the premises. He's had a testing time of it. Got involved in the Hotel Frangipani break-out, crawled in covered in brains. He's ... um ... currently *hors de combat*."

This was a delicate way of putting it. Fitz had been hosed down in the beer garden and had then, still stinking like a drain courtesy of his dip in the flooded basement, launched into an assault of unprecedented ferocity on the Jardin de Cygne's dwindling Martian population. He was now wrapped in blankets and unconscious in a corner. Peterson-Smith thought that for the first time since he'd met Fitz, the man had earned himself a decent drink.

On to other business. The UNHCR convoy survivors limping back into Freetown with machete mutilations and bullet wounds. News incomplete on the ambush, but it sounded like a bad one. Maybe 400, 450 dead. Nothing heard from the UN Res Rep. Hard to pin down but reports indicate a firefight related to a piano. Hotel Frangipani siege still ongoing despite breakout of some RUF units. SLA (Sierra Leone Army) in disarray. The NSLA (the breakaway New Sierra Leone Army) in disarray. Pro-government Kamajor militia on the rampage with unconfirmed reports of atrocities (in magical ceremonies) against civilians accused of being RUF infiltrators in mufti. Heavy flooding. More Nigerian troop desertions. Standard Chartered looted. Law Courts burned in 1990, rebuilt, currently re-burning merrily. More than 250 plus/minus expats moved by SLA units, helped by Executive Outcomes and SHEELD operatives, to hotels on the Lumley Beach Road, where they were awaiting evacuation to HMS *Clam* when the weather broke.

State House under siege. Museum occupied by RUF, all apparently wearing looted Bundu devil masks used by the Mende and Temne secret societies. Effigies of some porroh man called Papa Det appearing on street corners.

President Kabbah defiant, but still out of the country. Airport runway a write-off. Calling on OAU to intervene to restore order. OAU meeting in Windhoek, Namibia to try and resolve escalation of war in DRC. Unlikely to intervene in West Africa, not with the African equivalent of World War I raging in DRC. And with

Zimbabwe's loony Mugabe still driving the gravy train off the rails. Street battles in Harare. Etc., etc. Doom. Gloom.

God bless Africa.

When Dalziel terminated the call, after his usual comments about excellent work in formidable conditions, he withdrew to his cabin with a notebook and pen and began what his wife called "one of his thinking bouts".

The world that day continued to conspire against Sierra Leone in its bid for media coverage and the global eye. A second plane crashed in the USA, this time at Dallas Fort Worth, killing three and injuring 203. The Israeli-Palestinian peace talks degenerated to a thunderous background of street violence in Gaza and Hebron. *The Sun* newspaper announced that Prince William had announced that he was engaged. Then, at 18.35, the Pope died during a ceremony involving the Madonna Fatima.

The first homunculus began to exhibit symptoms of sleep deprivation at about the same time as the Pope fell over, knocking the Madonna Fatima (which had come all the way from Portugal and had been chosen as the symbol of the next millennium) from its ornately-wrought tray.

Rindert met the psychotic homunculus in the kitchen. It was standing in front of the fridge-freezer swaying its head from side to side in rhythmic, monotonously heavy sweeps that put Rindert in mind of a caged, stressed-out elephant.

Rindert, who'd come to the kitchen with plans of making butternut soup, stopped and wished that he was holding something with a little more offensive potential than a storm lantern and clippings from the Mission's cookery book.

The homunculus was not the worst he'd seen, not in the beauty stakes, but it was no oil painting.

Rather larger than most, it stood at a little more than five feet. The body was small and denuded, with the pot-belly of malnutrition. The head was large, fat and damaged – Rindert realised that it belonged (or more accurately had belonged) to the oldest of the Liberians killed in the field-test assault on Radio Butt Naked.

As always was the case with homunculi, the thing's physique and features had been modified with frightfully macabre exuberance. In this case with copper wire wrapped tight around its neck like the Burmese giraffe women or some madly over-enthused Congolese bangle-hag. There were nails sticking out from beneath the nose and the nails had been bent to resemble tusks.

The legs were slim and hairless. The sort of legs that whispered of erotic possibilities.

At the bottom of the legs were sneakers filled, not with feet, but with solder. Like the head, the sneakers were not new to Rindert. Abraham Lincoln had been wearing them prior to his road-side execution. One of Rindert's militia had appropriated them. And now here they were, adorning a particularly unlovely homunculus.

The footwear did not bode well for his patrol. Not if it was on a homunculus. Rindert hoped that Benjamin Franklin hadn't been wearing them. Realised then that Benjamin would not be wearing stolen property – his Baptist beliefs, though queer and unpolished, were deeply held. One of his men was dead though. Rindert hoped that Benjamin was somewhere far from here. And running fast to get a whole lot further.

The homunculus continued to sway its head and stand still. There was a sudden snort and a foul burst of gas belched from its nose tube. The head-swaying rhythm was unbroken.

Rindert tiptoed away from the kitchen to fetch firstly his rifle and secondly Jack.

"Wuthup?" Jack said. Not drunk, just absorbed in some intricate work that involved a pair of pliers and a set of false teeth.

"I think it's starting to go wrong. You've got one of your units exhibiting what I'd describe as erratic behaviour. Like a stressed-out animal."

"Theethuth," said Jack putting the false teeth into his mouth. "Jesus," he said again, then hurriedly removed the dentures and snipped at a pointed, painful piece of wire that was protruding. The dentures looked home-made. No clues needed for Rindert to guess where Jack had got the teeth. Rindert conceded that the man was clever with his hands. The engineering looked good.

"Cut my cheek on the inside. I'll get an ulcer. I'm susceptible to ulcers. And another thing. How come, whenever I pour a drink, a minute later there's a moth in it? Look at this glass. There's more moth in it than drink."

"You done?" Rindert asked. "One of your units is flaking out!"

Jack, with tears in his eyes, nodded.

Both men re-ascended the staircase to the kitchen.

"What happened to your gob?" Rindert asked as they climbed.

"Son-of-a-bitch pulled most of my teeth out. Black bastard!"

"Good."

The two men reached the top of the stairs, Rindert now in hunting mode, every sense alert and keen, waved Jack to silence.

"OK, shhh, here we are," whispered Rindert, seizing Jack's arm in a grip that was a vice and a bit more than a vice.

"Eek," whimpered Jack.

"Shhh. Look at this."

Rindert pulled Jack suddenly into the kitchen and levelled his weapon.

The homunculus was gone. The kitchen was empty. Dank with the smell of the rain, dank with the smell of rotting maize flour and dried fruit, it rustled with cockroaches and there was the sound of rats and the drone, the rather loud drone, of the fridge-freezer. But no homunculus.

CHAPTER THIRTY-ONE

Schindler's List

I want you to do the following.

1. Keep the buyers happy in the Bristol.
2. Hire some muscle to keep the Bristol safe. Use RUF. They seem to be screwing up less than the government troops and the Kamajors. If you've RUF on contract then the government won't start seducing the buyers. This is imperative. Keep buyers focused on auction. Imperative they don't start working for government, UN, guarding airports, evacuating civilians, etc. Block any such requests.
3. Secure a landing strip near the city, but not Lungi airport. Expect a Hercules. Night landing. Two or Three days time. I'm bringing essential supplies for the auction.
4. Get hold of a sat-phone that works and get it to Lalapanzi ASAP. That idiot Rindert bought defective sat-phone.
5. Don't screw up.
6. Rpt. Don't screw up!

This goes right you'll be rich. This screws up, I'll screw you up.

The faxed list was signed Dr P.

Schindler mentally checked the list.

1. Buyers happy (moping Colombians excepted). Wild but happy.
2. Bristol muscle. RUF? That would take some doing. Esther Speeks had cleared the square of the RUF families. He'd used a flame-thrower. In any event, the last thing the buyers needed was bodyguards.

   But The Croc was shrewd in his guess that there'd be requests for the buyers to help with evacs. Not a problem. No-one would get through to them while he held the switchboard.
3. Secure a landing strip. There was one. Used by an oil company. But it was too short for a Hercules to land in complete safety. The Croc might crash and burn. How sad that would be.
4. Getting hold of another sat-phone. Yeah, right! There'd been excellent sat-phones at the FCC. Blown to hell. The Hotel Bristol manager had said there was a sat-phone at the Jardin de Cygnes but it was used by the CIA and MI5. Or maybe MI6. Some kind of James Bond outfit. Would Esther Speeks go over there, Schindler wondered. Storm the place? Take the sat-phone? Speeks was normally up for any sort of craziness. But would he baulk at the prospect of hitting the CIA and MI5/MI6? That was the question. The answer was probably yes, he'd baulk. Not even Speeks would want to go head-to-head with James Bond. There was a sat-phone here at the Bristol. But he needed it.
5. Don't screw up. The nerve of the man! Schindler had followed every instruction to the letter. He hadn't screwed up.
6. Ditto. Rpt. Schindler hadn't screwed up, dammit!

Schindler had already decided to buy a couple of units himself. With their security, swords to hang over the heads of threatening

Crocodiles, he'd be immune. He might even buy three units. Send one over to England to blow the bossy bastard out of Kent.

Complete obedience, complete reliability, the homunculus units were a Schindler dream. Also the dream of every other man in the hotel, bar the manager and cook and the bell-boys who didn't have a clue as to what was going on. The girls and cleaners, of course, never thought much beyond the dollar of the day.

Brute beasts. Like every black.

CHAPTER THIRTY-TWO

Politics in the Museum

General Butt Naked and his men, boys and women and girls stole all the ambulances from Connaught Hospital at gun-point. Then they took the fire engines from the deserted fire station.

They then headed for the museum to pick up reinforcements for the trip to Lalapanzi.

The RUF cadre who had taken the museum was led by a close friend of Butt Naked called Commander Blue Book. Blue Book was a cocaine-based cocktail. Rather like crack. The commander was a firm fan of the highly addictive, rage-inducing drug

Blue Book greeted Butt Naked with complicated but traditional Sierra Leonian enquiries as to the health of his family.

Butt Naked said he didn't have a family – someone had shot them – and asked if Blue Book had any whisky. The Kamajor voodoo men who'd been firing at the Frangipani siege had put a round through Butt Naked's hip flask during his breakout. Butt Naked smelt of the stuff but was all out of whisky.

Blue Book, Butt Naked assumed, was seriously stoned.

Abruptly he backed away from Butt Naked, turned on his heels and then yipped about the museum, laughing and kicking out his legs in a threatening dance. He did a back-flip that might have earned him a medal at the Olympics. He returned from the manoeuver panting and still laughing.

"You know what that was?" Blue Book asked.

"No."

"That was the dance of the disgraced coward fleeing." Blue Book laughed some more.

Blue Book's cadre were laughing too. Butt Naked noticed, though, that there was a group of older men lined up against a wall. They were watching him, Butt Naked, with steady, focused, dangerous eyes.

Butt Naked's fighters were staring them back, eye-for-eye, tooth-for-tooth. Lean and mean.

Hostility danced like static in the air.

If that's the way they want it, Butt Naked decided, that's the way they'll get it. He was still touched with the battle hysteria and old men scowling were not a problem.

Butt Naked's men (boys and girls) were more battle-scarred, were on a roll, and were looking for more of it – of the violence. If Blue Book's commanders wanted to dance then they'd dance.

"What are you looking at!" yelled one of Butt Naked's boys at an angry-looking man in his forties who was propped against an ethnic statue. The man was wearing a suit and tie.

"Stop dancing around, you Blue Book nigger!" yelled Butt Naked. His shout echoed in the museum. "Get me some whisky!"

Weapons throughout the museum were raised simultaneously at the drinks order.

Butt Naked suddenly realised what all those dances of Blue Book meant. It was a misunderstanding. The RUF command thought he'd deserted the RUF by leaving the Hotel Frangipani.

These old farts giving General Butt Naked the evil eye were, he realised too, the RUF elite who had planned the coup. Hiding in a museum. It said it all. They were out of date.

Relics.

"Respected elders of our struggle," Butt Naked announced, buying time while he worked out a suitable response. "Fathers, Fathers of our Nation, I withdrew my soldiers from the Hotel Frangipani not because I am disloyal to the RUF but because I have business in Lalapanzi. Voodoo business. Powerful porroh business. I'm going to voodoo some serious butt."

There was a silence in the museum for a moment that felt long.

"Young man," said the suit-and-tie, who still was leaning against the statue, now flanked by two bearded men with Uzis. Experienced men. Hard-core RUF.

"You are a man of the world," said the suit-and-tie. "You must understand that we are gravely disappointed in your frightened escape from the Hotel Frangipani. You have abandoned our fighters and their women and children. You had the choice of running or fighting and you ran. I order you to return to the hotel, rejoin our fighters or face a court-martial."

General Butt Naked thought the proposition over for less than a second.

"I'm taking over the RUF! Me!" he shouted wildly. "I am now the RUF commander-in-chief. Anyone who disagrees can shut their mouths or expect consequences!"

"Young man, have you lost your mind?" said the man still leaning against the pillar. He looked complacent, kept his voice calm and quiet.

"No. I've found my mind."

"What you have just said is treason," shouted the man, now clearly angry. The two beards guarding the suit-and-tie were twisting and turning, trying to work out who was who and how many there were. Butt Naked had brought a lot of his people in through various doors. Butt Naked, young though he was, wasn't an amateur.

"Blue Book!" yelled Butt Naked.

"Yeah?"

Blue Book reeled back into view from behind a stinkwood sarcophagus. Stoned for sure. His eyes like dots.

"You've danced for these losers long enough," said Butt Naked. "Dance with me and we'll run this country."

"Whatever," said Blue Book.

"You're drunk," said the man by the statue, his eyes wide with fury. "You're acting like a crazy man. Like a man bewitched. This declaration of yours is madness! I'm placing you under arrest, and when you have sobered up we'll review your case."

"Smoke them!" yelled Butt Naked by way of reply, which is what his fighters did. The museum erupted.

Butt Naked's impulsive declaration of power, and the subsequent gunfight in the museum were to have dramatic consequences for the people and warring factions of Freetown. They were, in very real terms, ultimately to shape the nation

The most immediate result – once the shooting was over and the last of the older men had been cut down – was the termination of the RUF's inner council of policy makers. Also the RUF commander-in-chief. Also the RUF council of war. Butt Naked, on a whim, and in under three minutes, had achieved a job of work that the UN, the government, the Kamajors, the British, the Nigerians, the CIA and everybody else had failed to achieve in nine years. The utter destruction of RUF high command.

Blue Book's cadre dragged the bodies of their former leaders into the centre of the hall and made a pile of them. They looked terrified as they worked. Butt Naked's cadre, by contrast, were grinning.

Their general, butt naked as he was, was now *the man!*

Blue Book himself seemed stunned at the way things had developed.

"Why did you do that?" was his first question.

"I felt like it," was the general's response. "Felt like it. Did it. You helped."

"Did I?" Blue Book said. He honestly couldn't remember whether he'd opened fire on his commanders or not. The incident was a blank in his mind. He vaguely remembered being ordered to dance the dance of the disgraced coward fleeing. Quite why, he couldn't remember. Couldn't even remember that.

He moaned and scrubbed at his forehead with both hands.

"We're in serious trouble. Some kind of serious, serious trouble. Our people are gonna kill us for sure for this. Kill us if we're lucky. They'll chop us. You are one crazy ..."

"Relax, we're going to be fine. You know Samuel Doe?"

"Never met the man."

"Blue Book, you got to do some reading. How you going to develop if you don't even read?"

Butt Naked had been taught to read by a missionary from Finland. The general, like his junior officer, Commander Joe, had been enthused and had built an extensive library from looted buildings, still had bits of it, scattered here and there throughout the country. At times, when Butt Naked felt the urge, he'd read important sections of prose from *The Lion, the Witch and the Wardrobe* or Sven Hassel at comatose, obedient audiences. It was in a book called *Fishing in Africa* that he'd read about Samuel Doe.

"So who's Samuel Doe?"

"He was a master-sergeant over in Monrovia, OK? So early one morning in 1980 he takes sixteen men, goes over to the State House to ask for his back-pay, finds that the presidential guard isn't around and, bam, decides to chop the president, a dude called William Tolbert. And that's what he does. One minute later Tolbert's guts are out in the courtyard for the dogs and Doe's the new president of Liberia. Just like that. It's called seizing the moment."

Butt Naked decided that that was enough history for the time being. No need to mention how Doe got his ears cut off and had been beaten to death just over a decade later. Or that the torture was filmed. Or that the film had been seen by every bastard in Liberia with a video machine. That would just confuse old Bluey here.

"Listen up everybody. Here's the plan."

Butt Naked, self-elected RUF commander-in-chief, explained how things were going to work.

The bodies were to be burnt. The convoy was to truck out for Lalapanzi. There, they would collect zombies that would make them invincible. With this voodoo army they'd return, take the capital, everyone in the museum would be given an important job in the new government, the diamond mines would be shared out and the zombies would usher in a new age of prosperity. Everyone would be powerful and rich. And anyone who got in the way would be given a damn good chopping.

"You better be right about these zombies," said Blue Book with unfortunate volume.

"I'm right about these zombies."

Butt Naked pulled Blue Book aside. "They exist. One hundred per cent true. One of them tried to kill me with a car bomb a few days ago," he explained.

Blue Book did not look reassured.

"Blow you up," he mumbled. "And that's good news?"

"I know the man who makes them," Butt Naked soothed. "We go a way back. I got him his parts and you know what? The number of body parts I got him, I'm betting he's got a whole heap of zombies. I supplied him with food – fish, some real good fish, corned beef – him and I were sort of like business partners. Papa Det was real interested in him, too. That cold man, Papa Det!"

"Papa Det? But he's gone? Someone wasted that ace! He not been seen for months!"

"Who gives a fuck, Blue Book? Me? You?"

Blue Book nodded. Things were just going too fast for him. Maybe this was a drug-induced hallucination. He rather hoped it was.

"You saw that movie *The Body Snatchers*?" said Butt Naked.

"What movie?"

"*The Body Snatchers*."

"No."

"Well, you'll remember in that movie there were two white guys snatching bodies—"

"I didn't see the movie."

"Well I did. Stop interupting. I was like that. A body snatcher.

I'd get him the bodies—" A thought suddenly struck Butt Naked.

"Hey!" he yelled to the museum at large, "cancel that order on burning those bodies. We'll be snatching them with us."

"We're like old buddies, business partners—" Butt Naked resumed then stopped again.

Another thought had suddenly struck him. Not a good one.

There'd been a row he recalled. An argument over payment for some fish. Butt Naked had been totally drunk at the time, but he seemed to remember strapping Father Jack down to a pew in the chapel and taking out most of his teeth with a pair of the priest's own pliers.

He'd been ordered north the next day to castigate some rebellious gold miners. Couldn't clearly recall whether he'd actually taken the teeth out. Or had just dreamed he'd taken the teeth out. A lot of Butt Naked's life was a bit of a blur.

Whether he'd taken Jack's teeth out or whether he hadn't, Butt Naked decided that it was irrelevant. Jack was a Christian. Christians were big on forgiveness. Turn the other cheek. Open the lower jaw.

And if Jack wasn't forgiving, he had toenails and, Butt Naked presumed, still had his pliers.

Something could be worked out.

"You better be right about these zombies," mumbled Blue Book. "You wrong about the zombies then we're in trouble deep."

"Cheer up. Take a blue. I'm appointing you Minister of Offence."

"Not Minister of Defence?" Blue Book looked suddenly furious. "Who've you got lined up for Minister of Defence?"

"Minister Blue Book, are you some kind of pussy? An army's job isn't to defend. An army's there to kill and destroy and attack. Offence is the word. Not hang around defending."

"Cool," said Blue Book brightening. The new leader of Sierra Leone seemed to have his policies sorted out.

Blue Book asked slightly deferentially, "Do my troops address you as Prime Minister Butt Naked, or President Butt Naked? Or General?"

"Take a blue," he said. Buying time. Minister Blue Book took a blue.

While he did so, Butt Naked gnawed anxiously on a thumb. It was a big question. Prime Minister? President? General? Pope? Then, prompted by the smell of roasting meat, he yelled, "I said don't burn the bodies! Are you people deaf?"

"We're not burning the bodies, General," came a humble voice. "We're cooking the dead leaders' steaks and sausages. And the eggs and groundnuts. And some birds with long tails. And some monkeys."

"Food!" said Butt Naked with a brilliant grin. "The High Command always spoiled itself with food. That's where they'll have whisky. Bet on it. The indulgent pigs."

Blue Book smirked, the latest bluey was just frying his brains to the perfect temperature. The world was intense. The possibilities infinite. Butt Naked not a prime minister, not a president, not a general, but a liberating God. And he, Blue Book, was Minister of Offence. Not yet fifteen and already a leading politician.

God Butt Naked rose, slapped the hand of the first Minister he was to inaugurate in his giddy rise to power, and headed for the cooking.

"Calling me General will do just fine for the time being," said Butt Naked.

"We'll eat, then convoy out, General?" Minister Blue Book was back on form.

"We will. We will."

CHAPTER THIRTY-THREE

Dr Pleasant Goes North

Godfroi Mungo had two homes. One was in the small, depressed Cumbrian village of Thwaite.

Thwaite was a bleak, unlovely little place. Its bus shelter stank and was covered with misspelled graffiti, its one fish and chip shop was virtually always closed, and most of the buildings were 1930s terrace eyesores thrown up at minimal cost to house the men who maintained the railway track that snaked past Thwaite, via Oxenholme, to Penrith.

Only two features were attractive to the eye – Hoggs Hall, a huge (and hugely unattended) public school that sat aloofly on a hill overlooking the village, and the striking lines of Hill House, a smallish castle built by a whimsical Victorian coal magnate to please his equally whimsical wife.

It was in Hill House that Mungo did his living when the strains of work and his researches proved too much.

It was at Hill House that Dr Pleasant called, stiff and irritable after an eight-hour drive in clogged bank-holiday weekend traffic – dear God, the sheer number of caravans. The legions of traffic cones ...

It was already dark when he arrived.

His knock at the door was answered after a considerable pause by the porchlight flicking to yellow, cobwebbed life and a tiny woman, wrapped tight in an apron and wearing a mob cap. She took an age to unlock the door.

Dr Pleasant asked the woman if Mungo was home.

"Oh, no, love," croaked the woman froggily. She was wearing a cloying lavender perfume that, despite its pungency, did not obscure the sharp smell of mothballs. "He's at his other domicile at present, chuck."

Dr Pleasant peered at the woman with sudden curiosity. Her face was wrinkled and leathery with warts, her eyes a rather shocking blue, and she had neglected to shave what was rather a promising beard. Rindert had said the units looked like hell. The woman didn't look like hell, but came uncomfortably close.

"Are you one of them?" Dr Pleasant asked after a minute.

"One of what, my duck?" said the woman.

Her blue eyes swivelled glassily up at him. The lips puckered. In confusion? In thought? Was she about to blow out some green gas in the way Rindert said they did?

"There's no need to play coy. I know all about it," Dr Pleasant said. "I'm just curious. Are you one of them? You know, a homunculus?" Dr Pleasant winked conspiratorially.

When there was no response he continued impatiently.

"Oh, stop this pissing about. All I'm trying to find out is if you're a homunculus. One of his fucked-up Frankensteins."

"Have you been drinking?" asked the woman, drawing herself up and narrowing her eyes.

Whoops! thought Dr Pleasant. Not a homunculus.

He attempted a dignified and diplomatic withdrawal.

Dr Pleasant said that he hadn't been drinking. Apologised and said he'd made a mistake.

"Be off with you. And don't come back or I'll be calling the police," said Mungo's housekeeper. "You silly little man."

Dr Pleasant was doing just that, being off, when the final remark hit home.

Silly little man? *Silly little man?*

Pleasant stood six feet two and had a gut that would shame a sumo wrestler! This weathered toad of a warthog was small enough to stick in a pillow case.

The gall of it. The nerve. The ... the ...

Dr Pleasant, for one long second considered punching this ... this ...

Then he remembered the Mission. Moonlight was the objective. Not slamming his horny eisbein of a fist into this ... this ...

"Well, be off with you then," ordered the pugnacious figure guarding Mungo's door.

He back-tracked down the unlit path, muttering apologies, and lumbered for his vehicle.

Privately vowing that when this auction was over he'd hang Rindert up by his ears. Allowing an RUF RPG to blow up the moonlight, the bungling fool. Putting him through this ordeal.

Mungo's second house was in a remote, no, *a very remote*, part of Northumberland. Large and ancient, the building perched on the lip of a shallow ravine like a classic haunted house. Or a set for *Wuthering Heights*.

The nearest tarmac road was five miles away. Mungo's house, which was called Clouds, was approached by an occasionally-paved track that led over heather and bracken moors and through dark, conifer plantations that rustled and fidgeted when the wind whistled them to life.

In this part of Northumberland the wind did a lot of whistling. And when it wasn't whistling it was usually howling or raging. Or whipping about in a bleak and shrieking fury.

In wet weather the road was only negotiable by Land Rover.

Dr Pleasant had neglected to bring a Land Rover.

His rented minivan bogged down half a mile into the unexpected off-road venture and Pleasant, now in a state of fuming rage, climbed out.

He was in a stream, he realised. In the dark. Hadn't got boots. Was wearing brogues. Didn't have a torch. Was tired, still full of tea, starving, had been insulted. And here now in a river in

Northumberland. All because someone had screwed up.

"Rindert!" he bayed at the low clouds and the incessant torrents of chilling rain. "You bastard!"

Before beginning this excursion he had assumed that the north of England was just like Kent. Only more north. He'd not expected anything on this scale of ... he fumbled for the word and found it. Barbarity! This landscape was barbarous. Savage. Primeval.

Dr Pleasant half-expected to see Picts, Scots, hobgoblins waltzing past, smothered in woad, wearing horned helmets, carrying wicker men.

Not that he'd actually be able to see them. Not in this inky pitch and starless night. He began to shuffle along the track towards Clouds, tripping, stumbling, cursing in the dark.

"Now, who on earth could that be?" murmured Mungo at the distant clang of the bell.

Mungo was curled in a chair before a glowing coal fire, a glass of Madeira on the cherrywood table beside him and a leather-bound copy of Herodotus on his lap. Three clocks ticked on the walls. Each with thirteen hours marked upon their faces and thirteen hands that turned in both directions.

Rain tapped at the casement, wind fluted in the chimney and made the coals flare. It was a filthy night. Barometer still falling.

In the book Histiaeus was just tattooing a secret message urging revolt onto the scalp of a slave. The slave was then to have his hair grow back before being sent through enemy lines to his son-in-law. Orders accompanying the slave? Give him a hair cut.

Oh, sublime! thought Mungo. Quite sublime! Give him a haircut!

He chuckled softly and ruffled at his cat.

Mungo loved Herodotus. Loved all the Ancients. They had so much to teach and he had learned so very much from them. He returned to his contemplation of the book.

The room smelled warm and friendly. Toast, books, a delicately scented candle. Myrrh.

The bell jangled again. Reminding him. Gosh, he was getting forgetful in his old age!

Mungo pulled a fob watch from his thick dressing gown. The clocks on his walls were not for telling time.

3.20 a.m. Goodness, thought Mungo, I've allowed myself to get absorbed again. 3.20 a.m.

It was odd, he reflected, the way he forgot things when he was enjoying a good book.

And this was a very good book.

He turned the page and resumed his reading.

Outside, Dr Pleasant seethed and raged. He could see the light glowing a warm red in an upper gable. Why was the fool Mango not answering his door?

He yanked at the bell-pull again, this time with such force that it came loose and the bell crashed down on his head.

That did it. Enough of this horsing around.

Dr Pleasant produced his Heckler and Koch – the very same pistol he had nearly deployed in the Beck's Hill China Tea Rooms – stepped back from the door and sighted in on the upstairs window.

He then emptied the whole clip.

The window exploded. Ricochets flashed in on the gentle sanctum of Mungo. A clock burst with a chemical puff and fizz and then began to chime as if in pain. A telescope fell off its tripod. The volume of Herodotus stopped the round that would otherwise have pierced Mungo's narrow chest.

A hoarse voice bellowed up from below.

"Let me in! I'm not pissing about!"

CHAPTER THIRTY-FOUR

Come the Day

Mad Mike Schlessinger, CEO of SHEELD, replaced his radio receiver and called over his number two, Pieter Florin. The two men were in an office in a warehouse by the docks. Coffee was brewing on a gas stove, charts and maps were pinned to the wooden walls, there were thick boot-stained rugs on the floorboards.

Not precisely snug, but tolerable safety from the storm.

"News?" asked Florin.

Schlessinger grunted. "Jonny Petrus in Monrovia. Says there are Liberians coming our way. Supporting the RUF."

"How they coming? By sea?"

Schlessinger reached for the coffee pot. Poured for them both.

"Jonny doesn't know. Sea in this weather? I'd say unlikely. Not with the Royal Navy out there too. Land border-crossing? Strong possibility. Air? Doubtful. One thing for sure, though. We get Liberians throwing in behind the RUF and we're screwed. They'll win. The SLA's just not up to the challenge."

"You hear something?" asked Florin suddenly raising his head.

"Aircraft engine."

"Heavy transport."

"Liberians!"

Both men leaped to their feet and raced out of the office into the dank and dripping warehouse. "SAMs are over there. Look lively!"

Schlessinger and Florin wrestled the shoulder-fired SAM-7 anti-aircraft missile launchers from the packing crates and ran for the wall ladder that climbed to the roof. No troublemakers allowed on Mad Mike's shift. And that was for fucking sure.

Hotel Bristol. Dawn. Schindler speaking.

"Yes, I'm sorry to rouse you so early and without warning but I'm pleased to say that I've got the happy duty of announcing a happy moment. I think the news will make you ... erm ... happy. I'm happy to say."

"The auction did experience a brief hiccup, but obviously we're in the middle of a coup d'état or something. Actually, Christ knows what they think they're doing, whoever's doing it. Anyway let them get on with it.

"We're going to Lalapanzi now. The auction's back on. Chef's got, erm, some Bloody Marys and he's told me they're very bloody. Will sort any sore heads. Just what the doctor ordered. Sausages. Lettuce. About a ton of frozen peas. Soup. But we've got to be quick. The weather's breaking. The sun may be showing up today. We can all think about getting a tan. They'll be evacuating the ... erm ... foreign residents in all likelihood. SLA are regrouping. Anyway you probably don't care about that. What I'd like to say is ... I've got a surprise guest!"

"Show me a big hand for Dr Pleasant."

There was laughter, some applause, but mostly ribald, bleary jeers. Schindler's less-than-fluently-delivered speech had been conveyed at unfortunate decibels through a temperamental, static-ridden karaoke machine dragged from retirement for the occasion.

Schindler, encouraged by the support from his audience, ventured a final flourish.

"Dr Pleasant! The only man I know who has baled out of a blazing Hercules carrying a hundred litres of moonlight! And then dropped his Hercules straight into a four-star hotel full of foreign diplomats."

This last comment, if there had been someone present taking

minutes, might have been recorded for posterity with the adden-
dum: "Spoken with malice."

To Schindler's profound irritation the comment aroused
enthusiastic applause.

Schindler had been up all night guarding the landing lights
out at the abandoned PetroCo complex, swatting mosquitoes,
drenched in rain and waiting for the crocodilian swine to turn up
in his Hercules. Give him his due, Schindler had thought as lightning exploded and thunder roared, he's a mad one. To be flying
in on a night like this.

When the plane had finally put in an appearance somebody
had fired a SAM into it from the vicinity of the docks.

A palpable hit.

Schindler had watched the flaming machine pass overhead
not sure whether to weep or applaud.

Then he'd seen the parachutes. Like billowing mushrooms
revolving in the vicious gusts of wind. Now you see them.
Lightning. Now you don't. Thunder.

The Hercules lost height trailing smeary sheets of flame from
its left wing and disappeared in the direction of the Lumley Beach
Road. A short while later, while collecting Dr Pleasant and his oil
drums, there had been an enormous explosion as the aircraft met
the earth.

Or not precisely the earth.

When he returned to the Hotel Bristol it was to learn from
the manager that Pleasant's plane, just as Schindler had told the
hungover buyers in his stumbling speech, had landed on the
Hotel Sleep Tight.

The Sleep Tight, despite its ludicrous name, was a four-star
affair. According to the Hotel Bristol manager it had a bar in the
middle of its swimming pool, an Italian restaurant, a sushi bar
and a fitness centre. It had appeared on CNN as a CNN partnership hotel. It was also, the manager said, an assembly point for
foreign dignitaries awaiting evacuation by sea.

"We've got to keep my visit unannounced and discreet," The Crocodile had ordered Schindler over the phone from Beck's Hill. "No-one must notice my arrival. Low-key. Understand me, man? No screw-ups from your end. No screw-ups!"""

No screw-ups from Schindler's end. Why this constant carping about screw-ups? There had never been a screw-up from Schindler's end.

But if The Crocodile's idea of arriving unannounced, discreet, low key was to blitz half-a-dozen ambassadors and incinerate a CNN partnership hotel with a blazing cargo plane (in full view of a British warship, at the height of a tropical storm), then Schindler didn't plan to be around when the reptilian bastard pulled into town in an announced, indiscreet, high-key way.

At all.

More cheers distracted Schindler from his woes. The man had arrived.

Dr Pleasant mounted the piano-bar podium of the Hotel Bristol. He began his sales pitch for the assembled buyers by producing, then emptying, his Heckler and Koch straight into the discordant Karaoke machine. It exploded. Sparks showered Schindler.

"I cannot tolerate unfavourable feedback," said Dr Pleasant. "Which is why I never sell second-rate stuff."

There was booming laughter.

The Crocodile didn't know he was doing it when he spoke, or maybe he did, but he had the habit of being occasionally very, if inadvertently, funny.

The only people not laughing at the feedback gag (if it was a gag) were the sulking Schindler, Pepe and his Colombians. The Israelis, who knew the knack of blending in, chuckled and snorted. But they had been feeling impatient for things to resolve and the appearance of the fish-faced giant was reassuring. They felt suddenly gay and buoyant. With the current crisis in Israel, the sooner they had these units working on their behalf the better.

"You know me, gentlemen, and I know you," Dr Pleasant said in a husky, evil voice that carried through the hall perfectly.

The crowd stilled. Jokes over. Business news was coming.

"For the last few days you've been here at my expense. The fireworks were not my idea. I make no apologies for the wild kaffirs. It is in their nature to be wild and to misbehave. Nor do I apologise for the weather. I do, however, apologise for the delay."

"The units, though, you will find are very well worth a little inconvenience. They are very special. Very special indeed."

"I will spare you the speech about how the world is and how the world should be. I shall just say this: these units will make the world as it should be. As we all dream of seeing it."

"Drink your Bloody Marys, eat well. We have a day of bundu-bashing ahead. All done, we'll be clear of this country in three days' time."

Pepe stood up and asked a question.

"What is bundu-bashing?"

"It's bashing bundu. Bashing it hard. Any more questions?"

There were none.

The men in the Hotel Bristol ate, drank and departed.

The manager and staff, not to mention the girls, were sorry to see them go.

Paul Spong, the French photographer who had escaped the Butt Naked assassination car bomb and Hoppy Pongo's dynamite strike at the Foreign Correspondents Club, had seen the Hercules come in while staring hopefully at the skies from the rain-battered pool bar. It was slightly after 3.a.m. Spong was unable to sleep. Today, the weather forecasts said, the storm would end. Evacuation would be possible.

God, but it would be a relief to get away from this country.

Spong's first thought upon hearing the drone of engines was that evacuation was beginning.

His second thought, as the flaming airborne apocalypse pulled into view was, "*Merde!* Not again!" Then Spong leaped into the pool.

On HMS *Clam*, Dalziel witnessed the final flight of Air Dr Pleasant. As oily clouds of flame rose from the Hotel Sleep Tight he decided that this was it. The final straw.

Today, whatever the weather, he was getting the ex-pats out of Freetown. They'd been shot at, bombed, terrorised and now fate was throwing aircraft at them.

He would get them out, come hell or high water. Knowing Freetown, as he had come to know Freetown, Dalziel reflected that it would probably come to both.

CHAPTER THIRTY-FIVE

Convoy

Road activity that morning was intense.

Convoy One: The Auction-goers
It headed out of Freetown like a demolition derby. Bullets broke car windows, flattened tyres and whined off steel plates. The Freetown streets were an ugly, flooded maze of gutted vehicles, rubble, burning-tyre road-blocks and corpses. The auction-goers' convoy was headed by a Unimog, and the Unimog's machine-gun, mounted and manned by Esther Speeks, was constantly engaged. Anything moving, Speeks shot at.

The Crocodile cowered in the rear seat of a Mazda Proceed wishing he was in Kent. He still hadn't fully recovered from the SAM missile hit. Thank Christ he'd had the foresight to sit in the hold with a chute strapped to his back. Thank Christ, too, the pilots had known the Petroco strip was too short for a Herc to put down and had arranged the parachute drop. He wondered whether the pilots had baled out or just ridden the rocket.

Some ragged maniac emerged from a doorway, Dr Pleasant saw him briefly, hands up with a filthy white flag. Speeks blew the guy away. Dr Pleasant forgot about the pilots and sank lower in his seat wishing that he wasn't so bloody big.

Convoy Two: The Intelligence Community
Far more discreet, it nudged its way out of the car park of the Jardin de Cygnes. It contained Peterson-Smith, Fitz, the guards,

and Oliveira and his family, the latter clutching carpet bags and swaddled in blankets.

"I'm wrapping this nonsense up," Dalziel had told Peterson-Smith over the phone. "It's getting beyond a joke. Shut up shop and make your way to the Lumley Beach Road. RV at the Sofitel Mammy Yoko Hotel. We're about to land and secure it."

"Not the Sleep Tight?"

"Most definitely *not* the Sleep Tight," Dalziel had said grimly. "Break a leg."

And that had been that. Shut down. *Sayonara.*

Not, Peterson-Smith fervently hoped, *Auf Wiedersehen.* Or *Au revoir.* Or "See you again soon".

Convoy Three: Presidential, and in difficulties
Despite its earlier departure and initial good progress, the fire engines and ambulances had run into trouble half-way to Lalapanzi.

"I'm telling you Captain Rat, you don't get your torch-waving, body bags out of the road, I'm not going to do anything for you that doesn't hurt."

General Butt Naked's convoy was ensnared in an argument that had lasted what felt like hours. In actual fact the argument *had* lasted hours. Two and a half of them. Plus a few witless minutes.

Rat was an RUF newcomer, formally what was known as a sobel. Combine soldier, as in government soldier, and rebel, as in rebel, and you had yourself a sobel. A guy who'd joined the army, hijacked all the equipment and then had done exactly what he wanted, wherever he wanted, and to any degree.

Give Sobel Rat his due. Since coming out of the cold of free-lance work and joining the RUF, he'd really got organised.

From Butt Naked's perspective, the Rat had got his men in place, looked like a stone killer, but what this sobel sack of Rat didn't seem to understand was that Butt Naked was now the President of the country and Chief of the RUF.

Butt Naked had spent a lot of time explaining his new constitution.

Rat, who was wearing reflective sunglasses, kept throwing Butt Naked back at himself.

Rat kept harping on about his RUF Liberian backers and his contacts with the diamond brokers in Antwerp.

General Butt Naked, closely supported by his Minister of Offence, Minister Blue Book, had explained that Antwerp, Liberia and Rat didn't amount to any sort of opposition when faced with the voodoo army the general planned to lead him to power.

At one stage, while all key diplomatic players were hunkered down in a circle sharing a joint but pointing guns at each other, Rat had clapped his hands and dropped his pistol in the process.

Instead of signing on with the new government he had walked off and unexpectedly hauled a white woman out of a tent. With absurd deference, given that the woman had been stripped naked, Rat's men had all bowed, cheered and then discharged fire into the sky.

"Why don't you all stop it?" the woman had managed. "It's undignified. Please, I entreat you, I represent the United Nations High Commissioner for Refugees—"

"See? I've got me some serious connections with the UN," Rat had said. "Check this blanc out, man. I gives a call and Kaffir Anon will come running when he knows what I've got."

"You call the general 'man' again and he'll rain zombies on your butt like you'd never believe," put in Minister of Offence Blue Book. "You call him General!"

The naked white woman staggered upright and then was hit on the head with a Maglite torch donated to UNHCR by the American government and appropriated by Rat's squad. The Maglite was wielded by a young woman wearing a gas mask and a plastic rain-cape. She was stoned.

Butt Naked's brow furrowed in anger. These UN people were important. Once he was in his presidential palace holding total power, he'd need them. Everyone knew that if you were nice to the UN, the UN would be nice to you. Give you cars, money, support your presidency. The pussies! And here was Rat holding this woman hostage. That his own people had taken seventeen UN Indian peacekeepers hostage earlier that month was forgotten in the heat of the indignant moment.

"Rat," decided General Butt Naked, "I'm taking this woman you took hostage, hostage. You're not treating her right. You should give her some clothes. I'm on a handle. You understand what I'm saying?"

"No," said Rat. "What's this 'I'm on a handle' shit? Doesn't mean anything."

Butt Naked paused to think and wished he hadn't spent the journey drinking looted former RUF high-command Scotch. He felt muzzy. The joint wasn't helping.

He felt control slipping.

Rat had more men. Rat had the road. Rat hadn't spent the last week fighting. Just chopping, blitzing reffies (refugees) and capturing hostages. Rat's troops were fresher. And Rat didn't seem impressed by Butt Naked's plan to whistle up a legion of zombies.

"Let's start again," Butt Naked said. "I'm offering you the chance to join me and my zombies and take power. How would you like to be Minister of Education?"

"I never been to school," said Rat.

"Not a problem," Butt Naked declared magnanimously. "All you do is educate the people to do what we tell 'em to do. And if they're slow learners you and my Minister of Offfence here educate 'em a bit harder."

"Yeah?" Rat sneered.

"Yeah. There's a lot of vacancies for government positions at present on account of the fact that we shot the High Command. Wham bam. Shot them all."

Rat looked distinctly sceptical.

"Talk, that's all that is, just boasting and talk. You just all butt and no trousers."

"Minister Blue Book, please drag the bodies over here from the ambulance and show 'em to this doubting rodent here."

Blue Book and his fighters did so. Eileen Holden's eyes widened in shock. The bald, butt-naked pyschopath wasn't lying. There, arrayed in front of Rat in a muddy, bloody mutilated pile, was the entire RUF High Command. She also recognised the remains of UN peace broker Ahmadou Lye. So much for helping get the RUF to the table for talks. He'd been playing a callous double game, playing the UN like a piano, thought Holden.

But it was the dead RUF command that was top story.

Assuming the mad, naked freak was hallucinating about his zombies (and Holden assumed that as a matter of course) this could mean the end of Sierra Leone's nightmare of civil war.

Rat gaped. "You shot them?" he murmured. "You shot all of them?"

"They didn't get the picture. Didn't see the way the future lies. I give 'em destiny and they just throw it in my face."

"You in serious trouble," Rat said. "You have any idea, any idea at all, of what you've done?"

"Yes."

"We're expecting the first column of Liberians any time now. And then there's a second column coming in later. They see what you've done to their generals they're going to fry you."

"What Liberians?"

"The RUF Liberian High Command. It's been planned for months. They're coming in to support our people – those people –" Rat pointed to the dead, "take Freetown. Win this war."

"No-one told me anything about it."

There was the sudden sound of heavy engines.

"The Liberians." Captain Rat pointed towards a convoy of military trucks that had just rounded the bend in the road.

Convoy Four: The Liberians

There were a lot of trucks. Rat was sweating. If the men coming thought he was involved in the RUF leadership massacre he was dead. And being dead would take a while to happen. None of that while happy.

"Oh," said Butt Naked. "*Those* Liberians. Ah. Well, it's not a problem."

"Not a problem? Are you mad?" Rat was sweating again. If this Butt Naked was going to win, then Rat had better be on his side because he was obviously a man who didn't think twice about doing things. From the look of the shattered RUF leadership's corpses, definitely not twice.

"I'm as mad as I want to be and the reason for that is simple: I'm President," said Butt Naked.

Butt Naked? The Liberians? What to do? Who to throw in with?

Decisions, decisions, decisions for Captain Rat.

He saw the numbers of the Liberians, their new, expensive shiny equipment, and reached his decision.

Commander Joe pushed through the dripping bush with the remnants of the men, boys and girls from the Lalapanzi rout.

Commander Joe had, out of strategic interests, shot anybody wounded who would impede what he saw in his head as the "March of Commander Joe from Lalapanzi to Freetown". Every African Liberation figure had made a heroic march, according to Commander Joe's education.

Kabila had. Mao had. Long marches were important.

It was part of the way the system worked.

He'd also shot every single one of the Liberians. General Murder had been hung from the roof of Radio Murder (now re-christened Radio Joe). Joe's humiliating rape had been expunged in blood. And Joe was ready for more.

The people who marched behind Joe, were marching behind Joe. One hundred per cent behind.

When the great march began, Joe had a loping RUF quality to his stride. There was singing. There was a boasting competition which involved each fighter boasting about his or her accomplishments. If they didn't have any accomplishments then they boasted of deeds to come.

After the great march had found its loping stride inhibited by mud, roots, water and fatigue, it has become a trudge. As he slogged along in rain and mosquitoes, Joe's ideas became vague. He didn't like the way some of his fighters were bleeding. No-one had done that before in Joe's experience. Started going plum coloured and bleeding.

The first cases had begun shortly after the attack on Lalapanzi. It wasn't nice.

But he needed them all, bleeders and non-bleeders. For the great march.

Still, it was really dreary marching around when he could be firing up a joint, settling into a soft chair and running a radio station properly. He wondered whether he could pick up some new discs in Freetown. As for *Wait Till The Midnight Hour*, he never wanted to hear that damn tune ever again.

Dismal trudge.

Then Joe heard the growl of trucks and saw the twinkle of camp fires. He dropped and cuddled the wet earth. Behind him his cadre dropped too. Stoned. Tired. Sick. One of the bleeders was leaking blood from her eyes. Red smeary tears.

It was a revolting sight.

To business thought Joe. He applied his binoculars.

As soon as he saw the camp fires he knew they were Liberians. Sloppy. Over-confident.

Now for Blues, thought Joe. "Issue blues," he whispered. The whisper and the pills were passed back down the line.

"Every fighter take a blue book. Two blues. Three if you want them."

If ever there was a war waged on drugs, this was it. And Commander Joe, due to clever looting, had enough pharmaceuticals in his shoulder bag to take his people exactly where Commander Joe wanted them to go.

Which was to sort out more Liberians.

After that Joe's policy was unclear. Take Freetown. Explain the monster situation to General Butt Naked. Shoot the bleeders.

Buy some discs. Whatever. The future would sort itself out.

Eileen Holden had been born in County Cork but, as the saying goes, from a very young age had dreamed of Africa. In her small bedroom she had read books, feasted on the vibrant thrilling photos: Kilimanjaro rising above the Serengetti plains, dawn mists in the Bwindi Impenetrable Forests, smiles – those huge glowing African smiles – markets, sleekly muscled fishermen hauling nets of bulge-eyed fish in from the wild blue of the Indian Ocean.

Adventure.

As she matured, her reading shifted in focus. Steve Biko, Mandela, Nujoma, Sekou Toure, Slovo, the struggle for freedom, anti-colonialism, Third World debt, women's rights, AIDS.

An earnestness had settled on Eileen Holden. The frivolities of lions roaring at fat desert moons, of giraffes stooping at water holes, and drums athump in the jungle night were dismissed as childish fancies. A desire to make a difference took possession of her. A lust to hold out a hand to the starving children, to sink wells and build schools.

Holden's father, a glum, brooding, alcoholic Republican had rubbished her vision.

"Your place is with your own people fighting the Crown," he'd told her. "Not romping round the world to save the niggers."

God, how the man sat on the household like a bitter cloud. Always with a glass close to hand. Always with a paper article to be cursed, a TV programme to be shouted at, always something wrong to be yelled at with furious impotence. Mother pinched and fearful, younger sisters flinching from the dark rages of him.

But Africa, dreams of Africa, had sustained Holden as she grew, buoyed her like a rich, dark flying carpet.

And then Uhuru! University. A job with the UNHCR, a farewell to the claustrophobias of Cork, and with her heart as light as a kite, she first trod the earth of the Dark Continent.

Freetown. Sierra Leone.

And it had been godawful.

But never quite as godawful as it had been in the last week.

Rat's cadre had not killed her, not chopped her, not even beaten her. And, thank Dierdre of the Sorrows, hadn't raped her. But they'd pulled the Nigerian soldiers out of the trucks and thrashed them savagely. Then they'd shot them. Why beat them if you're planning to shoot them? Holden had wondered with wretched logic. What's the point of this? Of all this? It's not an ethnic war. Not one tribe against another. It's not even a war for diamonds. Though diamonds keep the cauldron boiling. It's a monstrous silliness.

Her refugees – the refugees she had personally and in defiance of UNHCR regulations assembled into the trucks – had been scattered like chaff.

She would never forget the sounds of that night. The hideous, pointless mutilations. The torches waving, the cackles and howls.

Rat and his ambushers had behaved like demons.

"They're from the hospital. They've been chopped already!" she'd implored.

"Well, tonight's their lucky night," Rat had leered. "They're going to get chopped again. Free of charge."

And now, after two days in a mouldy tent, there was this scene unfolding that promised further bedlam.

The naked man – the self proclaimed General President – and his people had, incredibly, laid down their weapons when the Liberians arrived.

Many of them had looked very reluctant to do so, but the naked man had seemed absurdly confident.

"I've got a good feeling about this!" he'd yelled. "It's going to be cool. What's the word for it? Diplomacy. Watch me at it! Learn from your General. I'm going to diplomacy their butts off!"

The man had then issued a series of high-pitched yelps accompanied by body twists that Holden recognised as voodoo. Of some sort. Though quite what sort she'd no idea.

Then the Liberians had seen what the diplomatic General President had done to the RUF leadership. They had looked first unbelieving, then outraged, then unbelieving again.

Their leader had actually wandered around in aimless circles clutching his head and howling.

It had taken him several minutes to calm.

The Liberian had then ordered that all the naked man's people be sat down cross-legged with their hands on the back of their necks.

The order had been carried out with extreme violence. Kicks. Blows from rifle butts. Hysterical yelling.

"You stupid, foolish idiots!" The Liberian commander had raged. "What do you think this is? This is a war of liberation the result of careful planning to place a RUF government in power. Not a gang fight! Not a game! We have been planning this for months. Months! We've got more reinforcements coming in by convoy any time from Monrovia. And who are they going to re-inforce? *Them?*"

The Liberian pointed at the corpses.

"Who ordered this outrageous act?"

"It wasn't me," Captain Rat stated hastily. "This man, General Butt Naked, said he was President and he's going to get zombies—"

"Zombies? Zombies?"

"Correct," said Butt Naked in a self-satisfied voice. He beamed. "I'm going to have more zombies than you know. Release us now and I'll make you Minister of Justice."

"What is this insanity? Zombies? Minister of Justice? I'll show you justice. Military justice. I'm convening a court martial. Get that defendant to rise. I'll justice you, you crazed, filthy, drunken animal!"

CHAPTER THIRTY-SIX

Carnage

Joe arrived at the same time Captain Rat was, with his Liberian backers, announcing that General Butt Naked was to face a chopping squad.

It didn't take much looking to see what was up. There were the hateful effete Liberians. There were the noble fighters of General Butt Naked. And there were a group of filthy lickspittle hounds wearing rain-capes helping in the preparation of a chop.

Under normal circumstances Joe would disperse his ambushers with care. Squads to the right. Squads to the left.

Try and make what he called a killing box of crossfire.

But in this instance there didn't seem to be time. Also he was too hyped up to care. The idea of chopping his general was blasphemy, pure and simple.

That and the blue conspired to create a burning lust for justice and retribution.

"Kill!" whooped Joe as his drug-maddened fighters swept out of the bush. "K-K-K-Killll!"

Esther Speeks in the lead Unimog arrived at the court martial a couple of minutes later. The road, the bush, the clearing for tents that met his gaze were in a frenzy. There were kaffirs all over the place, running around, rolling about, shooting, hollering, whirling swords, even throwing stones.

Hundreds of them.

First thought was to drive straight on through. It looked like a shit storm. But driving on through wasn't practical. The road was blocked by fire engines, ambulances and trucks painted green. Second thought to occur was to open fire.

Speeks beamed and did just that.

Behind him, the auction-goers piled out of their vehicles and followed suit. There wasn't much option, although for several minutes there was a confused and shouted exchange about alternative routes to Lalapanzi. One man was persistent in his claims that he'd seen a fork two klicks back and that he was sure a rerouting was possible.

Left alone, for one brief moment, Dr Pleasant sagged even deeper in his seat. Things were going beyond fiasco. No more in-country auctions, he resolved. From now on, it would be telemarketing. The Internet. Anything but in-country auctions.

He climbed out of his Mazda, sweating and tired but determined to see things through.

Who to shoot?

Where to start?

A man appeared in front of him shouting incoherently. Presumably abuse. Dr Pleasant succumbed to the ferocities of the moment, dispensed with the niceties of mechanised warfare and went to work with his fists.

CHAPTER THIRTY-SEVEN

Waiting, Fighting, Arrival

"Where the hell's everyone got to," fretted Father Jack. "They should be here by now."

Rindert had been thinking the same. According to the last conversation that had successfully carried over the defective sat-phone, The Crocodile had landed (albeit in a less than conventional fashion), and the auction-goers were ready to depart. ETA had been put at 17.00.

It was now 22.00.

Where were they?

Things had been increasingly tense at Lalapanzi Mission. The homunculi were becoming virtually universally unusual in their behaviour.

In the main street there was what Rindert would describe as a herd of them, wandering slowly around, their heads waving in slow, nodding perabola. There had been no specific incidents that spoke of violence, bar one.

The previous night, just as the rain stopped, there had been an outburst of frenzied whistling and trumpeting in the rooms that Father Jack had sealed off. The Ebola rooms.

Rindert had immediately raced down to locate and if possible terminate the source of the commotion. This hadn't involved waking up, clawing on clothing and blearily fumbling for his weapon. Since the incident in the larder, Rindert hadn't slept a wink.

He'd prowled the Mission armed with an improvised flame-thrower, Ebola being a hideous risk if bodily fluids flew as a result of gunfire. Why Jack had infected them with the deadly virus was beyond Rindert.

When not pacing on patrol, he'd sat flicking nervously through Jack's less arcane books.

He'd endured Jack's wittering conversation; the man's increasing stink of goat, all the while waiting for something. An incident. Like the eruption in the Ebola cells.

He'd reached them, and at first whatever it was that was raging about did its raging in the distant rooms. Rindert could hear it careering about, uttering its rage.

He'd wondered whether he should break the barrier of nailed planking and move in to clear it.

He'd decided against it. There wasn't anything in the Ebola cells that he wanted to see. And probably a great deal that he most definitely did *not* want to see.

Instead he'd waited to see if whatever was roaring around inside would come closer.

It took a long time. But then it did.

Something wearing the head of a nun and utterly blackened in dried blood had come thumping at him against the boarding.

"Look at me!" it had shrieked. "Look at what has become of me!"

"Of me! Of me!"

The apparition had then hurled itself roaring at the planking. After repeated attempts to break through it had finally given up, turned and thundered off into the recesses of the quarantined rooms. There had been the shattering of glass and a splash as the monster had hit the river via an unboarded window, Rindert presumed.

The incident had left Rindert in shock.

"The sooner Pleasant gets here with his moonlight the better," said Jack. "Will you just listen to those things?"

The invitation struck Rindert as particularly fatuous. There was no way to avoid listening to *those things*. Their hoots, whistles, clanks, keening and groans were increasing in volume by the hour. The cacophony rose into the night like a choir of the damned.

"How many of them do you think there are?" Rindert muttered.

"Hundreds, "Jack said bleakly. "Hundreds. I sometimes wish I'd not programmed them to reproduce, you know what I'm saying? Things could get out of hand."

Rindert stared at the alchemist. Had the warped freak just said what Rindert thought he'd said. Things *could* get out of hand?

"Come on, come on," Rindert said, pacing the boards of Jack's study like a caged cat. "Where are you?"

"I hope nothing happens to that moonlight," Jack said. He was spooning corned beef into his mouth, washing the muck down with swills of brandy.

"I hear you," Rindert said.

Peterson-Smith's convoy reached the Sofitel Mammy Yoko Hotel without incurring casualties. There had been one bad moment, when the road ahead had filled with vehicles full of thuggish forms chattering machine-gun fire and discharging shot guns. Peterson-Smith had cut his engine, turned off his headlights. The convoy had roared past and away. He'd caught a glimpse of the occupants. The Hotel Bristol crowd. A deranged-looking white man in the lead vehicle had blown Peterson-Smith a kiss and waved. A pallid Latino with a moustache had stared with what looked like desperation at Peterson-Smith. A fat man had goggled at him with watery, bulbous eyes. And then the convoy had gone.

Weird.

Other than that incident the drive through Freetown had been ghostly quiet. The streets abandoned, smoke-filled, flooded.

The Hotel Mammy Yoko was full of frightened people. It was

also, Peterson-Smith noted with relief, secured by British soldiers and Marines.

"Peterson-Smith, I presume?" said Dalziel, forcing his way through the crowds. "Good to finally meet the face behind the voice."

"Indeed," said Peterson-Smith. "And very much so. Did everybody make it?"

"Most. We had a bad moment when the Hotel Sleep Tight went up. Plane hit it. Thought we'd lost a lot of people there, but most of the Sleep Tight's guests weren't what you'd call desirables. Lebanese gun-peddlers, diamond dealers, according to a frog journalist. Most quality expats came here. Damn close thing, though. The frog says it was an inferno. Lucky man, that frog. Made it through by hopping into the pool. Sometimes pays to be amphibious."

"Excuse me, sir?" A soldier needed Dalziel.

"Mustn't chatter. Things to do," said Dalziel. "There's hot tea and sandwiches over by the bar. There's the bar too, of course, if you want something stronger."

"Bit early for me," said Peterson-Smith.

"Martians," breathed Fitz reverentially.

Dalziel looked at the American and blinked. The man stank like a polecat.

"Thought you said Martians, for a moment there," Dalziel shook his head in bewilderment. "Anyway, we'll soon have everyone on *Clam* and this horror story will be over."

Dalziel marched away to continue with his organising.

Eileen Holden had never been in a battle before. When asked about it afterwards all she could say was that it was confusing. Really confusing. Appallingly smelly. Smoky. Absolutely terrifying. And loud. Really loud.

But then Holden hadn't been watching the battle closely.

Naked, she had curled into a ball at the base of a palm tree and hoped that everybody would just go away. They hadn't.

Esther Speeks had been in plenty of battles. He rated this one as totally surreal. What got Speeks was the way no-one was running away.

Most battles Speeks had been in, virtually everyone ran away.

Most battles Speeks had been in, most people lay down, hugged the ground, hid behind trees, sought cover, advanced, followed rules, tried to employ coordination (usually unsuccessfully).

Not this battle. It was as if the combatants thought they were immortal.

"Look at that guy," Speeks thought in wonder. "That guy" was wearing a mask and spinning like a dervish, blasting from the hip. He ran out of ammunition but still kept spinning. Speeks saw blood pouring from the kaffir's ears.

"Your gun's dry, man. Reload!" Speeks had a tendency to offer advice. Even to the opposition.

Speeks was annoyed by the lack of response.

Speeks crouched up and put him down. One shot. Gone.

Another man veered into his gunsights, his pistol pressed against the temple of a naked white woman. Nice tits, Speeks noted.

"Drop the gun or I smoke the bitch!" yelled the man. It sounded like a line from some Hollywood movie. It *was* a line from a Hollywood movie. The RUF fighter had been itching to use it ever since he'd seen the *Red Thunder* video during training at the induction camp.

Speeks raised his gun.

The RUF fighter looked disconcerted. "Hey man, that's all wrong! You shoot me and my muscles tighten. Trigger's pulled. Bang! The bitch is smoke!"

The woman whimpered, flashed desperate rabbit eyes at Speeks, made a pitiful attempt to shield her genitals with her one free hand.

"Fucking amateur," said Speeks, popping the kaffir neatly in the eye with a perfectly aimed round. Muscle *tightening*? Everyone knew that an eye shot went straight through the brain stem. Result? Instant muscle *relaxation*. Trigger finger limp as lettuce in zip time. *Amateurs!*

The woman stared at Speeks in horror then reeled away, all attempts to preserve her modesty forgotten. Nice sprightly little pubic bush, Speeks noted. Dimples on her arse. He liked dimples. She was lost in the smoke.

A raking spray of bullets tore the bark off Speeks' banana tree cover, a leaf fell on his head, then – surreal, surreal! A monkey! On his head! The little fucker wouldn't let go. It was pulling his hair. Chattering in his ear. Blocking his vision.

There was a rush of kaffirs, five or six, all in a neat line, all heading for Speeks. A Banzai charge.

Speeks dropped his gun. With the monkey still on his head he reached for his flame thrower.

At midnight there was the blast of motor horn on the outskirts of Lalapanzi.

"Praise the Lord," yelled Jack who had been pacing restlessly and sucking his thumb. "They're here."

"And not before time," muttered Rindert. "They'd better have the moonlight or we're up a very nasty creek."

"Bullhorn them," said Jack. "Tell them to stay out of the village. Keep away from the homunculi. Till we've given them their moonlight there's no telling what could happen."

"Will do," said Rindert.

CHAPTER THIRTY-EIGHT

Dreaming Safaris (II)

"Ah, no!" Koransky cursed. Kutuzov cursed too.

The Aleph van was again sounding its horn in the hoot-hoot-hoot blare-blare-blare hoot-hoot-hoot imbecilic SOS design that meant it was time for the safari convoy to stop.

One blast of the horn, Koransky had suggested, would suffice.

No, the instructions had come back by fax. No! We shall use the international SOS symbol.

That is what safari people do.

And there it was again.

The useless dangerous noise indicated that there was more trouble in the Aleph contingent's bowel department.

Koransky found these regular instances of convoy halt, everyone out for mass projectile vomiting, confounding. His clients were supplied entirely by goods imported from Japan as strictly stipulated by the Aleph minister. None of the Aleph Dreaming Safari Goers had touched any local food. Nor had they touched any local water.

He couldn't imagine what was wrong with them. Perhaps it was the cod roe? Whatever it was, it was, in Koransky's considered opinion, an infernal nuisance.

Blare-blare-blare hoot-hoot-hoot blare-blare-blare.

"Convoy halt!" yelled Koransky standing up in his vehicle and waving his arms.

The convoy halted.

The cult members, still wearing their hats, fled their bus in an ugly, blundering rush and sought privacy among the tick-infested shrubs.

Koransky ordered his men to fan out and screen his clients. If recent experience was anything to judge by, the Japanese would be in the bushes for anything up to twenty minutes.

Best to secure the area. A lot could happen in twenty minutes this close to the border.

Kutuzov and the others slipped out of their vehicles, some into the road-side ditch and others into the dense vegetation on the verges where they began to assemble mortars, heavy machine-guns and missile launchers. They were good lads, Koransky thought approvingly. Ex-Spetsnaz. Afghan vets. Armed to the teeth. The best.

Only Koransky stayed with the vehicle. He lit a cigarette and inhaled the rough smoke gratefully.

That was when the Liberians appeared. There was a convoy of them. It looked like a convoy that meant business.

Koransky saw it grinding along. Heavy trucks. Full of troops. Or what passed for troops. He wondered how to explain his presence. The area in which he had stopped was officially classified as restricted. Thank God he'd deployed his men along the road verges.

Koransky stepped forwards. If nothing else, Africans, like everybody else, respected authority.

Sometimes.

"Greetings!" yelled Koransky with authority.

The convoy ground on towards him through the slushy mud like a dismal prehistoric caravan. The wheels fought mud, the convoy rocked as the tyres slithered to escape the ruts.

A review of the eyes glaring from the faces in the leading truck told Koransky that he was in the wrong place. And that the timing was bad. These people were doing something big. It wasn't a normal raid or a pointless patrol.

The vehicle was open-topped, impossibly crowded with soldiers and bristling with guns. Barrels pointing here, pointing there.

Give them a minute and all the barrels would be pointing at Koransky. After all, it was Koransky and his Dreaming Safari vehicles that were blocking their road. And the bit of road that Koransky and his Dreaming Safari vehicles were blocking was tactical, off-limits, and obviously in the way of an invasion.

So much for the $20,000 US Koransky had paid the army colonel in Monrovia for a clear road.

"Greetings!" yelled Koransky again.

The lead vehicle stopped. Everybody on the vehicle, and it looked like there were about fifty of them, was wearing bleach war-paint, clutching shells (sea shells, a powerful remedy against bullets) and, of course, the guns.

A man climbed out wearing the uniform of a major. Squat, heavily built, he was wearing sunglasses and had an armband on his left sleeve that read "RUF". He was holding a revolver.

"Who are you?" the Liberian major said.

"Dreaming Safaris," said Koransky with a smile. "We are here to enjoy your elephants. Your birds. Your lions. Have you heard of ecotourism? Safaris?"

"What's a safari?" said the man.

"Swahili for journey," said Koransky. "Tourists on a safari go journeying looking for animals and birds."

"Why?" said the man.

"Why? Well, because they like animals and birds."

"You are lying. No-one would indulge in such far-fetched and unreasonable behaviour. Who were you signalling to with your car horn just now? Spies?"

"I wasn't signalling," said Koransky weakly.

"I heard you signalling. Who are your collaborators?"

The Major was smiling. Not at Koransky but at what was going to happen.

He was playing now to the crowded guns of his lead vehicle. The men up there were beginning to sway and hum, all the while building their group spirit, their confidence. Koransky had heard that mob hum before.

Individuals were always committing stupid atrocities here. Hacking up illegitimate sons and daughters after their wives had accused them of impotency. Beating each other to death over the theft of a sieve. Raping three month old babies in the belief that having sex with a virgin cured AIDS. But when that humming began, the individuals began to merge into some kind of organically coordinated aggression. Serious trouble was afoot.

"Are you a spy?" the convoy leader shouted. He was continuing to play to the humming, rocking crowd. Losing himself and any kind of potential for logical conversation in the powerful throb of the swelling, impending and longed-for violence.

"We're bird-watchers," yelled Koransky. The whole scenario was insane.

"Who were you signalling to? Answer me or it will go very badly with you."

"I'm leading a safari in search of ..."

Ahh, to hell with it, thought Koransky. "Deploy! Kill the blackarses!" yelled Koransky in Russian.

"And about time," thought Kutuzov from behind his screen of ferns.

This was a situation that couldn't get better.

He depressed the trigger of his RPG.

Bang. Boom. Screams. Perfect RPG hit on lead vehicle, showering human forms into the air, burning like fireworks. No more humming and shaking. With the densely packed troops trapped in their stationary vehicles – and the vehicles were nose to bumper – the contact was a turkey shoot. The ineptly driven trucks were in that military dream: the killing box. Back-to-back trucks.

Gridlock. Meat and metal, masses of both, perfectly positioned to burn.

The Liberian orator turned in surprise as the first truck blew, and lost his life to a throat-slash of Koransky's knife. More RPG rounds roared from the bush. Thump. Boom. The rear vehicle detonated. It had clearly been carrying ammunition and the blast not only killed every man on it but incinerated the two trucks in front of it and Koransky's man who'd fired the rocket. Confusion. One by one the trucks and their cargo were reduced to flaming ruin. Kutuzov had never seen such a perfect kill. Twenty-five trucks. Say fifty Liberians to each truck. "Beautiful!" he thought. Well over a thousand hostiles down in less than two minutes!

Beautiful!

His men continued firing into the survivors who'd fallen or been blown off their trucks. A handful of Liberians made it into the bush, many were on fire and blundered, screaming, away like monstrous candles.

When it was pretty much over, the surviving Russians came out of cover and the Aleph contingent emerged from its bush toilet.

Several had forgotten to pull up their safari shorts. All were still wearing their bee-keeper hats, so it was hard to read their expressions.

They stared at the burning vehicles, the scorched, shattered piles of bodies, in silence.

Kutuzov noted miserably that the invasion convoy had not been destroyed without cost. Koransky was dead; smashed by flying debris. Six of his comrades had been engulfed in the explosions. Two more were wounded. All because of these spaced out Japanese loons and their SOS horn signals. Koransky would be sadly missed.

Which was probably more than could be said for the bee-keepers.

"We must continue," said the Aleph leader shakily.

Kutuzov turned away from the wreckage of his hero and mentor and eyed the clients he had inherited with cold-eyed interest. A pulse was throbbing at his temple. Some Liberian survivor with more balls and luck than brains opened fire somewhere near the rear of the smoking remnants of the convoy.

"Deal with that fucking blackarse," said Kutuzov. Three of his men went and did it. One man came back with a minor gunshot wound in his thigh. A skin scrape.

The other two had been killed. The luck of the "blackarse" had held. He'd escaped.

Two more comrades down. Kutuzov was deeply saddened. Then vengeful.

"I said we must continue. What are you looking at?" said the Aleph leader.

"Your jackets," answered the Russian.

CHAPTER THIRTY-NINE

Moon-Dip

"What happened to you?"

Dr Pleasant goggled balefully at Rindert from beneath a bloodstained head bandage.

"Where are all the buyers? We were expecting over a hundred. You've brought sixteen guys. Where's everyone else?"

Dr Pleasant blinked.

Jack interceded hurriedly. "We can get into that later. First things first, you've got the moonlight. Tell me you've got the moonlight."

Dr Pleasant said he had got the moonlight.

"Praise the lord," said Jack. "And pass the moonlight."

Together they manhandled the oil drums from the back of the truck (which Rindert dismally noted was stacked with groaning injured buyers) and at Jack's request trundled the drums towards a tank on the edge of the village. In its former life the tank had served as the Mission's sheep-dip. Local people would bring their goats and their sheep (and sometimes their children).

Since the change in Mission management, the sheep-dip had served as Jack's "moonwash".

"Pour one drum in," Jack instructed. "It's more than I'd usually use, but the manikins have been grievously short over the last few days. A little extra won't hurt."

The liquid glugged stickily into the sheep-dip, emitting as it did so a phosphorescent glow that bathed the men in sickly light.

As the liquid settled, it mixed with the atmosphere, eddied and rippled, then fumed like dry ice in water.

"That's odd," Jack muttered suddenly doubtful. "It doesn't usually do that."

"Do what?"

"Effervesce," said Jack, and hiccuped.

"Well it's doing it now," grunted Dr Pleasant impatiently. "What happens next."

"Bathtime," grinned Jack, doubts forgotten. It was queer, what the moonlight was doing, very queer. But then again, moonlight was strange stuff. And Jack was drunk. And Jack was in a hurry. He produced his kelp horn and blew out a rasping fog-horn toot.

"Here they come," said Jack.

"Dear heavens," muttered Dr Pleasant, taking an involuntary step backwards.

"What a sight!"

From the streets, the huts, the workshop, from the Mission, from the surrounding bush, the homunculi came.

They swayed, staggered, and jostled. They keened and whistled. Green, luminous fumes surrounded them. Eyes glowed as silver as the liquid that seethed and frothed in the sheep-dip.

Close to five hundred homunculi, not one identical. Many swinging their heads like pendulums in a bruised, dazed, psychotic manner.

"Oh, Franklin," mourned Rindert, as he caught a glimpse of that familiar Shoveller Duck head, now shrunken and deformed. It was still wearing its purple top hat. Its jaws rattled and chattered, its ears flapped and twitched with their own horrible life.

"Let's get back to the vehicles," said Jack. "Give them some elbow room. They're not right in the head quite yet."

"Like their creator," thought Dr Pleasant. The view went beyond grotesque.

Rindert and Jack, Dr Pleasant and the buyers who had survived the bloodshed on the road, did just that. They watched appalled as the homunculi took their bath and then, glowing faintly, emerged and stalked back into their huts.

When the last had taken its dip, Jack smiled brightly, clapped his hands together and announced that the homunculi would be asleep for the next thirty minutes or so. He suggested that everybody might like to repair to his study for a well-earned glass of Cape smoke.

"Then we can get this auction over," he added "And we can all go home."

"Amen to that," muttered Rindert. "But let's not forget the wounded."

"What? Oh, yes," said Dr Pleasant, who had in fact forgotten all about them.

The first thing Holden did when the fighting finally stopped was to not move a muscle. Not after that hostage thing. No muscles moved. Not for thirty minutes. During that time in between the groans, she heard the following conversation.

"Unbelievable, man, unbelievable."

"That gets it said. Where'd you get the monkey, Esther?"

"How many of our people left?" The dazed rumble was Dr Pleasant's. "Shout up now, if you're wounded, if you're down."

There were shaky calls. Counting.

"Twenty three wounded, sixteen unhurt."

"And the rest?"

"Fertiliser."

"Unbelievable, man, unbelievable."

Then a truck engine had started up.

"Hey, Speeks! There's a naked nigger stealing your Unimog!"

This announcement prompted renewed gunfire.

It stopped.

"Missed him. He ran off into the bush."

"Well, at least he didn't run off with my Unimog."

There was laughter.

How can they laugh? Holden had thought. How can they laugh at a time like this? After a fight like that?

"Hey guys, look here, it's Taylor!"

"What's left of him."

There was more firing.

"What you doing, Speeks?"

"I'm just finishing the wounded off. Might as well do the job properly."

"Yes, OK do it. We don't want to meet any of these people on the way back."

Chortled laughter. More shooting.

"Hey, government's here! Guy here's claiming he's the Minister of Offence." A shot. "Not any more he isn't."

More laughter.

"This little one says don't shoot him, he wants to retire and run a radio station. What do you reckon, fellows? Do we let him go and run his radio station?"

"What's he going to play? If it's rap I say we blow his balls off."

"He says he'll be playing Jimi Hendrix and Mozart."

There was a chorus of catcalls. "That a group?"

"He says he'll play anything you want."

"Healthy attitude. All right son, you run along, run your radio station. But no more choppings, got me?"

There was applause.

"All right guys, knock it off. We've an auction to get too. Let's patch our people up and haul out!" The men had left.

The second thing Holden did was appropriate a rain-cape to cover herself. It took a while to find one that had not been badly shredded. There were bodies slumped, sprawled and scattered everywhere, a very few were whimpering and twitching, most were deathly still. A long way away she could see a few figures staggering or running. But not many.

Feeling giddy, Holden continued to pick her way among the

slain, taking inventory. There was Captain Rat. Dead. The gas-masked girl who'd hit her with the Maglite. Dead. The Liberian RUF High Command. Dead. All dead. All of them.

She slipped and fell. The implications, the implications. This was it. The end of the RUF.

The end of the RUF!

And with them gone, Sierra Leone was faced with the brightest prospects for peace in more than a decade.

Holden decided to borrow a lorry from the dead Liberians, and then – it was a grisly business – searched through the bodies for the keys to the ignition. Over an hour later she managed to match a set of keys, not to a truck, but to a fire engine. She then set off to Freetown to spread the word, one thought rampant and exuberant capering about in her head.

The end of the RUF. The end.

CHAPTER FORTY

Meltdown

One o'clock in the morning and, while the wounded buyers slept in the Mission dormitory, sedated not with morphine but with bushweed and Cape brandy, Jack was well into his auction patter.

"The units are fortified with Ebola which if you are not aware is one of just two members of a family of RNA viruses called the Filoviridae. There are, interestingly, four subtypes of Ebola which is itself named after a river in the Democratic Republic of Congo, which was formerly known as Zaire. There's Ebola-Zaire, although if the Centres for Disease Control in Atlanta were to move with the times, that one should be renamed Ebola-Democratic Republic of Congo – not that it's democratic, or from what I've heard from my colleague Rindert here, much of a Rebublic."

"Then there's Ebola-Sudan, Ebola-Ivory Coast, and then there's Ebola-Reston, which for some reason has yet to infect human beings but which is present in certain cynomologus primates. Inadequate facilities have prevented me from identifying which subtype is present in the units, but all—"

"Can we skip medical school and just get on with this auction?" interrupted Dr Pleasant. "We've had a busy day."

"Of course, of course," Jack said, eager to oblige. "Anyway, they've got Ebola, which is typically amplified in a healthcare setting where bodily fluids are transmitted with relative ease. Here, of course, it was amplified in a homunculus-manufacturing setting."

"Mister, I don't think you heard the man." This contribution was from Ester Speeks. "We aren't here to listen to blarney."

"And you shouldn't be," said Jack. "And while we're on the subject, if you ever visit the Emerald Isle don't kiss the Blarney Stone. The curator can't stand the Yank tourists who come to kiss it. Of a night he pisses on the Blarney Stone. It's true! That's what you get if you do it. Lips smeared with Irish piss!"

This sally actually got some laughs. But not from Speeks.

"If you don't start talking sense I'm going to incinerate you," explained Speeks. He levelled his flame-thrower as evidence.

Dr Pleasant hastily cut in. "Let's not do anything premature. We're in a confined space and we all know what a flame-thrower can do in a confined space. But Mr Speeks has a point. Jack, will you please get to the point. And the point is what's the point of them having Ebola? What's the competitive advantage?"

None, actually, thought Jack, not to anyone who isn't completely off his rocker. The whole contamination thing had been a grotesque accident. Contaminated body parts, provided by who else but General Butt Naked. The whole Ebola angle made the units a complete liability. They could snag on a thorn, a nail, trip on barbed wire, get gnawed by a rat or nibbled open by ants or cockroaches.

The animal and plant kingdoms seemed to instinctively recognise that the homunculi were dead despite their capacity for movement. Flora grew on them in the form of moulds, fungi, small orchids and even, in one instance, a fern. Fauna, of the verminous sort, tended to chew them when they were immobile.

Then there was the risk that the homunculi might inadvertently cut themselves with their razor-blade teeth, or their shears, or barbed wire or whatever, and spray death-giving bodily fluids in all directions. It was a major reason Jack wanted to dump them ASAP. Take the money and run.

He had another taste of brandy and coughed importantly.

"The Ebola factor – and I call it my little extra ingredient –

makes them extremely effective as bio-warfare tools," Jack said. "Order them to burst asunder in one of your PLO camps." Here Jack was talking to the two surviving Israelis, desperate to win some friends in his gruesome audience. "Next time the ragheads are having a peace conference in Sharm El Sheik or wherever, send one in, get it to explode in the conference room. Those Saudis, Iraqis, that Hamas guy with the squint – all those people are history."

"That Hamas guy with the squint *is* history," said one Israeli. He knew. He'd helped. Just ten days ago, though it felt a lot longer.

"Yes, well. Whatever. The units are also perfect for donkeying dope. Self-destruct facility if they're intercepted. There are some Colombians here, right?"

"Wrong," intoned Dr Pleasant gloomily. Pepe and his men had been shot dead by Captain Rat in the closing moments of the battle. The loss was weighing heavily on Dr Pleasant's mind. Muccio would be less than impressed when he heard the news.

"Well, erm, no Colombians, is that the case? Pity," continued Jack, wiping his sweating hands on his grimy trousers. "Moving along, these units will repair themselves if damaged and they'll also, if instructed, repair each other."

Jack, on Rindert's advice, had agreed to downplay the ability of homunculi to manufacture new homunculi. On the grounds that a self-perpetuating supply would be bad for future business. The two men had decided that as soon as the homunculi had their moonlight and had stopped evincing signs of potentially homicidal psychosis, all successfully auctioned units would be instructed NOT to make any more homunculi and that should this order ever be countermanded, then the homunculi were to explode. That way, Rindert had explained, any buyer bright enough to consider going into the homunculus manufacturing business would be killed instantly.

"You can expect unquestioning obedience," said Jack, showing a queasy grin.

"What else?" Jack drained his glass. "They're highly intelligent.

We showed them a picture of the target, showed them a city map, told a unit of, erm, units to steal an ambulance and a UN vehicle for the second field test. And gentlemen, that's *all* we told them. Go to Freetown, we said, steal a UN car and blow up this RUF general called Butt Naked. Take the bits away in the ambulance, we said. That's all we said. And the units improvised and did it. Which I think you'll agree is pretty remarkable."

Jack poured more brandy and then, fed up with his speech, suggested that everybody go down to the village square for a practical demonstration.

Everybody agreed.

Everybody was fed up with Jack's speech.

And everybody wanted to see what these units, these homunculi, were capable of doing.

"Gentlemen," Jack announced with a theatrical flourish, "I give you the future: I give you the Homunculus, mark 1!"

The buyers were now seated on folding chairs with their backs to the Mission. Illumination was provided by a row of storm lanterns and flaming torches. The buyers stared intently at the hut door from which the priest was summoning his creation. The atmosphere was tense. Electric. Thunder rippled in the distance.

Jack said, "Come!"

A figure emerged from the shadowy hut, moving slowly, jerkily. There was no smoke coming from its nose.

It approached the seated men. Some buyers leant forward to see more closely. Most though drew back. There were gasps and muttered curses.

It was a horrid sight.

The homunculus stopped.

"Not bad eh, gentlemen?" crowed Jack.

The homunculus wobbled.

One of its legs fell off, then an arm.

The homunculus tottered.

Then the homunculus folded in on itself and pitched forward. There was a crackle of fire and its head exploded. Jack yelped.

There was a brief silence from the buyers.

"Was that meant to happen?" one Israeli asked.

"Yes, quite normal," said Jack improvising frantically. "I, um, I asked it to do that because I wanted to show you the repair regimes. I shall now instruct another homunculus to repair that damaged homunculus. You will be amazed."

"I'd better be," growled Speeks. He still had his flame-thrower.

"Gentlemen, I give you homunculus repair! Come!"

A second twisted nightmare-figure emerged from the hut into the square. Rindert recognised it as the unit that had had its neurotic attack in the larder. The homunculus reeled around in an unsteady circle.

Then it melted.

Just melted, like wax in a furnace. Dissolved into a puddle from which stuck wires and shears, solder, a small solar panel and a stack of cogs. The head sat on top of the gluey pool for a moment like a very rotten cherry on a very rotten cake. Then the head fizzed and exploded.

"What is this? Guy Faulkes night? What the hell are you playing at, Jack?" roared The Crocodile.

Jack ran desperately into the hut. His torch could be seen playing about within. But Jack did not come out.

There was a bellowed yell from within the hut. Just one strangled word was discernible: "Why?"

The buyers shifted uncertainly, in some cases, irritably. What was going on?

"What's all this bullshine, Pleasant?" asked Speeks.

"Go in and get him, Rindert!" ordered The Crocodile, his face thunderous, suffused with rage.

While Rindert obeyed his master's voice, Dr Pleasant turned on his buyers and from some reserve deep inside, summoned up a chuckle.

"Everything will be fine. That I am sure of. Ho. Ho. Ho."

Like a rattle of firecrackers the quiet of the village was broken by a series of small fizzing, popping explosions. By now everyone recognised the noise. It was the sound of homunculus heads exploding.

Queer lights flared in the windows of the huts – vivid purples, ghastly greens, soft uncanny blues.

Jack emerged suddenly from his hut and raced madly down the street away from the buyers towards the sheep-dip. Rindert followed in jogging, dogged pursuit.

When he reached the drum, Jack shone his torch on the hieroglyphs and symbols. All was made painfully clear.

Dr Pleasant, the bungling, crocodilian oaf hadn't brought distilled moonlight. He'd brought starlight concentrate. Mungo, for some reason, had given him starlight concentrate. The result, as any alchemist knew, was anathema to a homunculus. Like water to magnesium. All his dipped units had simply melted. Disaster! Fiasco! Doom!

Why in the name of the seven celestial conjunctions had Mungo given Dr Pleasant starlight? Why?

CHAPTER FORTY-ONE

Mungo

The answer to this question was sad, brave, and simple. After his window shattered and the bullets had rained in, Mungo had risen unsteadily to his feet and wandered around his study in a state of raw shock.

He had then heard more shouted demands that he open up. That his visitor was in no mood for fun and games. The voice had then calmed and declared that its owner regretted structural damage and was – ho, ho, ho – here on legitimate and mutually profitable business.

Mungo, listening to the awful voice, had temporarily lost his reason.

As the figure outside stopped laughing and began to hurl itself at Clouds' stout oak door, Mungo had wandered panic-stricken through his rooms in search of a hiding place. He had eventually concealed himself in a large copper kettle that he used for thickening moor mist to soothe restless phantoms.

It was here in the kettle three hours later after an infuriated, crashing, bear-like search of the house that Dr Pleasant found Mungo cowering, blinking and fearful beneath his nightcap.

"Out!" Pleasant had roared.

Mungo's legs had failed him. He was a gentle, academic man, frail and otherworldly. Never had anything like this happened to him. He had found himself paralysed with fear. A thin-limbed, nightcapped rabbit faced by a bulge-eyed, rabid stoat.

When the alchemist had evinced no signs of vacating his kettle, Pleasant had hauled him out and for good measure hurled him across the room into a rack of queerly carved ebony fishing rods. Mungo used these for catching dreams and lost thoughts. There were many lost thoughts floating about on the moors. Some very old and very lost indeed. Mungo with the help of his rods had caught many and had an extensive collection. Those of use to their owners he would post back. The seemingly empty envelopes would arrive by mail prompting puzzlement on the behalf of their recipients. And then they'd think of things forgotten. A spring day long ago, the smile on the face of a child, sharing bites of a crisp apple with a lover, a cricket match played out on a long balmy summer's evening.

Darker thoughts, or thoughts from the dead or from antiquity, Mungo would bottle either for study or to prevent harm. Thoughts could be dangerous.

After he'd thrown Mungo across the room, Dr Pleasant had then kicked Mungo into insensibility.

When Mungo had come out of his swoon it was to find himself tied to a chair in the cellars with a light playing in his face.

His visitor on the other side of the light was invisible.

"I'm here for moonlight and I'm taking your Land Rover," the visitor had said.

"But why?"

"Because I need the moonlight for a bunch of homunculi that are screwing up in West Africa. Because you wouldn't answer the door. And because your road's an absolute and bloody disgrace. You should be utterly ashamed of yourself. It's a traffic hazard."

"Please don't shine that light in my eyes. I know all about you."

"Like hell, you do."

"But I do. You are a dark and troubled man. I have herbs that might soothe you, which might help you find peace with what you've done."

"I'm completely at peace with what I've done. That's why I need your moonlight. I'm planning to do more of it."

"Yes, I see that now. My herbs are probably of insufficient strength to help. But tell me first about the homunculi and just why you need the moonlight."

What had happened next came as no surprise to Mungo who was a master of the subtleties. What had happened next went completely unremembered by Dr Pleasant.

Dr Pleasant, from behind his interrogator's light, had told him everything. From behind the light, in a flat, monotonous voice, Pleasant had explained the lot. The buyers, the auction, the RUF RPG, about Jack, what he knew of the homunculi, and his vision of the units as weapons of assassination, political murder, genocide, profit and the ultimate extermination of the Bantu race. But not the San Bushmen. Dr Pleasant had a soft spot for the persecuted desert folk. After all they'd acted as trackers for Koevoet in the bush war against SWAPO.

Dr Pleasant had no idea that he had been hypnotised by the subtleties of Mungo. Indeed he was only a minute away from cutting the bonds, standing the alchemist up, helping him to his bed and making him a sweet cup of tea.

Then Mungo, who was over 600 years old, ran out of luck. He felt it coming at him in a numbing rush up his left arm. Heart, he thought. The beating, the kicking, the fear. Mungo knew it was over for him.

He dispelled the hypnotic web that he had cast over the demonic South African. There was still time to do one good thing to offset the darkness. Mungo sensed that it would be more than a good thing, perhaps a thing of wonder.

"So where's the moonlight?" Dr Pleasant growled.

"You will find it in drums beside the barn. Red drums."

"Good," Pleasant had said. "You're going blue. You've got pills somewhere I can get you? Looks as if you're having a heart attack?"

"Yes," Mungo had managed, face ghastly taut beneath his nightcap. "You have killed me, sir."

"Well, sorry. But you're not the first and you'll not be the last. Red drums? You're sure they're red?"

"Red drums. Yesss ..." said Mungo.

And then Mungo had jerked in his chair and had gone.

The Crocodile had goggled at the ancient ash that remained in a neat pile in the chair.

But not for long. If that's what happened to dead alchemists, then that's what happened to dead alchemists, he'd thought.

Different strokes for different folks. And there was a bonus. At least he'd not need to hide the body. Just find Mungo's vacuum cleaner, Hoover the chair. (Most of the dust was held tidily beneath the nightcap). Then toss the vacuum cleaner bag into that river he'd driven into.

Neat. Tidy. The way he liked it.

He'd done the housework, collected the red drums, transferred them from Mungo's Land Rover to his van, then had used the Land Rover to drag his van from the river and, after three hours' sleep in the cab, had driven back to Kent. And when that had been achieved he had gone to a phone box in Hunters Wood. He had avoided Beck's Hill, where, following the incident outside the China Tea Rooms, he was wanted by the police for aggravated assault. From the Hunters Wood phone box he had secured a Hercules transport plane from a firm he knew in Guinea Bissau. The Hercules had not come cheap. The people in Guinea Bissau knew that urgent orders for Hercules transport planes were never issued by people who didn't need them urgently. They'd soaked him, but good.

All in all, it had been a long couple of days for Dr Pleasant.

And the days had been lengthened by the sure knowledge that he was in for more of them. Two things buoyed him. At least he had not operated in West Africa before. There was little likelihood of him being recognised, shot or jailed for his past efforts on behalf of the apartheid anti-communist struggle.

And at least, he'd thought, the auction (thanks to his super-human efforts) would be a triumph.

Yes, a triumph.

CHAPTER FORTY-TWO

Customer Relations

"Yes, well, thank you for coming all this way," chortled The Crocodile. "The auction was perhaps not the glowing success I had envisaged. But I feel sure you'll agree that the last few days have not been entirely without interest. I for one won't forget bailing out of the blazing Hercules in a hurry." Ho, ho. Chortle, chortle. "Yes, I think we have all had some experiences that were new to us."

Rindert had to hand it to The Crocodile. The buyers were staring at him with cold, furious eyes. The man was, quite literally, talking for his life. And here he was launching into some comradely, chuckling, we're-all-in-this-thing-together routine.

"What about our costs, Pleasant?" snarled Speeks. "This little jaunt of yours has cost me a fortune."

"You and me both," chuckled Dr Pleasant. "A pretty packet. Ho, ho, ho."

"Yes, what about our costs?" said an Israeli.

The other buyers chimed in.

"I came this close to having my head blown off!" shouted Speeks, holding his fingers six inches apart to show how close he'd come to having his head blown off. "There's twenty men upstairs suffering from gunshot wounds. There's more than sixty dead and I'm not counting the kaffirs! I've had to kill hundreds of kaffirs! I blew up a Panhard. It's been pissing with rain! And this food you're serving – this fish – isn't fit for human consumption!"

Dr Pleasant spread his hands wide.

"Gentlemen, gentlemen, please. Indulge me a little. Hear me out. I'm very well aware that everybody has incurred expense and inconvenience and I am very anxious that you should be fully reimbursed—"

"Reimbursed?" yelled Speeks.

"—and fully compensated," continued Dr Pleasant. "How does the sum of $1,000,000 per man sound?"

"Sounds like bullshine!" said Speeks raising his flame-thrower.

"Wait!" An Israeli held Speeks back. "You are seriously offering $1,000,000 per man? You are aware that if you include the wounded we are talking about nearly 40 million bucks? You say you have that sort of money?"

"Gentlemen, for a number of years, as you know, I worked with the CCB – that's the Civil Co-operation Bureau – in Namibia suppressing the *swart en rooi gevaar*. The red kaffirs. We were given carte blanche in our freedom struggle. We had full access to the Namibian diamond fields. Best stones in the world. And it would be no exaggeration to say that if every single man who unfortunately died today was still alive I could compensate them all too. No exaggeration."

Which was of course, not true. It was a hell of an exaggeration, a fantastic exaggeration. Dr Pleasant had expended considerable sums on the Hercules and had no more than £32,000 left in his Beck's Hill Lloyds savings account. Stocks and shares amounted to perhaps the same again. If he sold his house in Kent he might realise half a million sterling. He did have diamonds – quite a few – but they were his. And they were going to stay that way.

Instead of money, however, he had a plan. Dr Pleasant was a man who thought on his feet. And a rather good thought had just come to him. A way to get out of this thing not just alive, but rich and with his reputation still intact. Just so long as these fish bit at the bait.

There was discussion among the fish.

Then the fish bit.

"Bluff called, Pleasant," said Speeks. "But we don't let you out of sight till we get the stones. First thing tomorrow we're out of here. You're coming with us. First sign of bullshine then you get it."

"You can bank on me," chortled Pleasant.

There was actually some answering laughter. The Crocodile was, inadvertently, being funny again.

And there wasn't a man among his audience who didn't want to be a millionaire.

The next day dawned on a subdued Freetown. There had been very little firing in the night. The Hotel Frangipani siege still muttered away, but both besiegers and besieged were losing impetus.

The Kamajor militia were nearly out of ammunition. The Hotel's RUF guests likewise. The pronounced failure of the promised reinforcements to arrive from Liberia and the mysterious disappearance of the High Command was weighing on the collective RUF mind. There'd been talk of brokering a surrender that didn't involve getting chopped.

On the streets, civilians were beginning to emerge and make furtive, scurrying forays in search of food, cooking oil or matches. None were sniped.

At a little before noon, the sole remaining representative of the UN and the official international community drove into town in her fire engine. She skirted a smouldering piano, drove to her office and commandeered a loudspeaker. Then she took to the streets to bring the glad tidings to the people, helped in her mission by the fire engine's bell.

"It's over!" yelled Eileen Holden again and again. "The RUF command are all dead. Their Liberian allies are dead. The rebels are finished! It is safe again. Safe again!"

The spectacle of Eileen Holden naked but for a rain cape and with her hair slathered in blood, shouting joyously into her speaker from a bullet-pocked fire engine was not as dignified as a visitation from the likes of Nelson Mandela or Kofi Annan. But she received cheers. Few at first. But as the day wore on, more. Then a little procession formed behind her.

There were still no snipings.

The procession swelled.

By nightfall, despite isolated incidents of violence, there was dancing in the streets. Or more precisely, splashing in the streets. There were water fights. Many of Freetown's residents were still too traumatised to leave their houses and bolt-holes. But if the last decade had taught the people of Sierra Leone anything, it had taught them resilience.

The people on the streets were bouncing back.

It was a dream come true for Eileen Holden. Residents of Freetown cheering her. Offering her wretched little gifts, cola nuts, a pineapple, a box of matches, bunches of hastily picked flowers. Cheering her. Cheering themselves. It was history in the making. The rebirth of a nation. Uhuru!

HMS *Clam* was underway on a course set very firmly for Conakry, Guinea, the captain grimly determined to rid his vessel of the civilian taint.

Aboard were all the foreign residents, journalists, traders, along with an almost unrealistic quantity of government-affiliated citizens of Sierra Leone. Only one British national had been left behind. Graham McDougal, the Scots haulage company boss. He was still anxiously awaiting the return of all the vehicles he had rented to Pleasant's auction-goers.

The money he had been promised had been considerable. The money he'd been paid minimal. Beggars and choosers. With Freetown in freefall, he'd been a beggar. Pleasant's people had done the choosing.

If the vehicles didn't return, then McDougal would be a beggar in more than metaphorical terms, he reflected. Standard Chartered's Freetown branch might be a smoking, water-logged ruin but banks had memories that went beyond temporary rampages.

If McDougal had known about Dr Pleasant's nocturnal activities subsequent to the million-dollar promise he would not have been a happy man.

While Speeks and the other buyers slept the sleep of the just plain knackered, Pleasant had tiptoed out of the Mission with a satchel slung over his beefy shoulders. In the satchel was Rindert's C4 explosive which he then proceeded to attach to unobtrusive places on the vehicles.

At about the same time that McDougal was making a meagre breakfast of bananas and tinned cream at the Sofitel, and wondering when he'd get his fleet back, the buyers were climbing into their vehicles and making the wounded as comfortable as was possible under the circumstances. The Crocodile was chuckling, Speeks was still looking dark and threatening, but most of the men were just feeling tired and anxious to be off.

Pleasant's announcement that he'd forgotten his overnight bag was greeted with groans.

"Won't be long! Soon have this show on the road!"

"You better not be long!"

As soon as he was within the sheltering walls of the Mission, Pleasant pushed the magic button.

CHAPTER FORTY-THREE

Unpleasant

"What the bejesus was that?"

Rindert and Jack were despondently contemplating the immediate future when the blasts occurred.

A flaming tyre hurtled through the window and shattered Jack's work-bench

"The Crocodile," Rindert said after cautiously peering through the broken glass, "has just solved the problem of the disgruntled buyers."

"He's blown them up?" Jack said "Did he get them all?"

Rindert nodded from the window.

"Reckon so. Though there's a lot of smoke."

Lalapanzi's main street looked like Mogadishu on a particularly bad day. At least ten of the huts were on fire. What with the RUF attack and The Crocodile's version of customer relations the village had lost its untouched plaster, wedding cake look. Its walls were now as pockmarked and scarred as any other self respecting settlement in Sierra Leone. The flowerbeds looked as if a buffalo herd had stampeded over them.

"The man's a force of nature!" said Jack, awe in his voice.

"He's a loony is what he is." Rindert reached for his gun. "We've got to get rid of him, before he gets rid of us. Ah hell! Someone's pinched my ammo clips."

Someone. The Crocodile. This wasn't looking good.

"*Nil desperandum*, Rindert, *nil desperandum*. I'll handle this," Jack whispered and winked.

The door opened and in strolled Dr Pleasant rubbing his hands. He looked well-satisfied.

"We'll have no more whinging from them," said Dr Pleasant.

"We certainly won't," confirmed Rindert.

"Put that tyre out. It's stinking the place up," said Dr Pleasant. Rindert poured water on the tyre.

"So?" Jack said brightly, clapping his hands together and cracking a hideously enthused smile.

"So what?" grunted Pleasant.

"So when's the next auction?"

Both the South Africans stared at Jack. Neither could believe what they were hearing. Was Baron Frankenstein completely off his rocker? Wasn't one auction enough for him?

"What man has done, man can do again," Jack continued relentlessly, still grinning his revolting Fagin grin. "Hey and OK, so we've had a few setbacks. Through no fault of your own, I hasten to add, you brought the wrong stuff. Melted my homunculi, but that's not the end of it. I can make more units. All I need is some moonlight. Get me some moonlight, a few body parts and Bob's your uncle and Fanny's your aunt as my uncle Bob used to say. Not that my aunt was called Fanny, mind. That would be too much of a coincidence."

Off his rocker, thought Rindert: nuts, a madman, a ranting cheese-faced loon.

"Well, come on fellas, look lively, Where's this indomitable Boer spirit we're always hearing about?" Jack leered. "Mungo's not going to fob you off with starlight again, now is he? Not now you know the difference."

"Two problems spring to mind *vis a vis* your totally insane suggestion," said Dr Pleasant.

"Problem one, I have just killed all my buyers. It'll take months, if I'm lucky, to get any new ones."

"And problem two?"

"Mungo isn't going to fob me off with more starlight and that's for damn sure. In the course of our business transaction he was, how should I put it? Killed. Yes that's the right word. Killed."

Jack's grin vanished. He leaned back on his desk. But the work-bench was no longer there. It had been destroyed by the flying tyre. He reeled, then steadied himself.

"You killed Mungo? The best alchemist in Europe? The oldest alchemist in Europe?"

"Yes," said Dr Pleasant.

For Jack this was not a disaster. Rather the reverse. It was a chance. And the chance was a chance with a capital C.

Mungo, despite his unrivalled skills had been a prissy, fussy little do-gooder. He had drawn up codes of alchemical ethics, he had had all sorts of qualms and cautions that were, in Jack's opinion, holding back alchemy's progressive and natural developments. He had dominated the whole science for at least five centuries. Well overdue for retirement.

Everyone in the know knew that Mungo had even developed the Philosopher's Stone, that gold-soaked bunny that swept tantalisingly before (but ever beyond reach of) the younger greyhounds in the alchemical racetrack.

No-one had ever developed the Philosopher's Stone.

No-one but Mungo.

And what had Mungo done with his Philosopher's Stone after he'd developed it? Turned base metals into gold? That was the whole point of the Philosopher's Stone, in Jack's opinion. But no. Mungo hadn't. He had written a dry monograph recommending that every member of the Guild of Gentle Alchemists pursue the achievement of the stone. But he himself hadn't even used his stone. Not true. He'd used it once. He'd converted a sprig of heather to purest gold. He'd never used it since. Nor had he told anyone else how to develop the stone.

Stupid, Jack thought that. Really, really stupid.

Mungo could have paved the streets of London with gold. He could have built himself a palace in Bimini, a rocket to the moon. He could have had legions of houris waving their slinky curvature before him in obedient dance and dangling sweet moist grapes above his withered lips.

Instead, in his monograph, he'd said that the possession of power was actually a weakening influence if the power was used, and had droned on about the dangers of destabilising the global economy.

What grated most with Jack, though, was Mungo's performance as head of the secret but influential League of Gentle Alchemists.

The League, at Mungo's urgent urgings, had blackballed Jack. Had denied him entry.

The insulting and inconvenient repulse had followed an interview during which Jack had shown Mungo some of his more venturesome homunculus designs.

"You are mentally ill. Your pungent odour is characteristic of the more dangerous manifestations of schizophrenia. Your designs reflect your illness. You have also been trying to do what hurried avaricious young persons today call 'fast-tracking'. You have been cutting corners and associating with porroh men and spirits of malice. You are a shame to this honourable profession. Etc., etc. Blah, blah."

The only constructive comment Mungo had delivered was at Jack's humiliating departure from the quiet sanctuary of Clouds.

"If you must have the thing that was Papa Det as a partner, take this as very wise advice. Keep it confined in a very, very cold environment. And only ever disturb it when it has been weakened by Mars in ascendancy and Sirius in a state of ineffectiveness. Then offer him – no, it – milk. Otherwise you will invoke Papa Det's wrath. I mourn for you. Truly I do. You have such talents." Etc., etc., blah, blah, etc."

Etc., blah.

Tedious, conservative, but Mungo's recommendation had been sound. He'd had a lot less trouble from Papa Det following Mungo's advice.

And now this Dr Pleasant had done what centuries of life, inquisitions, disease, war, fire, and plain bad luck had not.

Put Mungo out of it. Killed the immortal. Created a vacuum.

A lot hung on the answer to Jack's next question.

"Which house did you kill him in?"

"Thought you'd gone to sleep for a minute. What does it matter? The one in the middle of nowhere. With the lousy road."

Perfect, thought Jack.

Clouds.

Ten-to-one no-one even knows he's dead. Stuck out there. Now all that was required was to get rid of Dr Pleasant, get hold of a false passport (just in case any home-improvements nut had been digging up the gardens behind his former Muswell Hill house) and take possession of Clouds before the League of Gentle Alchemists learned it was vacant.

But first, Dr Pleasant. If Rindert's disarmed gun was anything to go by Jack was on a tightrope and this bulge-eyed horror could start sawing at the strands at any time.

"Mungo dead. Killed you say?" Jack affected a look of disinterested dejection then brightened again.

"How about a steak breakfast?" he suggested. "I've got a stack of steaks, thick ones, upstairs in the freezer. Namibian fillet. The best. If one of you gentlemen would care to go up and fetch them I'll be lighting up my stove and we can get a decent meal into us."

"I'm still putting this tyre out," grunted Rindert. Burning tyres were the very devil to extinguish. And he didn't like Jack's freezer. His neck was twitching.

"How about it, Dr P?" Jack said, with an ingratiating leer. "Nice thick steak? Plump?"

Dr Pleasant thought about it. He had intended to just throw these two screw-ups out of the window and clear off to check the shattered convoy for valuables. All the buyers had been packing diamonds, gold, cash. It had never been a credit card sort of auction. Something of worth would have survived the bangs. Since he'd decided to kill all the buyers Dr Pleasant had been rather looking forward to the treasure hunt.

But steak sounded good. The previous night's fish and corned beef (combined with the covert nocturnal C4 placement) had given Dr Pleasant dyspepsia but had also left him feeling hollow.

A decent steak, thick, burned on the outside, raw within, that would be just the job. The juice. That sizzle. That smell.

"I'll go," said Dr Pleasant.

"Wouldn't want to put you to inconvenience," he added with a chortle.

Hearty breakfasts. Condemned men. A good slab of steak. Then both of the screw-ups out of the window. The treasure hunt. Out of the country. Try somewhere new for a while. After the Beck's Hill traffic warden incident and that God-be-damned journalist, Basil Rudge, Kent was no longer the haven it had been. Maybe Costa Rica. He'd got a postcard from Black Jack Stephansky. Stephansky had written that Costa Rica was real nice.

"Where's the freezer?" asked Dr Pleasant, carp-like, lunging in greed for Jack's steak-baited hook.

When Pleasant had lumbered out of the room in search of the fridge-freezer and the soon-to-be-griddled ox flesh, Rindert turned viciously on Jack. His eyes were smarting from the tyre smoke.

"You mean to say we've been eating this poxy fish, this foul hippo fat muck and all the while you've had steaks in the fridge-freezer? Are you a sadist?"

"I was lying. No steaks in that freezer," said Jack, thinking that he'd need money for Clouds.

"I wonder whether those buyers were bringing cash?" Jack said.

"No, Diners Club. Barclaycard. Trade goods of cinnamon and frankincense. Are you an idiot? Of course they were carrying cash. And help me with this flaming tyre. I'm chucking it out of the window."

There was a peculiar brazen crash. It came from the direction of the kitchens.

"What was that?"

"Don't ask," said Jack.

There was a brief burst of gunfire. Then a hellish human scream. Then a hellish inhuman scream. Then a brief mixture of both.

Then the peculiar brazen crash again.

And silence.

"Was that your fridge-freezer?" Rindert asked, tyre forgotten. "What the hell do you keep in that fridge-freezer?"

"Papa Det," said Jack.

CHAPTER FORTY-FOUR

Wrapping Up

Where possible, on HMS *Clam*, the evacuees were given cabins, or failing that, hammocks, blankets or bed rolls. Dalziel, and the captain had both given up their berths. As had all Dalziel's junior officers.

Ironically the least crowded room on the vessel was the brig. It was occupied by just one man. Fitz. Confined at Her Majesty's pleasure following a richly deserved charge of drunk and disorderly.

Dalziel, in the only offensive action he had been able to make during the entire Freetown crisis, had floored Fitz with a devastating blow after Fitz had invaded Wiley's "rabbit hole" demanding to be put through to the President of the United States so he could tell him to "kiss my covert ass goodbye". Wiley, the radio operator with Naval Intelligence, had obliged but without success so Fitz had ordered Wiley to order him up a whore, a fishing road and a cabin in Montana. "Where nobody goes," Fitz had added, lurching to the twin rhythms of the Atlantic waves and the Martians he'd consumed at the Sofitel Mammy Yoko Hotel.

Dalziel had been passing with the latest fax from home weighing heavily in his chest pocket. Derek had been busted for possession of Mary Jane in Brittany while sacredly running past a police station. The little twerp.

Dalziel had overheard Fitz's instructions to Wiley. Had taken action.

One colossal punch to the pongy Yank's head. Lights out.

Damned knuckles hurt like billy-o, but it felt good to be proactive for a change.

The last buyer to arrive at the auction had no idea that there was an auction.

But then again he had no intention of paying for anything.

He turned up as Jack and Rindert were packing their bags into the back of Rindert's truck and preparing to bid forever farewell to Lalapanzi and a heavily-armed hello to Freetown. Despite the ferocity of the C4 blasts, well over eight million dollars worth of gold and stones – even bank notes and bearer bonds – had been recovered.

This was due to two happy factors. Firstly, all the buyers who had been killed during the battle with the RUF had had their portable purchasing power redistributed by the surviving auction-goers.

Secondly, several of the buyers had had the foresight to store their collateral in fire-proof safes, titanium-fortified belts or stalwart steel boxes. Rindert and Jack had spent many hours putting the welding equipment furnished by the Christian American Charitable Foundation to more profitable use than fair trade.

They were, as they packed to depart, both very rich indeed. Rindert, who knew diamonds, and diamond smuggling, was richer than Jack. He'd found a quantity of them tucked into a secret hole in Esther Speeks' boot but had decided not to mention it.

Jack had also lost out on the I'll-choose-one-then-you-choose-one system of sharing out the mutually discovered stones.

Jack went for size. Rindert unerringly went for quality. By the time the 50–50 fair share-out was concluded, Rindert was about two million ahead.

Still they were both rich. Very rich.

The visitor was not.

He was covered in mud, soot, caked blood, staggering with exhaustion, and alone. Lacking transport following the gunfight and his abortive attempt to steal the Unimog, he had walked the whole way to Lalapanzi. He was out of food. Out of whisky. Also out of ammunition.

"I'm here for your zombies," said Butt Naked by way of introduction.

"Sorry," Jack cackled shrilly, giddy with his wealth and the ordeal that had made him rich. "Fresh out of zombies."

"Listen," said Butt Naked in a conciliatory tone. He shambled closer. "If it's because of what I did to your teeth, then I'd like to say sorry about that. I never meant to do it."

"You never meant to do it?" Jack squawked. "If you never meant to do it, why the hell did you do it?"

"What's all this?" Rindert asked, bemused. He looked the newcomer over carefully. "You're Butt Naked. Thought we'd killed you."

"Yes, I'm Butt Naked. I'm the President but you can call me General. Jack and me are comrades."

" You people know each other?"

"He got me some things," Jack said lamely. "I just didn't want to mention it, knowing how you merc guys feel about the RUF. Didn't want you to, you know, shoot me. Or anything."

"We were business partners!" announced Butt Naked throwing a grazed and filthy arm around Jack's neck. Butt Naked's muscles were like steel. He grinned and squeezed. "We were like brothers across the racial divide, man. There was nothing I would not do for this man, man."

"You pulled my teeth out!" choked Jack. Was this monstrosity going to break his neck? He could. Jack knew he could. He wilted.

"Listen, you were getting on my case about the fish. I got you some fish. Really good fish. You got on my case about it. I was drunk. Anyway, forget about that. That's all in the past. I'm thinking now of the future. I'm going to make you Minister of Science. Just let me have your zombies. I really need them."

"I'm telling you there aren't any zombies! If you'd come here the day before yesterday you could have had five hundred. But they've gone. They've melted. Poof! Gone."

Butt Naked digested the news.

"You sure?"

"I'm sure."

"Without the damn zombies how am I going to remain President?"

"The answer to that is, you're probably not," said Rindert.

"Sure you're sure? No zombies?"

"Sure."

"Sure?"

"Sure!"

"Ain't that a kick in the nuts," said Butt Naked bleakly.

"Why don't you wander off?" suggested Rindert waving his empty rifle.

"OK," said the President brokenly.

"Wait up, I've a better idea," Jack suggested, thinking about his dentures and the incident with the pliers in the chapel.

"You're probably in need of a drink after your walk. There's whisky up there on the third floor. It's in the freezer. You know what a freezer is? You do. Well it's in there."

"Hey, Father Jack," said Rindert. "You're a priest. There's been enough mayhem. Cut the kid some slack. I'm sure after what he's been through he'll shuffle off and start a farm. Grow peanuts. Do something wise."

"You mad?" Butt Naked hauled himself erect and turned on Rindert with blazing eyes.

"Grow peanuts? I ain't no peanut grubber! The world only just started to hear about President Butt Naked! You hear? I'm going to Butt Naked their butts to hell! I'm going to out-butt their butts! I'm gonna—"

"Freezer. Whisky. Third floor," said Rindert tiredly.

CHAPTER FORTY-FIVE

Sayonara

The phone rang in the Akihabara computer warehouse. The Defence Minister picked up, listened for a while, then flung the receiver at the wall. He missed the wall. The receiver plucking the telephone after it like the trailing tail of a kite broke the window and sailed off and down into the crowded street where it stunned a fried octopus doughball vendor.

It was generally accepted among the Aleph elite that the Defence Minister, who bulged with steroid assisted musculature, didn't know his own strength.

"It's Kutuzov. He works for Koransky. Our pet Russian."

"Good news?" asked the Minister of Transport.

"Bad news!" muttered the Defence Minister. "Fever."

"Not fever again?"

"Fever. Again," said the Defence Minister.

"Everybody?"

"All of them. Dead."

There was a long silence.

Then ...

"Argghhh!" screamed the Science Minister. "Sea cucumbers. Fools. Eels!"

Chubachi collapsed foaming, writhed, clutched wildly at the desk which tilted, spilling the green teapot onto his head. He spasmed some more. Then stilled.

The Minister of Transport waited for a while – the Science

Minister's love affair with pentobarbital was known to have unplanned results. Eventually, with no resurrection apparent, he approached the convulsed body, fumbled about with the flabby wrist feeling for a pulse. Pulse there was none. The Minister of Transport put on a solemn expression and pronounced Chubachi dead. Of a massive stroke, he guessed.

No-one rushed forward to attempt mouth-to-mouth resuscitation.

It took some time and many meetings but, following the demise of Chubachi and the zealots in West Africa, Aleph foreign and domestic policy swung radically away from Ebola hunts and death-ray designs.

There was still talk of *Saishu Sen*, the final war, but by the end of the year, with Tokyo gripped in frost and twinkling with avariciously commercial Christmas lights, such talk was largely for the sake of form. Form and ritual.

With Chubachi gone, and a tidy income still to be made from computer software design, Aleph lost its fire, its apocalyptic zeal. It was never to be a normal organisation. Its members were never going to be normal.

But *Saishu Sen* was relegated to a more conventional globally religious status. The Christians, and they were a significantly dominant world religion so perhaps they knew best, thought that the end would come not with earthquake machines but with some woman called the Whore of Babylon, beasts with seven heads and brazen trumpets.

It struck the Aleph steering committee as an unlikely scenario. But the principle was sound.

God would start the end of the world. Not man. And definitely not Aleph.

Most Aleph members privately agreed that it was better that way.

A few hardliners held out, but they were suppressed (microwaved actually) by the newly ascendant Minister of Transport.

The last thing he wanted was a final war. Not while his daughter's artistic career was taking off. And in such a promising fashion.

Though obviously upset that her safari design work had been wasted, she had eventually been persuaded to eat again, leave the toilet, and had subsequently risen to new artistic heights following her release from the padded cells of a private Aleph hospital that was normally reserved for containing new recruits who had decided to leave Aleph and wanted to go home.

She had told him that she was now doing her first music industry-related work. Designing a cover for the band Limp Bizkit.

The album – Limp Bizkit's debut album, she said – was named "Chocolate Starfish and the Hot Dog-flavoured Water." Her design was, in the Transport Minister's opinion, innovative and brave. It depicted asexual Negro children coloured green. They all looked thin and starved, which the Transport Minister found particularly ironic and humorous. After all, apart from the one standing and proffering the chocolate starfish, all the green starving Negro children were lounging listlessly about in limpid water. Water that was full of bobbing hot dogs.

How clever to pick up on the essential truth that all foreigners were intrinsically incapable of feeding themselves without Japanese guidance.

It was enough to make a Daddy really proud. She'd make, in time, an excellent Aleph Minister of Transport.

His daughter hadn't, in fact, designed the album cover, but as Rindert had said to Father Jack so many months previously in the haunted Mission, when he'd first met the homunculus, that was Japanese for you. No respect for patents.

CHAPTER FORTY-SIX

Good Bye

Rindert and Jack arrived at immigration, Heathrow, without undue difficulty.

But it was touch and go whether Jack' s forged passport would survive careful scrutiny. Rindert's regular Freetown forger had been evacuated by HMS *Clam* and Rindert had had to improvise.

While Rindert had improvised he'd had to post Jack at what was left of the forger's front door.

Not to fend off RUF, sobels, or Kamajor witch fighters waving cutlasses. And certainly not to keep the police at bay. There weren't any left. Rindert's problem was the celebration.

People were frolicking and parading in the streets. Throwing flowers. Waving simple clay or palm-frond figurines of Mama Holden (a white porroh woman who'd singlehandedly sent the RUF to hell and who had flown on transparent wings above a red elephant through the streets to cry "Freedom for the people" with a voice like a trumpet.)

There were cheers for one and all.

Unless they looked cornered and afraid at the new power shift.

Anyone unwise enough to look cornered and afraid lit the mob's blue fuse. They were butchered. Bits of them were waved about in triumph and offered to Mama Holden.

Body parts stuck on sticks aside (the "Freetown liberation kebab") there was, by the inventive and ambitious standards set by Sierra Leone, relatively little violence.

Just optimism, brimming optimism.

Executive Outcomes was back in town. SHEELD had brought in a new generation of security consultants, mainly French Foreign Legion deserters who'd been involved in a blood feud that got out of hand in Djibouti and who needed a rapid change in air.

It was rumoured that HMS *Clam* would be returning soon (carrying most of its refugees who, following bureaucratic obstacles in Conakry, had decided to come back too). It was also said that the British were finally going to be landing again.

The dancing and singing and the chants of "Mama Holden!" had been a serious distraction in the passport-forging process. If Esther Speeks had been doing the intricate work, he would no doubt have stopped, cleared the streets with short but accurate bursts of fire, then done a proper job of Jack's passport. But Speeks was, if not dead, at least limping bootless for the Liberian border. Vowing murderous revenge. The only man to survive Dr Pleasant's little surprise.

Rindert, not being Speeks, had not killed indiscriminately with placid, sociopathic efficiency. He'd just grimaced, endured, struggled and become more and more and more annoyed.

He had almost finished when a huge, fat, wailing mammy had thundered in to shake his hand and ask for money and matches. She was clearly intoxicated, reeked of palm wine and in her jubilant lunge to embrace her liberator spilled Rindert's ink. Tense from lack of sleep and his recent exertions, Rindert had snapped and launched a volley of fast swift hooks to the fat woman's gut. Putting the woman down had been an extraordinary business. So fat. So vocal. It was like trying to punch out a hippo.

Rindert had just been trying to throttle her – her neck fat, thick as a tree trunk – when a white man in paramilitary uniform had punched Jack flat and entered the room, firing intimidating bursts through the ceiling. Plaster fell on Rindert, the woman, and the passport.

"Ah, fa crying out loud!"

"What's what in here? Rindert! Versus what? The Incredible Hulk?"

Rindert had recognised the voice. Mad Mike Schlessinger. CEO of SHEELD.

"Listen Mike, I'm trying to do a passport and this—"

"Yeah, well hurry it up! I'll sort this—"

Schlessinger did it, while speaking. A perfectly aimed blow to the back of the woman's head. She'd subsided like a mud-slide.

"—out. But I want you out too. There are some weird questions being asked about that auction of yours."

"I'm not hanging around to give you any weird answers," Rindert had said. "All I'm trying to do is forge this passport for my colleague – the redheaded guy you just brained – then I'm out. And he's out. No more auctions."

"That's the right idea. We're cleaning this place up. Got some Legionnaire vets in to help. Time for some urgent democracy before the English come back with their rules and Geneva Conventions."

There was gunfire in a distant part of the city.

"Any food on you?" Rindert had asked, trying to change the subject. Sounded like Mike and his French deserters were planning some bullshit coup. Rindert wanted none of that.

"Plenty. And I'll enjoy it later. Now finish your forgery."

"We killed all the RUF. Doesn't that earn a bite to eat?"

Schlessinger'd thought about this and softened. "Have some biltong." He'd dug a twisted fibrous length of springbok sinew out of his trousers.

While Rindert gnawed at the pungent sun-dried meat. Schlessinger's eyes had narrowed. He'd got to the point.

"We've been having these little guys, suicide bombers in ambulance uniforms scurrying around and blowing themselves up. Hard to see quite why. But there's talk they'd win the Third World War if you order them right. If you've got the right money to buy their allegiance. You know anything about them?"

"Not a thing," Rindert had said finishing the biltong. He put the final touch to the passport.

Like the biltong it was rather a botched job.

Fortunately for Messrs Campbell and Geffries careful scrutiny of passports at their time of arrival in Britain was not a Heathrow immigration priority. At least not with Jim.

There was an ongoing A1 situation – another La Guardia staffer had touched British soil and the British official was distracted, hungry with anticipation.

The Yanks had already started retaliation. Three Heathrow cleaners had actually been strip-searched. Time to show the Yanks who really ran the world's busiest international airport.

"Enjoy your visit," Jim, the immigration official said, but all the while his eyes were elsewhere. If the La Guardia Yank was carrying mace, she'd be doing more than bending over and spreading her cheeks. She'd be doing time. The airport police were taking no more nonsense. Not after Mr Horseright's ordeal in JFK with the emetics and the transparent and constantly supervised toilet, constructed to thwart people who smuggled drugs internally in the DEA-affiliated "poop room".

On his honeymoon too.

Parting Ways

"No more of this homunculus stuff? Promise?"

Father Jack stared up at Rindert's face and met his gaze.

"Promise," lied Father Jack. "What's your plan?"

"Buy a game ranch in the Free State. I've had a place in mind for a while. Catch up with my bird-watching. Clean sheets. Peace. Just the odd poacher to shoot, help keep my eye in. I've a mind to breed black rhino. Magnificent animals. And you? You really going to buy Mungo's place? What was it called? Clouds?"

"Yes. I'll buy it, try it for a while. I need a bit of peace."

"Well, it doesn't sound healthy to me. Enjoy Clouds, then, if you can buy it. But I'm serious, no more nonsense. Or I'll shut you down."

"No more nonsense," vowed Father Jack, lying again. With access to Mungo's stuff, his books, his moonlight recipes, the sky was the limit.

No, body parts were the limit. He'd have to find a way round that.

The two men shook hands but it was half-hearted. Everything they'd known and done together had been too weird. Too painfully unsuccessful. And although both men were rich, the wealth itself hadn't formed a basis for an enduring camaraderie. Much less a friendship.

They parted ways.

Final Words

It is always tempting to butt in when you are an author who has just finished a book.

Editors advise against the habit, but Stephen King does it all the time and it hasn't hurt his sales figures any.

So what the hell? I'll be bold and do it too.

I'm proud to say that *Homunculus* is probably the most bizarre work of fiction ever to emerge from the African continent (African presidents' memoirs and autobiographies excepted). The characters in this novel are, upon occasion and as you might have guessed, fictitious. But not completely. Actually they're bits of people I've met, pieced together homunculus-style.

A lot of characters in this book are rather more real.

General Butt Naked exists (unless someone has shot him or his overtaxed liver has exploded) but he does not hail from Sierra Leone. Just over the border in Liberia. And he is (or was) a dyed-in-the-wool bastard. Restoring the ecological balance, there is an anti-RUF "Born Naked" unit in Sierra Leone. Born naked. Fight naked. Die naked. That's their motto. And they're the *good* guys.

Choppings, monstrous legions of doped-up adolescents, Kamajor witchdoctors wearing sea shells and waving swords, the St Peter's church massacre, eight-year-olds with kalashnikovs. All strange, as Ripley would say. But true.

Doubt me, then check your paper, surf the Net, look for Sierra Leone (which ironically was one of the first nations to sign up to the UN treaty on the rights of the child).

Raping virgins to cure AIDS? Widespread. Ongoing. Babies qualify as virgins. There's bad stuff going on.

The happy ending – all the villains getting sorted out in one hectic auction weekend? That's fiction.

Sorry.

The General Murders, the Blue Books, still prowl, scrap, lope about and their legacy is carnage, misery and rubbish. "I've never in all my life seen such horrors – not in Rwanda, Burundi, Zaire or Central America." That was the verdict of Reed Brody, a director of Human Rights Watch. If Sierra Leone is out-horroring Rwanda, then it's a place to skip when you're planning your next tropical holiday.

And blood diamonds are still a semi-crazed West African rebel's best friend.

Shoko Asahara and his followers did indeed fry each other in microwaves, claimed their earthquake machine destroyed Kobe (circa 6,000 dead), Sarin-gassed the Tokyo subway (16 dead, 5,500 injured) and sent people off and away to bring back viral plagues with the idea of wiping us all out. They also attempted to levitate. Sweating sociopathic loons, they hopped about on tatami mats, thrusting themselves skywards with painful thrusts of the elbow. Thought they were flying.

And yes, I fear they did campaign for political power, releasing balloons shaped like the guru's head. And they jogged about on bus roofs dressed as pink elephants.

I saw them doing it.

Even more disturbing is the fact that their membership *is* on the increase. Some Japanese citizens actually *want* to come on board!

Koransky I bumped into during a journalistic jaunt in the Bolivian Amazon. He was a deserter from the Russian army, looking for gold. While he wasn't finding any (which was all of the time), he augmented his income as a rainforest tour guide. He didn't actually shoot his pestiferous clients. Just hopped into the boat and took off while they muttered about his lousy carrot soup in their dripping tents beside the caiman-haunted Beni River. It took them three weeks to get back to civilisation. Three weeks! They got by on insects. No doubt thinking how they'd kill for a drop of carrot soup.

The South Africans are readily available. Go to any African war zone. Or save yourself the bother and just fly BA or SAA to South Africa. You'll find them all over the place. Try a bar in Kwazulu/Natal after a Rugby match. Many South Africans have put aside the guns, have embraced the new regime, the "rainbow nation" and peace and harmony is what it's now all about. Some haven't. Their stories are tall. But often true.

Dr Pleasant is a fiction, but a gentleman working with apartheid's Civil Co-operation Bureau did do his bit for civil co-operation by body-bombing SWAPO rebel fighters out of planes over the Skeleton Coast and suffocating captives with muscle relaxants. The same gent poisoned the Dobra wells (unsuccessfully) and did rather appalling things to lots of people. He's not in jail. Had an engaging laugh. And could conceivably be living next door to you.

The syphilitic mice were someone else's idea. But that happened too.

And the homunculus? The homunculi?

People have been trying to alter life or create life since they first found that they could. Or imagined that they could. The creation of a homunculus (lit. little man) is a consistent bee in the alchemical community's creative bonnet. Has been for years.

And, of course, alchemists pre-date the efforts of sensible mainstream genetically modifying science by quite a lot of years. And rather a lot of centuries.

Jack, who is entirely fictional, and not remotely sensible, is currently busy at work on grander stuff than Dolly the sheep, destroying essential ecosystems with experimental GM alfalfa, looking at aborted human foetuses with a view to human fertilization, or cloning frogs destined for white-cloaked scientific, experimental nastinesses.

Jack is at work right now. Right this now.

Rummaging through Mungo's files; ignorantly releasing all Mungo's bottled and waywardly-dangerous moor-caught thoughts; stinking like a goat; looking for what he thinks he needs; chucking what he thinks he doesn't; bottling this; decanting that. Accidentally releasing the other.

Wondering where to get those all-important human body parts.

All in the effort to create ...

... The Perfect Man!

For details of what goes horribly and predictably wrong see the forthcoming volume, *Homunculus II*. More of the same. Only this time in England!

Unless of course this book bombs.

In which case you'll never hear another word from me upon the subject again.

Cheers!

Hugh Paxton
Windhoek, Namibia.

Acknowledgements

I'd like to thank my publisher Mike Barnard for his help and encouragement and to offer apologies to his wife Jayne for taking up his weekends in order to get this book sorted.